11/9

AND THE TERRORIST
WHO LOVED
BONSAI TREES

PHILIP KRASKE

11/9

AND THE TERRORIST WHO LOVED BONSAI TREES

encompass
EDITIONS

Published by Encompass Editions, Kingston, Ontario, Canada.
No part of this book may be reproduced, copied or used in any form or manner
whatsoever without written permission, except for the purposes of brief
quotations in reviews and critical articles. For reader comments,
orders, press and media inquiries:
www.encompasseditions.com
or
www.philipkraske.com

FIRST EDITION 2019
ISBN 978-1-927664-09-4
Cataloguing in Publication
Program (CIP) information available from
Library and Archives Canada
at www.collectionscanada.gc.ca

cover design by Ismael Medina

encompass
EDITIONS

To 9/11 Truthers everywhere.
Be of good heart. History will be more
grateful than our contemporaries.

AUTHOR'S NOTE

Paul Klippen's story continues from my last novel, *City on the Ledge*. Not to spoil things for later readers of that novel, in the present one I am intentionally vague about his exact doings as a diplomat in Ecuador.

Bonsai [Jpn *bon*, lit., basin or pot + *sai*, to plant]: a potted plant (such as a tree) dwarfed (as by pruning) and trained to an artistic shape.

Merriam-Webster English Dictionary

Civilization is a fragile bungalow precariously poised on a live volcano of barbarism.
Will Durant,
Fallen Leaves

PART ONE: THE START

1
It was Any American Street.

The 100 block of Charlesdrew Street in Jersey City, New Jersey, displays at its midpoint a line of elegant three-story brownstone duplexes that border a cracked sidewalk, which itself borders a pot-holed street. On its east side cars are permitted to park, and because the area is heavily populated, they line up tail to trunk like circus elephants. Above them, a spidery black sprawl of electrical cables disperse power to dwellings of every conceivable type: wooden and brick, condos and triplexes, arty townhouses and artless clapboards, all pressed one against another down every street. They crowd out trees, which peek above the buildings from the center of each block, hoping to soften this cramped urban motley with some greenery. Lying directly across the river from glamorous Manhattan, Jersey City was an odd place for American History to point her saintly finger, and much less at the brownstone at 126 Charlesdrew, the converted offices of a small Internet-advertising firm called Hallerbee Net Research. But she did: on that sunny Tuesday morning, the ninth of November, when Trudy Schelling entered Hallerbee as its new employee and exited thirty seconds later as America's number one new terrorist.

She was poorly cast for the role of villain; a mighty effort of inventiveness would be required to make her one. Born in northern Louisiana twenty-eight years before and raised in Lincoln, Nebraska, she was short – just over five feet tall – and had a pleasantly doe-like face and an athlete's build come by honestly: she had been an All-State gymnast in high school and the top star in vault, floor exercise, and parallel bars on her team during her first two years of college – at Cornell on full scholarship – until a shoulder-shattering fall on the balance beam ended her career. It also left her with an odd stride: her left arm swung diagonally in front of her torso as if she were sawing wood.

Furthermore, nothing about Trudy was even distantly villainous. She was devoutly religious and a regular at Mass. Trudy was so kind, so shy, so polite, so honest, so serious, so low-key, so sweet – so square

– that her worst vices were spending money on her collection of bonsai trees and playing online poker. A statistician by trade, she was a skillful player and usually ended the month four- to five-hundred dollars to the better, a fact seized on by her critics, for nothing gives off a whiff of the illicit like a "lady gambler." In reality, Trudy felt guilty about taking others' money and wished they could all just play for points or championship cups. She gave her winnings to charities and the Church. Victim of two gropings in college, she was wary of men and had even called three of them "creeps" to their faces. This was the only real insult in her arsenal, but to her it covered every miscreant in the pantheon of human evil between litterbug and axe murderer.

Purse and nylon good-shoes bag – she drove wearing her tennis shoes – both slung on one shoulder, silver-gray pants loosely outlining her hips, pink cotton blouse peeking out of her dark-green jacket, she got out of her three-month-old Nissan Micra and punched the button on the door handle to lock it. The car, pearl-white, was squeaky-clean both outside and in, for she washed and vacuumed it every two weeks on Fridays. She was a methodical woman.

Now she pushed her beautiful mane of thick blond hair – her best feature – back over her shoulders and with her peculiar wood-sawing gait took eleven steps to cross the street; I have counted them because, slouched shabbily in my seat, I was recording her on my phone from my own car, which was just behind hers. (The Jeep Cherokee parked there all night had vacated the space, on cue, just as Trudy turned up the street. I admired the smoothness: very professional.) And wouldn't you know it? Just before reaching the sidewalk, she hesitated, pulled the key out of her purse, turned around, and, one eye closed to aim the remote, locked the car again. Well, name me a bloody fool who doesn't do that now and then.

Two steps down the sidewalk, she stopped again, this time out of surprise. For a man now came down the steps of Hallerbee: a Catholic priest in his black habit, and carrying a small black grip: about seventy, slender, deep-set eyes, a thin khaki-gray crewcut flat as a tabletop. For the moment, let's leave it at that.

The Rainmaker. I had seen him before, in Cancún, Mexico, some five years earlier, and had hunted him ever since; he was, in fact, what had led me to that morning in Charlesdrew Street. It seemed he really was a priest. For disguises are rarely well-chosen and tend to fight their users as pieces of poorly-matched furniture do. But now that I had a good look at him – the desert pallor, the chinless flat face – it was evident that this man lived and breathed the ancient aridity of the priesthood.

He climbed down the six steps with rickety jerks of his elbows – his knees were stiff and arthritic – and turned down the sidewalk towards Trudy.

"Oh my gosh!" Trudy exclaimed. "But, but you don't work here. Who are you?"

The man's smile showed only a crooked line of lower teeth. "I'm Father John Paper – for what's it's worth to you," he replied. "I'm afraid there's been a death in your office, my dear."

"Oh my gosh! Who?"

"His name was George Harley."

"I don't know him," said Trudy. "I don't know anyone there, really. Today is my first day."

"The poor man collapsed right here on the sidewalk – surely some kind of heart ailment. A couple of your coworkers helped him in. I was passing by, and I thought I could help, but, alas…." He lifted his grip briefly. "I happened to have my things with me. I administered the extreme unction while they were doing a heart massage."

"Well, at least he got that."

"You must be Gertrude – the new girl." Another professional smile and a jerk of his head back at the house. "They're awfully concerned that this is going to make a bad impression on your first day. Well, I must be running along. Lots of –"

"Please, Father John – your blessing?"

This request shook The Rainmaker. His rectangular face fell open, his lipless face a blank hole.

Trudy felt immediately that she had embarrassed him. "Well, if you'd rather not…"

But the priest recovered. "Why, of course, child. Yes, that would be most fitting. In the name of the Father, the Son…." And as he lifted a gray hand and gently rubbed a cross on her uptilted forehead, he raised his other hand, the grip hanging by his thumb, behind Trudy, towards the blue window-tinted van on my side of the street: a policeman's traffic-stopping flat palm. I moved the camera slightly. For on my side of the street, three or four vehicles along, the driver's door of the blue van had slid open. Now it slowly closed, as if the man inside were offended.

"Thank you, Father."

"Your faith is important to you, child?"

"Oh for sure, it's the center of my life."

This also staggered the priest. I couldn't hear the conversation, of course – the windows were up – but even so, it was clear the man was truly moved. "Do you go to Mass?" he asked.

"Almost every week. And I confess every year at Easter."

"Well!" the priest exclaimed. "Well, that's fine, that's…that's very laudable, child. Well, rest assured that our Lord will take good care of you."

They parted. Trudy didn't like the sound of that: *Our Lord will take good care of you.*

She didn't like the man getting out of the van and watching her, either. Now he was crossing the street to her. Walking up the six steps to the front door of Hallerbee, she reached into her bag and grabbed her stun gun and flicked the switch to turn it on. She rang the doorbell, panic rising in her because she could hear the man behind her hopping up onto the sidewalk, then the lowest step.

"Come *on!*" she pleaded softly. With a buzz, the door opened, and she darted in, shoving it closed with her foot. Now another man loomed up before her: athletic-looking, dressed in a kind of green-black uniform, not quite like a janitor: smarter. He towered over Trudy, but most people did. His short hair seemed to make his little ears stick out even more.

"Hi. You Gertrude?" he asked with a grin.

"Yeah, sure am. Whew! There was a guy…."

And now the man snatched a huge hank of her hair.

"Hey, what are you doing?" Trudy squawked.

"Okay, got her," he called up over his shoulder, hauling her farther into the house.

"On the sofa, Sandusky," answered a man's voice from that direction, dry as an eye-doctor's.

The man pulled her three steps that way, then sank to his knees under the hoarse bray of Trudy's stun gun, which released 10,000 volts into the most unfortunate testicles in the history of maleness. He melted to the floor, releasing her. Shoving her hair back, Trudy looked around: to her left, a largely barren living room with a chewed sofa lying wounded at an angle, missing its little legs on one side. Some half-dozen oldish people, either asleep or dead, lay or sat slouched in old armchairs and the sofa, and the one that gazed back at her had the dull look of a doll that had lost its stuffing, his filthy pant cuffs turned up in order not to drag on his shoes. A thirtyish Chinese woman sat on the floor against the sofa, looking at Trudy as if irritated by her arrival. It was only later that Trudy realized that she was frightened for her.

"Shit! Shit, Sandusky's bought it! Move move move move move!"

In front of her, at the top of the stairway, was none other than Steve Hallerbee, an electrically jaunty man with a pointy jaw and V-shaped grin. During the interview over a good steak lunch in Manhattan, he had constantly exclaimed, "That is *so* interesting!" which had all but unnerved Trudy. Now he was dressed in the same jumpsuit as the first man, and Trudy realized now that this was not janitorial garb at all, but military: his pants were tucked into tall jackboots. He and another man were carrying someone upstairs by his arms and legs.

The front door, of course, was no option. Trudy dashed past the foot of the stairway and down the hall. Her shoes seemed to make a horrible, creaking clatter on the bare floorboards. At the far end was the back door of the kitchen – which, two steps on, she saw, was held shut with a fat chain gripping the door handle tight to an unused shelf support on the wall. She turned right into the first doorway.

"Trudy, hold up. I got something for you. A gift for your first day," called Steve Hallerbee in a voice that not even his dog would have believed.

By reflex Trudy was polite. "Great, can you bring it down?" she called, slamming the door shut.

She found herself in a small functioning office. The massive metal desk, scarred and battered, held a big laptop computer facing the desk chair as if awaiting its orders, and a chunky printer set on a board that slid out of the desk.

"She's in the office!" yelled Hallerbee.

Another voice: *"What? Get her, get her now!"*

Footsteps thundered everywhere.

Trudy had already tipped over a round, metal wastebasket and set it lengthwise between the door and desk, and now snatched an unopened block of printer paper from the desk and jammed it – stomping it down with her foot – between the wastebasket's bottom and the door. The door handle turned, the wastebasket budged an inch, the paper budged an inch, the desk budged a lengthwise inch – and then stopped against the wall opposite.

"C'mon, Gertrude, this is all a misunderstanding," the man panted, banging on the the door. "Open up."

"I'm calling the police and you creeps are going to *get it!*" Trudy snapped over her shoulder, hitting the security button atop the window sash and sliding it up. "And by the way I said to call me 'Trudy.'"

"We *are* the police," the man, shoving hard against the door.

"Oh, like I'm gonna believe *that!*"

"It's jammed," Hallerbee said to a second one who now arrived. "It's jammed solid."

"I'll tell you what," said Trudy. "Slide your i.d. under the door, and I'll take a look at it."

"Okay, just hang on. I'm getting it out!"

Trudy snatched her purse and good-shoes bag. She climbed onto the window sash and looked down: it was a six-foot drop to the little space between the Hallerbee brownstone and the next one.

"All right, now just take it easy. Here it comes…."

Which was all Trudy heard before jumping out and sprinting towards the back patio.

The back wall was three feet taller than she was, but she charged it, rammed a foot against the bricks, leapt up and cleared the top by belly-flopping over.

They would see her out the kitchen window at the back of the house, but they had to unchain the back door first.

So Trudy was forty yards down the alley, at its very end, when a bullet hissed past her ear and hit a passing city bus on the fender, just behind the back wheel. At the bus stop just ten strides up the street, she jumped aboard, and blurted to the driver that she had gone to her company on Charlesdrew Street to start her first day of work and a guy had grabbed her and everyone looked like they'd been drugged, and maybe some were dead – all of which must have been convincing because the driver let her stay on the bus. One elderly passenger gave her his seat. Another, a bulky, motherish lady with pointy glasses, thrust a package of tropical-fruit drink into her hand.

When Trudy had caught her breath, this latter passenger heard her out and gave her directions to a police station. Trudy rode three blocks, walked another, and went to another bus stop. She boarded the first bus that came, rolled her phone into a castoff newspaper, set it under her seat, and got off.

After that, she changed buses again and rode all the way into Manhattan, on the sound principle that when one loses a job the best thing to do is to jump right into getting another.

Thus had Gertrude Ingrid Schelling, the bumpy name by which the entire planet would soon come to know her, kicked off 11/9.

2

NOVEMBER 9 (TUESDAY)

Of further events on Charlesdrew Street that morning, little need be said.

All the world knows the story of how the five men entered the Empire State Building – 9:07 A.M. on the security video – and patiently went through security, little halos shining above their swarthy features. They rode an elevator to the fourth floor, the highest one of the base of the building that directly borders the sidewalk. This floor held an office that had been vacated a month before by a Norwegian shipping-container representative; security alarms had been taken out. There they forced open a temporary door to the space, opened a window on the 34th Street side, dropped a string tied to a weight out the window, and with the help of a confederate down below drew in two ropes, each heavier than the last. The second was a robust inch-thick cord that could have clutched a yacht to its dock. They drew up a smallish block and tackle, and attached it to an exposed ceiling beam. With this, they drew up two of three wooden crates from the van, each big enough to hold a household air conditioner.

The men never opened them. When the good guys did, some hours later, the two already hauled up would prove to hold, in one crate, a number of tools and a variety of electronic meters, and in the other, some type of gizmo with a lot of electronics. It occurred to someone – the skeptics, known as "11/9 Truthers," would later wonder why – to run a Geiger counter over it immediately: "It nearly blew the needles off the machine," said one officer.

It would quickly be dubbed a "baby bomb," according to FBI sources, and held enough punch to vaporize everything in a radius of fifty meters and, more to the point, destabilize the hundred-floor building and topple it into the street.

The men had prayed first; this needs mentioning. An accountant who was walking up the stairs for his morning exercise heard the long mooing of "*Allah-u-akhbar*": "God is great" in Arabic. Or as reporters from the more conservative TV programs quoted, "God's great." The other murmur of the terrorists, heard by a passing pest-control man of Egyptian background, was "*In cha Allah*": "May the will of God be done."

On this lovely Tuesday morning, however, God's will took the burly form of NYPD Officer Havershall Hicks, thirty-six years earlier named for a great-great-grandfather born into slavery on a Virginia plantation, a cultural detail widely trumpeted by day's end.

With a single four-story glance at the Keystone Kops moving job before him, "Shally" Hicks formed a low opinion of both the movers and their technique. He didn't like the flurrying arms of the man in the street who was urging his colleagues to pull the second box up fast. He didn't like the man's tight, purple-and-green woolen sweater or his bushy beard. He didn't like their school-bus-yellow rented mini-van parked half on the curb. He didn't like the size of the box or the way it was tied on, so that the box rose corner-downwards. Nor did he like the man's milky smile at him as he waited for his friends at the top to pull the box in and undo the knot.

The scene simply begged for the judicious eye and judgmatic disposition of New York's Finest.

As reporters later sedulously reminded everyone, Shally Hicks had nothing against Muslims: his own brother had converted to Islam five years earlier – a fact mentioned by the president in his eulogy of Hicks. Shally and Hassan (formerly George) still had their munchies in front of the TV for the Saturday NBA game, just like always. Hassan now drank only Coke, but still served Shally his Heineken as cold as ever. No, Officer Hicks was just doing his duty when he asked Raschid al-Bousapha to get his papers – permits, licenses, the usual – out of the truck. And he certainly didn't deserve the bullet in the gut that he got for an answer.

The jig was up, and four floors above, the other five men knew it. They sprinted down the stairs, grousing so bitterly among themselves that on the third floor, a stock-broker executive – by no means a wilting violet – let them pass and decided that an elevator was the better part of valor. The men walked out past security and jumped right into the yellow van, which al-Bousapha thoughtfully had waiting for them right outside the door.

Shally Hicks had a partner on his beat. Officer Leonard Kanely had by now run out of the convenience store – without having paid for his fruit pie – when he heard the shot and screams. He came running, saw poor Shally lying on the sidewalk beside the third crate and saw the yellow van with green lettering on the side jump away from the curb and race around the corner. He ran to his partner, snatching out his radio on the run, and radioed for an ambulance. Then he radioed headquarters and described the van and its last-seen direction down Fifth Avenue.

While the bad guys are burning rubber, let's note a point made about the matter of Leonard Kanely. 11/9 Truthers would soon point out that Kanely had been partnered with Hicks only two weeks earlier, coming off a suspension for a small-time corruption charge – he'd taken money from illegal immigrants for not turning them in – that should have lasted much longer. Furthermore, his radio call fell on deaf ears. An oddity of 11/9 is that the call does not show up on recordings and was never received by squad cars. The ambulance that came for Hicks seemed to appear simply by chance.

Back to the action. The New Jersey State Police, who had somehow got the alert, spotted the brightly-colored van as it exited the Lincoln Tunnel into Jersey City. Two local units were presently on its tail and more were coming. A helicopter, careful not to trouble charging airliners on their glide paths, also hovered nearby.

Raschid al-Bousapha swerved into Charlesdrew Street. (I had discreetly left by then.) By now three squad cars were following him; one sped down the alley behind the brownstones, hoping to cut off the mini-van at the intersection with Bernel Street. But halfway down Charlesdrew, al-Bousapha jammed on the brakes. His men shoved open the back doors and opened fire with three handguns, as the squad-car videos later revealed. Expecting as much, the two police quickly swerved sideways and formed a barrier, the officers crouching behind their cars. Calling to his men, al-Bousapha ran up to 126 Charlesdrew, firing his chunky automatic at the door lock as he ran. The other five men ran inside with him. A few seconds later, they heard the sickening sound of gunshots as the first of the Hallerbee employees met their deaths.

The standoff had begun.

And from there, as everyone remembers: threats, bullhorns, telephoned demands, panicked evacuations of surrounding houses; policemen crouching, reporters purring, tiptoes hurting, photographers squinting. "Seemingly," "reportedly," "apparently," "allegedly" – all the wet nurses of modern journalism rose to the task of covering a live crisis. SWAT teams unpacked lockers, Special Teams stretched muscles, local police chiefs sipped bad coffee, the White House expressed concern. Chin-stroking specialists from every fief in specialdom gathered at each end of the 100 block of Charlesdrew Street, where a little carnival of professionalism crackled and hummed, all at the service of the Public Good and the extinction of Public Danger.

And as the minutes ticked past, speculation spread its great white wings, soared, banked, wheeled, swooped and glided on every network TV show in the land. "Best bets" were postulated, "scary versions" articulated, and "worst case scenarios" despaired over. Newscasters echoed them, reporters tweeted them, and coffee-mug-gripping experts formed panels to flesh them out:

They'll ask for a deal with the Israelis, said an ex-CIA officer.

We do not negotiate with terrorists, said an ex-Marine commander.

The material objective is to make them see the hopelessness of their situation, said a hostage expert.

A surgical strike, recommended an Air Force pilot with AfPak experience, though he admitted that "collateral" might be "an issue" for owners of nearby houses.

A floor plan of the brownstone was miraculously discovered, swiftly brought forward and delicately analyzed. *Now I would imagine, Karen, that the hostages are being detained* here, *in the kitchen at the back.*

But what if these men are hopeless – desperate – to start with? the anchorwoman objected. *I mean, what is the state of mind running through these guys' heads? And the scary thing is this could happen on any American street. That is all of us in that house.*

Any American street. Around the country, this melodic, wondrously dehiscent phrase burst and flung its seeds across the land. *Any American street:* yours, mine, the newscaster's, your best friend's. Terrorists rife as termites could come running up to *your* house firing a gun and breaking down *your* door.

If this can play out on any American street, we need terrorism protection, not just some poor cop on the beat with a pea-shooter. He doesn't stand a chance, bawled a congressman from New Jersey, forefingers puncturing our ancient ideas about vigilant cops on the beat; the experts nodded like doctors considering a diagnosis.

And then – everyone was cut off in mid-opinion – a young woman burst out the front door of Hallerbee and staggered down the front steps to the sidewalk, just barely managing to keep her feet: her hands were bound together with a strip of cloth, and her shoulder-length hair hung down in front of her face – an Oriental face. She reached the sidewalk and limped into the street. A heroic police officer jumped the barricade and sprinted towards her – 126 Charlesdrew was the fifth house down from the Warble Street end – but to no avail. A gun barked in the house and the front bay window shattered: two shots hit her in the back. Her legs collapsed under her, she fell forward, and her hair swept like a parachute over her Vietnamese beauty – Ellen Nguyen, according to the company webpage photo – a lovely chiseled face with broad cheekbones that angled down to a fragile chin. Two shots in the general direction of the cop – Nate Niedemeyer, later decorated – forced him to dive over a parked car and stay there for the duration.

On went the circus. Spectators speculated, photographers photographed, experts ex-spurted, and the gruesome scene with poor Ms. Nguyen was replayed over and over, always with the titillating caveat that the video was "gruesome" and that "parental discretion was advised." Soon Ms. Nguyen, her hair tumbling over her like a magic spell, became more icon than person.

Hecklers – just from the sound, I'd call it Hecklers any day of the week, said the ex-Marine, and for the moment nobody speculated on how Hecklers had bloomed among terrorists who had run inside carrying handguns.

If this Asia-oriented woman found it within herself to get out, that means that the terrorists are thin-slicing their hostage surveillance in order to secure their positions, said the hostage expert. *I would say this means they are disarrayed.*

The terrorism expert dismissed this. *These are hardened terrorists. They've been through the camps. They know every situation in the book. They're in there sipping a Coke and waiting for our negotiator to start bending.*

Our homeland has become the new battlefield, said the congressman gravely.

A news bulletin handed to news anchors revealed that the Border Patrol had been looking for some half-dozen men who had cut through a chain-link fence in Montana, and they had advised the FBI that these were probably the men: both their number – six – and "ethnicity-type" matched.

And arriving on any American street, added the anchorwoman darkly.

Then an excited assistant ran to her side and handed her a paper. Yes, the FBI had just confirmed that they were in telephone talks with the terrorists.

A group of Hallerbee i.d. photos popped up on the screen, including Trudy's. Reporters also began to profile them: their work histories, families, hobbies – everything. They knew that Steve Hallerbee – bearded, and not the one that Trudy had met – had two children and that Ellen's parents had immigrated to America in 1979, after the fall of Saigon. The information gave the victims personalities and did much to fill out the narrative.

Twelve hard-working professional young people in the prime of life, intoned the congressman. *I wonder which ones were assassinated as these terrorists-losers ran into the house.*

Then, sixty militarily precise minutes – another item that would later drive 11/9 Truthers nuts – after Ellen's escape, it was the bearded Steve Hallerbee who made a break for freedom. Only Truthers would wonder how he and Ellen Nguyen had managed to open the heavy front door with their hands tied behind their backs. 11/9 Conspiracy Debunkers – they, too, would organize quickly – replied that the locking mechanism had already been shot off; to which Truthers counter-replied that something of considerable size and weight – an armchair, for example – had surely been placed in front of the door to keep it shut. At any rate, you had to admire the reflexes of the TV technicians at the control panels. No sooner had the front door opened again than television screens filled with the awkward, down-the-street shots of the building.

Hallerbee descended the steps hastily but sideways, as if able to bend just one knee. His hands behind his back, his head bobbed groundward as if on a spring. Commentators would later wonder if he hadn't been beaten earlier. He took three long strides, passing Ellen Nguyen, and then two shots to the back of the head blew his face off. He dove head-first into the street, his lower jaw ripped backward by the force of impact.

Now two bodies lay in the street.

The hostage expert remarked that the "window" for a negotiated resolution was closing and expected an attack.

The disgusted terrorism expert again disagreed, saying it was foolish to try anything against "trained terrorists" in a situation like that. *By now they've got the whole place laid out with explosives. Your only closure is by negotiation.*

The anchorwoman was startled. *Explosives? Could they be carrying explosives?*

Are you kidding? exclaimed the ex-Marine sardonically.

It seemed that no terrorist worth his beard was without a charge or two of C-4. And as if by magic, "explosives" now became the watchword. The terrorism expert said that they surely had explosives and the "extensive knowledge" needed to use them.

Yes, everyone assumed that the house was set to blow up. The anchorwoman hoped that all the neighbors had been evacuated. The congressman assured her that they had, "or someone doesn't need to come to work tomorrow morning."

Now the crowd – even the cameraman – flinched. Two distinct shots were fired in the house.

One was probably just an echo, said the ex-Marine.

Could that have been the sound of the last hostages meeting their worldly end? the anchorwoman wondered.

The hostage expert said he doubted it. *At this point, hostages are the only card these guys have got vis-a-vis.*

Unless they blow the place up, said the terrorism expert.

Unconfirmed rumors had it that the Special Forces were going to storm the building. Did reporters see any unusual movement on the street? Well, yes, they did. The police cordon had been "reconfigured" – that is, moved back to the other sides of the intersections. A police armored car had entered what used to be the press area, and some half-dozen armed agents were climbing in – a local SWAT team, however, not Special Forces. One agent had tied a white flag to the windshield wiper and tied the wiper vertically into place: their rifles might be loaded, but their intentions were peaceful.

The SWAT team armored car drove slowly – "a leisurely, tour-ist-in-Paris pace," as one news magazine would later put it – down Charlesdrew, angling to place itself up on the sidewalk, between the brownstone houses and the two bodies in the street.

Damn right, said the congressman, and the anchorwoman looked at him sharply. *I don't care. This is America. That could be any American street. Those people have a right to their dignity. We can't have two dead bodies lying on the street, poisoning the dreams of a hundred thousand children for a generation.*

Had the pick-up of bodies been negotiated? One police spokesman replied cryptically that this was "ongoing."

The terrorists, for their part, took the move with churlishness. They fired four shots at the windshield when the armored car was just two houses away. The armored car stopped at this point, as if indecisive. Two minutes passed – again, exactly two minutes to the second, which troubled skeptical Truthers like an itch they couldn't scratch. Then it began to move forward again.

The terrorists, however, being mere terrorists and not seasoned football players, had taken the bait. They never realized that the armored car was merely a diversion.

Because now the Special Forces – later identified by Pentagon sources as an elite "Team A" – were speeding up the alley in their own armored vehicle. Just as they reached it, "Team B" blew up the back wall along the alley – "breached" was the military's term in every journalistic mouth for the rest of the day – just in time for Team A to roar through the hole.

They didn't get far. Because the terrorists, just as the experts had said, had mined the house with explosives and now blew it off the foundations; the houses to either side were destroyed as well.

The dust cleared; sadness filled the void of excitement. By the time the six o'clock news aired, the terrorists had been identified to a man: three Iranians, one Saudi Arabian, and two Syrians; it seemed they had left their passports behind in their safe house some miles away. Their ringleader was Raschid al-Bousapha, an Iranian whom the CIA had on their files as belonging to the Revolutionary Guard.

And Gertrude Ingrid Schelling, some very incriminating papers and computer pendrives found in her Newark apartment, was named the seventh terrorist. The Hallerbee website photo of her face, unsettlingly pleasant with her blond hair creaming off her shoulders, soon appeared everywhere. Here indeed was the missing link in the plot.

She was surely the one who had brought in the explosives.

She had prepared everything at Hallerbee, a fallback hideout in case the Empire State Building plot went wrong, for as every plumber's son knows, women are often used in such secondary roles in Muslim terrorist operations.

By the next news cycle, many more "unconfirmed" details had come to light; myriad sources from American intelligence, normally hostile to the media, were gossiping more giddily than a team of cheerleaders. They reported that her recruitment had taken place in France, where – this was true – Gertrude had worked for three years before returning to America just a few months earlier. She had links to Raschid al-Bousapha going back about two years; they had been lovers when she lived in Paris; they spent two nights a week in discotheques; there were whispers of "multi-party sex."

On one network panel after another, terrorism experts puffed out their cheeks like dentists depicting your future if you don't repair that bad molar, and affirmed that she was that most deadly species of terrorist: a "sleeper."

And she was still at large, ready and able to attack on "any American street."

3 **AUGUST 27**

"That's right, Mr. Deputy Assistant Under Secretary of State for Political Whatnots: you are to beg off on your round of smart Georgetown cocktail parties and have a pissy great Friday down the pub with me," I commanded, then dangled the carrot: "I might even pay for a round!"

So on a soggy Washington evening in August when rain is far more welcome than the muggy sun, and twenty minutes late for my own invitation, yours humbly, Max Venable, lumbered into the bar, still reading a student's paper folded back in one hand. I sniffed the air – a mix of popcorn cloy and bar fug – realized that I was actually now *in* the place and looked over my reading specs till I spotted Paul, took a bearing and set my feet going, reading more as I felt my way along, muttering quaint excuses through the military and lobbying classes clustered around the U-shaped bar talking to each other and looking at their mobile phones. God, how I hate those little buggers.

"Who the bloody hell is General Shek?" I demanded of Paul, reaching his booth. I waved the paper. "Not a bad essay for an undergrad, but damned if I can place a General Bloody Shek."

"Chiang Kai-shek?" Paul ventured.

I grabbed my beard. "Oh, bloody Christ. Oh, what a bloody great fool I am. Where's my bloody –" I patted pockets madly till Paul slipped a pen from an interior pocket.

"Allow me, Professor."

Sitting down opposite Paul, I snatched it and dashed a comment, then stuck Paul's pen probably halfway into my mouth, thinking. "Makes more sense, actually – now that I know who General Bloody Shek is. I'm a sucker for proper style and grammar, you know. And none of that canned stuff off Internet. Analysis of America's reaction to the Chinese Revolution: kind of a general theme – thought I'd give the kids one to stretch out and run with. Poor lass can't help it if nobody told her that the Chinese put the family name first. Give her a B+. No, bloody Christ, with her poor parents paying 50 cracks a year. Bloody scandal what they charge for a scribble of education in this country." I wrote *A-* at the top of the page and stuffed the paper into the wilds of my leather satchel.

"Keep doing that, and they'll have your ass, Max," said Paul, wisely cleaning off his pen on a napkin.

"Sod the lot. Yale will take me tomorrow for twice the money, oh yes." I called to the waitress and ordered a Guinness. "Well! Onwards and upwards! Mr. Deputy, I hope I find you well? Cindy is getting her sea legs?"

Four years earlier, his wife Cindy had injured her spine in a freak accident, slipping on ice as she got out of her car. But all was not lost. With daily growth-hormone shots injected directly into the injured part of the spine – an uninsured experimental therapy that used up the larger part of a diplomat's paycheck – the spine was reviving. Paul related the latest on her progress – sixty unaided steps in a row – in regaining her walking legs.

"She uses crutches around the house," Paul finished, "no more wheelchair. Does her rehab workout twice a day for an hour. Never misses. Maybe in a year she'll walk more or less well."

"Well done her, bloody hell. She'll be out jogging with Washington bureaucrats before we know it. About you, however…I do not see the usual Klippen buoyancy."

"No?"

"Oh dear, no, old fruit: we are troubled. We are on at least our second whiskey and third basket of popcorn, mobile phone turned off to the world, top button undone, cufflinks off, and those shoulders are far too hunched to be those of a typical carefree State Department official with half the world squirming under his fleshy palps. No, I would say we are under some type of cloud."

Paul only chuckled and shook his head; he always does when I pull the secret-agent stuff on him.

I knew him well enough to see it. We had actually been friends since our college days, when Paul was a Rhodes scholar in Old Blighty. Now that he was in Washington, he and I met often for a drink or dinner at his place or mine – his Cindy was a Brit, my Sheila a Yank – and *yes,* he had listed me on his contact sheet as a friend, and *yes,* with the straight admission that I had worked for ten years in MI6 before becoming an academic scholar, currently here at Georgetown. The bloody CIA reads these things, of course, and sod the lot of you too.

I almost forgot: descriptions. Paul Klippen had started his forties but a year earlier, with a slender build and a well-cut face topped by an enviably lush head of dark-brown hair. Roundish glasses with fine frames complement the angular set of his cheekbones. His brown eyes have a kindliness, even a sleepiness, that women love – this according to my wife, who claims expertise in the matter. At Cambridge, I had heard, said sleepiness had assisted him in the enjoyment of a fair share of womanhood. Yet they also disguised a man who could pull a sixty-hour-straight whack of meetings, paperwork, travel and research when he needed to, which was often in his new job. He had been brought from the embassy in Ecuador to play Mr. (Bottom-Rung) Big in the new administration.

Your writer is less picturesque. Place me two years older than him, my accent from within the London M25 ring road: the comfortable Essex-type of Englishman who lives for a decent glass of port and a well-stocked household library. I have a beard that I wear against my will, but it covers the scars – from getting my cheeks punctured and then poorly repaired – on an otherwise Adonic face. What else? An untamable sagebrush of hair, thin slice of nose, rather wide hips that make me look stocky. In addition to the scars, some mashed fingers, one that twitches from side to side like the second hand of a broken watch, and a limp from a damaged knee – all these due to the min-istrations of a Mexican drug cartel in the Yucatán a few years earlier that ended my run with MI6; more on that later. The Office, with institutional pity, put me out to academic pasture. Now I'm an odd-ball expert in Caribbean languages, folk culture and history. Oh, and throughout this account you may picture me wearing an off-the-rack suit, dignified despite the odd wrinkle, largely because it's the only disguise in which I don't look out of place. Paul, by contrast, wears his own suits impeccably, and with particularly clever ties.

Well, that's done. Back at it.

"Why are you correcting a paper on the Chinese Revolution?" Paul asked. "Isn't your specialty the Caribbean?"

"Oh, this bloody course I'm giving: History of U.S. Foreign Pol-icy 1945-1973. Pregnant prof, nobody available for cheap, notes were all ready, thought it might be fun to brush up my World Wars anyway. Lovely group too: ask good questions, don't let me blather on too much. Venezuelan lass with a chest worthy of Mount Rush-more. Good fun."

The waitress, probably a student herself, came with my Guinness and a fresh popcorn basket – it was free – and I gave her a nice tip. "Old love, do us a favor and don't wander back unless we call for more popcorn, okay? If we require further attention, we'll fire a gun out the lee port."

Her delight with the tip melted into concern. "Uh, this is a non-firearms establishment, sir."

"I said, 'out the *lee* port,' old love."

A puzzled smile. "Oh. Okay."

"Probably doing her Master's thesis on artificial intelligence," Paul said with that lovely deadpan humor of his. "She'll have both our jobs in ten years."

I examined the set of my Guinness and decided to let it ferment a moment. "You are being followed, is that the trouble?" I said to Paul, whose head jerked the tiniest bit. "Really, old fruit, I would have thought that even in Washington you could have dodged bullets for a year or two, being such a deep old cuss. I'm disappointed, oh yes."

"I'll pay the next round, then."

"You should. Divorced blond lady, top of the curve of the bar, right? Nothing like fake-reading for checking out a room quickly."

My back was to her, but Paul could see her out of the corner of his eye: a woman in her late thirties with a dark-blond wash of hair over a tall collar, her coat laid over a barstool.

"You sure?"

"Please, old man: one sailor recognizes another."

"Is she with the guy beside her?"

"The one she's talking to? No: a pretender to the throne, poor bloke. I'd say she's married but not too much – working on divorce. She seemed to be enjoying the bloke's attention too seriously."

"You're an amazing man, Mr. Venable," Paul observed.

I frowned. "Old fellow, observe: the well-blown hair, unsheathed brolly hung on the bar at the ready, the open stance, the rubber-soled walking shoes?"

"And her marital status?"

"Her age plus the rings on her *middle* and *pinky* fingers emphasizing the crying absence of the one between. What does *that* say to you?"

"She wants to meet me?"

"An amateur's conclusion. I'll take her bearings later on. She could be useful to us." I tested my Guinness to see if it had settled; it hadn't. Paul says that when I test the Guinness, I look rather comically like a man walking on thin ice. "The question really is, can I be seen publicly with you?"

"Go to hell. Thing is, I don't know why all the attention. She isn't Secret Service or anything. I only spotted her because I turned the wrong way in the Metro and had to backtrack."

"Like the red-haired lass who gave you the come-on in the Helsinki hotel?" Paul's eyebrow jerked up, to my delight. "There are people, Mr. Deputy Assistant blah-blah-blah, that would like to know how flexible your morals are. You're disappointing them, by the way."

I enjoyed Paul's befuddlement while I inspected the Guinness again: success. "Ah!" I said. "Nothing like the first sip of the evening. Poetry in suds."

"Max!" Paul said impatiently.

"You're right: brass tacks." I worked the foam out of my mustache. "Remember my old hobby?"

It took Paul a moment; this had been a running topic between us ever since I had left MI6, though I had not mentioned it for a long time.

"You mean, tracing 'Rainmaker'? You've found something?"

"More than something, old man. I've found *him* – generally if not physically – the man's bloody security clearance is up in the clouds somewhere." Another sip. "And more to the point, old fruit, in finding *him,* I've also come across *you.* Which is why I dragged you down to the pub here: I wanted to see what kind of surveillance you're under."

"Keep talking."

"I have this friend from 6, Ian: lives up in Penrith, just south of Hadrian's Wall. Hacking's just a sideline now, after he uncovered a major financial scandal carried on by some of our minor royals a couple of years ago. Hacked his way through a half-dozen well-perfumed banks and showed his minister they'd been charging for pets as household staff; and they hadn't paid even a bloody tenth of what they should in taxes for twenty years. Needless to say, he was quickly bought out and pensioned off. Just 35, the lucky bloke."

"One of these guys that wears a chain and has tattoos down his arms, I suppose."

"Ian? Hardly. A dart-thrower, plays wearing a tie. Runs a second-hand bookshop with his wife." Another sip. "Well, having gone down many dead ends looking for Rainmaker, I had an idea and checked it with Ian: perhaps there's a Rainmaker sending reports to some congressional committees – say, Foreign Relations. He doesn't, it turns out, but Ian hacked their phones, and – *eh voila!* – Senator Dorothy Crick has a chat going with him by text message. I only see her side of the dialog; it seems the good senator can't be bothered with such trifles as encryption."

"Dorothy Crick? She chairs Senate Foreign Relations. He reports to her?"

"Not quite report, no. This is something – *Cómo se dice?* – of a different nature altogether. This is some type of collaboration – on what, I'm not sure. She may not use encryption, but she's careful not to give anything away."

"Maybe talking about some legislation, or funding."

"No, not quite, old fruit. It's the damnedest thing. I really can't make head or tail of it. But she often refers to the 'Doers,' you see, and both she and Rainmaker seem to belong to the group."

Paul chewed popcorn for some time before answering. It's one of the pleasures of our friendship that dead air makes neither of us uncomfortable. "And their dialog included a reference to me?"

"Indeed it did, old man, on several occasions. It seems they want you to join their club."

4 NOVEMBER 9 (TUESDAY)

Trudy Schelling stood under a small forest of signs in autumnal colors that read with alliterative ecstasy *Fall Fashion Fun Flair!* She was looking through corduroy dresses and skirts on a rack in a midtown Manhattan boutique; it was the third shop that morning. She had her reading glasses on, her hair tucked up under a new Yankees baseball cap, and kept her back to the door and shop window. Though not yet christened a terrorist, she was a fugitive. A lot of people – not the police yet, but they would soon follow – were looking frantically for her, probably some watching monitors of the streets. In this, she remembered, she had an ally. Since summer, a group of anarchist radicals called the Guy Fawkes, indignant about the ubiquitous electronic surveillance in New York, had been going around the city spraying paint or putting stickers on the lens of the cameras, and doing it at a rate much faster than city maintenance people could repair them or the police catch them. They were even doing it on subway platforms, and expressways around the city. It was getting so bad that NYPD spokesmen refused to say what proportion of cameras had been affected. They merely expressed satisfaction that the fine for tampering with them had been raised to twenty thousand dollars.

She fanned through another rack, looked at her watch – hardly eleven, time moved so slowly – moved to a thick collection of woven leather belts and ran a hand over them as if they were the long hair of a little girl. She remembered the lunch with Steve Hallerbee – "Boy, he sure turned out to be a creep," she muttered – and him talking proudly about how his oldest child had been accepted into a school for "gifted" children. She worried about the man she had shocked. She hadn't meant to get him in the groin – she had aimed for his thigh – but, well, he was a creep too. What kind of a guy would grab a girl by her hair? That wasn't even fair.

"Can I help you find something today?" a clerk asked her, coming over. She was a tallish, box-like woman with heavy shoulders and hair dyed purple.

"Um, do you have any caps like this?" she asked, taking off the cap and letting her hair jump down to her shoulders.

"No, we don't sell caps, but you know…." Now the woman reached over and pulled her hair forward over her shoulders. "You ought to wear it down like this. You have great hair."

"Thanks," said Trudy, snatching her hair up and rolling it and stuffing her cap down on top. "But, um, it's not washed."

"Still – looks great." Her voice was blatantly inviting. "Come back some time and we'll go out for coffee, okay? I get off at three."

Trudy was out the door in a flash. She hated pick-ups. She hated the whole romance game which had never, ever gone well for her. The only guys who wanted to get to know her a little were either losers or men who were short and felt uncomfortable with taller women. But none of them ever much suited her, and she resented that her short stature was an attraction. At times she had consented to sex because she was lonely, but she rarely enjoyed it, and she feared that men wanted oral sex, just the thought of which made her sick. She always finished with the feeling that she had performed poorly as a lover.

Now she walked briskly up through mid-town Manhattan, trying to look as if she was going somewhere. She was surrounded by noise and teeming streets, but every sharp noise startled her. Sliding glass shop doors heaved themselves open as she passed, making her flinch, and long claws of air-conditioning reached out and swiped at her. It was a warm day for November, and her skin felt oily, like a freshly-caught fish.

For an hour, she watched events on Charlesdrew unfold at Yaitha's Shake and Cake, crouched in a booth deeply enough that she could not be seen from the street but could still see the TV above the front counter, Yaitha's jiggling dreadlocks moving back and forth beneath it. She ordered a latté and a piece of what was probably wonderful pecan pie – she could hardly concentrate enough on the flavor. Her purse held a little stick of cream, a collapsible toothbrush, house and car keys and her wallet with 93 dollars and some change. She didn't dare use an ATM now.

Her bifocals had correction only for reading so that she didn't have to keep taking them off to talk with someone. Glasses changed her face, turning it from doe-like to mouse-like. She had also bought a sweater with a hood, and a small knapsack. It now carried her purse and good shoes. She made sure the stun gun was turned off and placed it for easy use in the outside pocket. It was for emergencies only.

She lingered at the café – saw Steve Hallerbee murdered and the house blown to smithereens, which gave her a start. Yaitha came over and asked rather pointedly if she wanted to order anything else. Trudy left.

Then she saw a coffee shop that had a "Help Wanted" sign, and was encouraged by the post script added below in a jagged scrawl: *IMMEDIET start.*

Mad About Coffee had blocky brown armchairs and a reek of coffee and sweet rolls that enveloped her like a bear hug. Behind the counter, a wiry young man with large brown eyes wiped the foam off the top of the cup with one hand and with the other gave her a clipboard with blank job applications clamped to it. "We can sure use the help," he said with a spiky Maine accent, looking her over as if she were a race horse. "Yeah, you're just about right: short and quick. Put down you have previous experience – whatever, serving ice cream, bar waitress. Do that, and you got a job. Don't worry: I'll train ya in. It's easy."

Trudy filled out the application, using the name Helen Swoboda, her best friend in Nebraska.

The man took it to a door marked *Private* and sang as if tempting a three-year-old with candy, "Ri-i-ta, guess wha-a-a-at: I got an a-a-a-app. You're interviewin' today, right?"

"Hell, yes!"

An obese woman dressed in a company uniform waddled out and took the clipboard. Like most people with enormous bodies, she was of indeterminate age, though probably under forty. Her arms waggled out at her sides like the broken wings of a bird, and her walk was a bow-legged shuffle, like a kid trying to skate for the first time. But she seemed friendly, her grin like an islet amidst a rolling sea of flesh and folds. "Hey, I'm Rita," she said, swinging her hand up somewhat sideways in greeting. "Come on in. I'm real basic." She sidled back into the *Private* room. "This is a really cool place to work and we are just incredibly flexible," she said over her shoulder.

"That sounds nice," Trudy said politely.

"You're 25, huh? I'd have said 22. You tryin' to make it on Broadway, like Cam?" She dug a thumb back towards the doorway.

"Oh no, I'm just, I'm just going to try out a few different things."

The little office had stark metal shelving up to the ceiling on three sides, these filled mainly with packing boxes from which cups, napkins and stirring sticks overflowed the flaps as if trying to escape. The one open wall had a poster of *The Lion King* on which someone had scrawled "RITA" and drawn an arrow lest the inference were lost. Trudy was glad there were no windows.

To sit, Rita had to side-step around the end of her desk and then hold an intense, squeaking, scuffling negotiation with the table and the chair. She shuffled one way and the other like a person trying out a new dance step, and finally maneuvered the chair around and under her buttocks, and let herself down on it. She was so fat that she sat forward from the back of the chair. Her purple "Mad about Coffee" polo shirt lay over her torso in an undulating mass of hills and dales and hollows and layered ridges. Her wobbling triceps, Trudy estimated, were as big as her own thighs.

"Okay, so I'm real basic," Rita repeated, looking over the application, "and I'm just gonna ask you some super-basic stuff so I can get to know you a little." The head popped up. "Wanna cookie?" she said, reaching for a plate of them on a shelf.

"Yes, please," Trudy said without enthusiasm. She took a chocolate chip the size of a small pizza and as thick as her thumb.

"Hey, you gotta loosen up, honey!" Rita laughed suddenly. "Just think of this as the funnest job interview you ever had."

"I'll try," Trudy said, and tried to work up a laugh. "It's just that, y'see, ah…" She put her head down.

"That's okay, you can tell me." Rita might have been her mother.

"I, ah, I had a little trouble this morning."

"Oh my god! Did some male commit harassment on you?"

Trudy nodded into her lap. That was better than anything she could think up. "On the bus."

"Were you touched?"

"*Touched?* No, I was pretty mad."

This didn't register on Rita. "I mean, did he do physical contact?"

"Yeah, you know…the usual stuff."

"Did you notify the police?"

"Oh no. It was just a few seconds. He was getting off the bus. I couldn't even describe him."

Rita reached for her desk phone. "That doesn't matter. The bus has security on it. These incidents must be reported. If you say someone committed unwanted physical intimacy on you, the police can take the guy down."

It took Trudy a great effort to convince Rita that she would rather not report it.

"All right, okay. I respect that," she said with obvious disappointment, putting down the phone. "All right, let's do our interview. You just take your time and give me your answers." Then she leaned to one side and took from somewhere in the middle of a tower of stacked trays, a sheet of paper encased in a smudgy transparent-plastic folder. At its top was a Mad About Coffee logo. "Okay, Helen, just real basic now." She read: "Do you consider yourself a personal-relationship-orientated-type person? If so, how much?"

5 **AUGUST 27**
Paul waited till the waitress had deposited a new supply of alcohol and popcorn on our table. "So how do you know about the Helsinki lady?"

"Miss Helsinki seems to have been some kind of bait – see how crooked you are. Someone in the group called Jack doesn't trust a man who doesn't cheat on his wife. For the longest time, Ian couldn't trace who this was. But finally, by comparing computer servers, cell phone receiving towers, hotel records, credit-card records and the Good Lord knows what else, he got it: Jack Mirage."

"The financier?"

"The very same. And when he's not sinking someone's currency or bankrupting a government, he's quite the playboy himself. The trouble is, you aren't. And it bothers him when someone else doesn't share his sense of sin, sounds like. Bloody Christ, man, what the bloody hell gets into the rich?"

"They're not like you and me, as Scott Fitzgerald said." Paul raised his glass. "God save us from the curse of wealth, Max."

"Hear the good gentleman!" We clinked our glasses together.

"So the lady at the bar that's following me is probably sent by this group," he said. "But not sent to pick me up, surely."

"Trying to see if you're up to something with someone more interesting than me."

"Useless exercise, though: they surely have my phone watched and knew where I was going."

"Oldest trick in the book, old man," I said dismissively. "You have a friend call you at a certain time on a certain day, the listeners think you're going to go bowling with him, and you leave your phone with him and slip away for an hour of carnality."

"Ah. Point taken. MI6 seems to make for dirty minds."

"Indeed. The odd thing is that Senator Crick is defending you. For whatever reason, she wants you in. She says and I quote, 'Jack thinks a little too much with that damn sausage of his.'"

Paul laughed. "That sounds like the good senator."

"You know her?"

"From a couple of meetings. A ripsaw made human."

"According to Ian, she holds out hope that you'll have a liaison with someone – more to satisfy Mirage than anything else."

"But why me?"

"From what I can tell, it's due to your machinations in Quito."

Paul shook his head. "I heard on the grapevine that's why I was promoted to Washington. My god, that little caper's turned out to be the best thing for my career that I ever did," Paul said.

Let me explain briefly. When Paul was at his last diplomatic posting, in Quito, Ecuador, he was ordered by the ambassador himself to defeat a national strike that looked to improve conditions and pay for field workers on banana plantations. And indeed he put together a plan and threw himself into it – held some 200 meetings in Washington among a dozen different departments. He never liked the operation, however, and so looked on with complacency when the CIA head-of-station took it over and made a hash of it. He even managed to pin the full blame for the debacle on the head-of-station.

"It was indeed, old man. And that is just what the Doers want: a man without scruples when it comes to furthering the aims of his country."

"Sounds like I'm better off without them," Paul said, taking a handful of popcorn.

"You might well be. But there's the rub, old man. I need –"

A shout from the bar distracted them: "We bring back the draft, and in two years we'll have a fighting force that'll kick China's ass back to kingdom come!" one declared.

"Damn right, sir!"

"How simple it is to be a soldier," I murmured, turning awkwardly and watching them. "Just follow orders, blow the other bloke to kingdom come, and call it serving the country."

"I can't stand them," Paul admitted quietly. "The swagger, the arrogant certainty, the bloated budgets – they have way too much money for their own good."

We both sat back in the booth for some time without speaking. My right index finger flicked to one side and another. At the bar, the military officers began arm-wrestling. Paul's shadow lady was the judge, leaning down to see if the back of the hand really touched the bar.

"She should have left some time ago and been replaced," I observed, turning back. "Either she's poorly trained or working alone to save on expenses, which means she's private sector. I'll follow her when we leave."

Paul sipped his whiskey. "You were talking about the rub."

"A delicate matter, old fruit – delicate indeed," I said. "Dorothy Crick and the Doers are the only connection, after my years of searching, that I have been able to make to Rainmaker."

"And they want me in the group."

"They do."

"And if I were, it might give me the chance of helping you find him."

"That is it in a nutshell, yes. And depending on what the Doers actually do, you might make a decent run of it. They sound like a powerful group. And this Rainmaker – Ian can't touch him. All of that legwork on Jack Mirage? It didn't work on Rainmaker. Not even a tinkle. Ian can't get a line on him anywhere."

A roar went up from the military men as one of them won the match. Paul rolled his eyes. "You'd think he'd saved a baby from a burning building."

"Indeed."

"So I'd better start accepting invitations from strange women?"

"No, not really. But I have a little scheme in mind: we might sit down with the next Miss Helsinki they send – me as a state-security type and you as you – and suggest in rather heavy terms that she's a foreign spy. Might be good fun."

"And we might get some useful information."

A waitress passed by and I asked her for the check.

"More to the point, old fruit: it would be a simple way of getting Jack Mirage to accept you. If he thinks you're resisting temptation because these women might be honey traps, he might make an exception in your case."

"And allow me to enter this group."

"Precisely. From there it's a short hop to Rainmaker."

Another long silence filled with popcorn and suds. Silence is also a conversation, as Buddhists say, and I value my silences with Paul as much as the words. "Max, just one thing. I'm happy to help you find this Rainmaker guy, but…but not for you to take revenge, understand? That's out. Once you find him, what? Because to be honest, this obsession of yours has never seemed to me all that healthy."

"Good point, good point, old fruit. It *is* a splinter in my finger – but you've never sat through torture and watched the fellow directing the fun sip a piña colada." I drank more Guinness and let it work in me. "Actually, it would depend on the circumstances, but mainly what I'd just like to do is show up in front of him, give him a good shock – because half the shock is just the knowledge that five seconds before that I could easily have turned him into apple sauce. The other half is that I know who he is. And if I do, so most likely do others. He's blown."

"That's all? Blow his cover?" Paul asked skeptically.

I needed patience. "Paul, old fruit, you don't know what cover is to a man like that. It's their meat and drink. It's their platform up above the common herd. I present myself before his dropped jaw, show him I've tracked him across the world to this patch of ground, without even the help of 6? His world will crumble around him, oh yes."

Paul shrugged. "High-up guys love to brag about their clearance, that's for sure."

"As to what I'd really like to *say* to him, just something a bit… cheerful: 'Don't worry, old fellow. You see, I did come out all right, after your fellows beat the living shit out of me.' Call it frog-marching him down Memory Lane."

Paul opened that lovely smile of his. "All right, sounds good – healthy."

We finished our drinks. "We'll talk another day, old man. Head for home, and I'll take a bearing on your shadow. And by the way, if you could do something, say, something bureaucratically dirty – take credit for someone's work, get someone fired or transferred to the bloody Bureau of Weights and Measures – I bet that would do something for your reputation with the Doers. They seem to appreciate venality."

6
FIVE YEARS EARLIER
My injuries and the little score I had to settle with Rainmaker – this being before I heard from Paul that he carried the grander title "*The* Rainmaker" – form a small but essential part of my story, and deserve a brief explanation. Besides, I do enjoy the telling: it's the only James Bond-worthy thing I ever did in all my time as a spy.

Let's go back to a simpler day and time: my body trim and whole, my face shaven. The scene was a discreet CIA office in Manhattan whose sign outside read something like "Mucka-wucka and Sons, Accountants."

"Other ancillary branches of the Yucatán Group, such as South Mérida labs, Cancún chemical wholesalers and Campeche distributors, are mid-level priorities that on an immediate basis must go back-burner to our Priority-Level-Four operation," droned an incoherent CIA lady, "which must be kept on focus for ongoing projects in other theaters."

I kept my bureaucrat's menthol demeanor intact, though I nearly jumped out of my chair. Cancún wholesalers? Nobody was supposed to know about them because that was *my* bloody network – ten strong – and I had not told anyone; it was completely "dark," as they say in the trade: no e-contact at all. Everything was verbal or written. I'd insisted on a complete blackout because my people were in sensitive positions and truly indispensable. You can't turn coca paste into sniffable stuff without chemicals, and my most important agent kept me informed about who was buying them in northern and eastern Mexico and how much; and because nobody buys anything direct but through cut-outs, other agents told me where the liquids actually went; yet others told me about the money transfers for all of this. It had taken me three years to develop the network, and my request for exclusivity on running it had been respected because it had supplied solid intel for just short of two years; it had resulted in one major and three minor shipments being snatched *and* destroyed still in Mexico.

I'd had a feeling that the Cousins were dogging my tracks: several weeks earlier, a bored Chinese-American fellow in the back row who had attended my Miami lecture on the Yoruba culture of Cuba (my cover back then) had shown up a month later on my flight to Mexico City.

And now the droning CIA lady – Carol Unger, according to the probably false i.d. hung around her veined neck – was saying that she needed the i.d.'s of *my* agents in particular because they wished to "reconfigure the network as a whole" in order to better service their new agent, who was a "Priority Level Four." She said all this with the tranquility of one asking for directions to the nearest petrol station. Needless to say, I said no – just a slate-black monosyllabic no. I would not turn over sources. At best, I could close down the network, given a week or so; some of my agents were harder to contact than others.

"I'm afraid that won't do, Max. Our Level Four is afraid that they would continue activities on their own and hurt his effectiveness."

"I believe that what you mean, Carol, is that your bloody Level Four is also doing some dirty work for you, and my agents might hear about it." I neglected to add that I had already caught a few scents in the wind myself.

"That question goes above my pay grade, so I'm going to have to tell you that I cannot answer that." (An irritating habit of Americans is that, to give you bad news, they put as many verbs in it as they can: *I'm going to have to tell you that...*)

But I was right – as I learnt from a 6 colleague some years later.

For it would turn out that amongst those sucking up the cocaine money was a Mexican real estate mogul who worked for the American Cousins. He was sending delectable paychecks to Syrian Turks fighting the Assad regime – the so-called, "ongoing projects in other theaters." He did this because the American Congress refused to fund them, the Syrian Turks being cousins, brothers, in-laws, friends, drinking buddies if not one-and-the-same with the local al Qaeda branch, and plenty of toys already sent to the brave Syrian Turks had been turned on Yanks in other "theaters," by which the Yanks mean "places." But the Cousins, always bleeding hearts where a decent militia is involved, had taken it upon themselves to make up the shortfall, tapping the mogul. The trouble was that my network, destroying cocaine by the ton, was cutting down his cash flow. Hence the need to "back-burner" our work; that is, scotch it completely and make sure that those who knew too much met their Maker.

(This sublime financing, incidentally, ended rather spectacularly after about eighteen months: the mogul had on retainer a local crew who did strong-arm jobs for him – for example, when someone didn't pay their monthly rent – who turned their arts on the mogul when he himself became too casual about meeting the payroll.)

"Besides, Max," Carol went on, "they're just paid agents. They know the risks."

I needed a moment to control my anger and reflected on how Carol had spread her lipstick too high onto her thin upper lip to make it appear bigger. "Carol, old love, paid or not, mercenary their aims or not, *nobody* deserves to be double-crossed. That is not in the contract, not even in the small print. It's bad enough our cutting out on them. How would you like the Company to stop *your* paychecks?"

"They have their normal jobs too!"

"Whose pay they find inadequate. Which is why they take risks for us. My point stands."

In this, I am happy to add, I was supported by my fellow agent-runners in the room.

Carol, with professional superiority: "I'm sorry, Max, but this is Priority Level *Four*. The next level we're talking about WMD and nuclear emergencies. I mean, people run risks for big money, and sometimes it doesn't work out."

"Bloody easy to say in an air-conditioned room with little bottles of mineral water lined up on the table, oh yes. Do you have any idea what would happen to my people if they were found out? Think blow torches, Carol. Think cables and grip hoists. The bloody Inquisition has nothing on what those crackheads do when they want to make a point about *chivatos*. And let's remember –"

"Don't you dare lecture me! I've run agents in Cairo, Beirut and Talinn."

"And how many of them did you burn, Carol? More than ten? Less?"

"Well, if I did, I have to live with that *every day of my life!* Operational necessities take precedence!" She was shouting now, the hypocrite fully on display. "Or do I have to go to your supervisor?"

"You can go to the bloody queen if you don't forget to curtsey. Your people agreed that my network is dark, dark for good reason, and this is exactly why. I will shut it down for you, and I will warn my people of extreme danger if they deal with anyone else. And I will throw in the lie that the heat will eventually die down and I will return in some months – thus holding out the prospect of future paychecks. That is all I can offer and it is bloody well good enough for your bloody Level Four."

Well, there was more arguing, not worth typing out. I made my excuses, left at the coffee break, and flew direct to Cancún to tell my agents to go to ground; they knew the drill because I rehearsed it with them every time we met. Unfortunately, I was kidnapped in Cancún, two blocks from one of my agents; I'd had the good sense to park some ways from his house.

The three kidnappers wished to know – wait for it – the names and locations of my agents; I declined to answer, or at least answer truthfully. Over two days, sundry methods of torture were performed on me with an amateur's skill and a maniac's verve. I've already mentioned my present ailments; to them I only need specify that my right knee was ruined when it was prodded into bending in the same direction as my elbows. To delay further exercises, I agreed to look at photos of people and identify my agents. For this, I was hooded, tied up with inch-wide zip-ties that would have subdued African gorillas, and taken to a large house in an elegant neighborhood of Cancún – folded up in the trunk, by the way, which added to my knee's woes. I was loaded from the trunk onto a rolling office chair and, once unhooded, sat squinting into a laptop computer set on a broad kind of workshop table. I managed to work my damaged leg onto stabilizing bars running diagonally between the legs across its center, though my ankle laid atop a sharp run of rusted burrs in the welding. But my ankle bravely bore the pain for my knee.

Two of my captors were Mexicans with their clipped Spanish accent, and the other, their leader, an Argentine whose Spanish had the bounce and swing of Italian. He also spoke a rough-hewn English, which he used with me, though I would have understood his Spanish better.

This latter fellow was called "Hano" by the Mexicans; good enough for them, good enough for us.

Hano showed me photos, most fairly grainy and taken from a distance, on the laptop. Some were my people, some not. My strategy was simple. I had to give them some agents, for they had already i.d.'d about six. Those that I could contact quickly, I said yes. Those whose line of contact was dodgier, I said no. For I was going to escape from these buggers, oh yes. Already I had let go of a half-dozen plans. They had but to put me back in that trunk, and that was the last they would hear of me. I had nearly escaped when they pulled into the garage.

On and on. Once I said yes to a man I didn't recognize, and they merely noted it. Another time Hano swatted my already-torn cheek and said, wiping the blood off his hand, "But he is a mechanic of cars, little pig! You need we give you more teach about the true and the lies?" He was a born torturer, Hano: narrow eyes, flaxen buzz-cut, hands like bricks, the brown squint so deep between his colorless eyebrows it could have held a penny.

And then, into this drama, a dozen soft steps came down from behind and a man in a flat Midwestern accent announced dinner.

Hano grunted and turned around. He groused at his two cronies, who jerked the chair out from under me – I fell on my zip-tied hands – and kicked me under the table. I caught a glimpse of the Midwesterner going up the steps and could have sworn I was looking at the back of a priest dressed in a black habit. In a moment, they had all disappeared up the steps, through a sort of broad cut in the cement wall that led up to a heavy door, which they opened and closed hastily – or guiltily: not everyone in the house knew what was going on here.

I rested, groaning on my side, for perhaps two seconds, then I got to work. With some effort and much pain, I hoisted myself up to lie on the bars that I had rested my leg on. I found the sharp series of burrs and, all my weight pressing down on them, rubbed the thick zip-tie on them. With a puzzled pop, it parted. Seeing nothing better around me, I did the same with the tie on my ankles. My knee decried the injustice, and the process took longer, but finally the tie gave in.

I dragged myself out from under the desk and stood up on my good leg. I was in some type of basement room. It was only four or five steps wide, but quite long – probably running the width of the house. A collection of wood-framed paintings leaned against a wall, a thick curtain rod stood beside them. There was a pile of rolled-up rugs, a Cancún soccer-team flag to carry to games, and an old wheezing shoulder-high refrigerator. A Ping-pong table occupied the far end, and it must have been used often because nothing lay atop it except a pair of racquets, one set diagonally on a ball. Now and then I felt a judder, not quite amounting to a sound, of cars passing, somewhere above and nearby.

First I needed a crutch, and the only thing that would do was the curtain rod. It was a thick wooden thing about as tall as me, and I steadied myself with it. Fine and well, but as a weapon with which to take on four men, it was lacking. I could break it in two, use the tines, but that would be noisy. Damn it all. I had gone through weapons training and learnt that nearly anything could be used to cut, gash, stun – but here my options were practically nil. I opened the refrigerator: bottles of white wine and beer.

Cursing, I was considering wrapping myself in one of the rugs and giving the illusion of having escaped, when footsteps approached the door up the stairs. I clumped to the wall beside it just in time before it opened.

"Rainmaker, you want any beer too?" called Hano. "Rainmaker" – Hano had spoken to him by phone often – had turned up my lies about agents the previous day, and was clearly the employer of the three strong-arm boys. By the way, my hacking friend Ian later traced the house itself to its owner: the Bureau of Industry and Security, the intel arm of the U.S. Commerce Department. Sod them as well.

"Just white wine, if you have it, Hano, thank you," called the thick Midwestern voice. "No red, please – gives me headaches."

I considered shouting, but that would have been for naught: there were no honest cops about – at best some maid or cook whom I would only turn into someone who "knew too much."

Hano shut the door – I heard the pert click of the bolt – and started down. I felt a nudge at my leg and looked down: the little soccer-team flag. I released the curtain rod, letting it fall with a plop on the rolled-up rugs.

"How you doin', Maxie?" Hano sang. "You cohmfor-table here?"

I snatched the soccer-team flag and raised it, ready to bring it down on his head. But the aluminum shaft was only two feet long and had no weight – none at all. The footsteps clopped downwards, like the ticking of a clock. I reversed my grip and put the palm of one hand behind the flag-end of the shaft, the other gripping it with one finger curled over the top as if the pole were a billiard cue. The refrigerator was directly in front of the stairway, but I had been lying to the same side of the stairway that I was now standing on. I knew Hano would look that way.

"Hey, you must to be hohn-gry. If I get some leftovers, you wanna –"

As his face cleared the corner, I drove the flagpole through his near eye. It traversed his brain diagonally and must have pierced the brain stem; it killed him cold. He fell backward against the corner of the stairway wall, and from there he slid down onto the lowest step, legs crumpling under him. Arms flat behind him, his torso tipped gently forward over his legs till the end of the pole touched the floor between his knees, turning his head sideways as if in question.

Satisfying. But now what? I still needed a weapon.

I searched the man – he wore a fanny pack on his hip – hoping for a gun, but found only my wallet, my mobile phone, his mobile, and, in the button-down pocket of his shirt, my passport. I stuffed them in my pockets, looking wildly around. How long would it be before someone came looking for him? Not more than a minute.

Then my eye fell on a door at the Ping-pong end of the room. I grabbed the desk chair and sat in it and rolled myself backward with my good leg. I hoped to find a bathroom or tool-filled closet, but the door opened on a garage with a black BMW parked in it. What a goddamn bloody fool I was. This was the car I had arrived in and from which I had been *wheeled* into the house on the desk chair!

I rolled backward to it, checked the driver side: no keys. But leaning against the wall as sweetly as a street hooker was a wooden shovel handle that reached to my waist. I grabbed it and, using it as a cane, walked up the slight ramp to the normal-sized door beside the broad garage door. To my relief, the normal door opened, and I stepped out onto a dark narrow lawn that ran between the house and the twenty-foot-high wall that bordered the street. Ivy covered much of it; bits of broken glass like a city skyline shone at the top. The sliding door for the garage entrance was closed, of course, and I clumped along over the grass towards the center of the house, where a scraggly light spilled in through the narrow front gate in the wall. It would be locked, but there was usually a button hidden in the ivy beside it that opened the door.

"Buenas noches, señor," said a polite guard, stepping down from the front porch. His arms cradled a shotgun that was nearly as long as he was short. In the dark, I could see only his silhouette, the long gleam of the rifle barrel, and the outline of gold in one of his front teeth.

I replied with the same, and with Essex urbanity remarked that the night was a little cool.

"It's freezing," the man complained.

Behind him, through the living-room window, I could see the dining table: the two Mexicans and, clearly, Rainmaker dressed as a priest. They sat with their heads bowed, as if in prayer. Indeed, it was a prayer: now all three raised their heads, and Rainmaker crossed himself with that spare tracing and kiss of the finger that denote a true Catholic. And for the life of me, he did it just like the priest he was dressed as. Salt-and-pepper hair, rectangular chinless face, deep-set eyes that looked like little black seeds.

So you're the one, I told him silently. *I will see to you, my friend. I have your contact's cell phone, and he called you with it, and it's amazing what the right people can do with information like that.*

One of the Mexicans, hooking his arm on the back of the chair, yelled towards the room I had just left. A maid in light-blue uniform came out of a doorway and began picking up trays of appetizers and replacing them with bowls. Another maid ladled soup into the bowls. It seemed that my escape had lasted as long as the entrée.

"Why are you leaving the house through the garage?" the guard inquired.

"I got lost!" I chuckled. "What a big house!"

"Caramba! It's true. I still get lost when I enter. My master has an enormous house," he added proudly. "Where are you going now, sir? You will not stay for dinner? My wife is an excellent cook."

"Yes, it's a pity," I said, knowing the importance of small talk in Latin America. "I'm afraid that I have to go to the airport."

"Would you like me to call you a taxi, sir?" the man said eagerly, already reaching into his pocket. I had hardly answered when the man snapped into his mobile phone, "Chanchi, mándame uno *ya!"*

And Chanchi was a resourceful fellow, for I had scarcely stepped onto the sidewalk when a taxi came tearing around the corner. I took a last look through the front window and saw one of the Mexicans throw his napkin on the table and stalk off towards the basement door.

Awkwardly with one hand, I managed to thumb a bill out of my wallet and held it out to the kind guard.

"Oh no, sir, I cannot accept that. It has been an honor to help a gentleman like you." He opened the door of the taxi, helped me in, handed me, with muffled amazement, my "cane," and, making sure that though I stretched myself out somewhat on the back seat my feet were inside, cautiously closed the door. There's nothing like the Latin sense of honor.

The driver, too, drove loyally and asked no questions, though puzzled by my orders, and after a hour of dashing around town scratching the sides of mailboxes with his car keys, breaking off low-hanging branches of avocado trees, and stuffing the requisite three plastic bags into chain-link fences – all go-to-ground signals to my crew – he took me near to my safe house, to which I limped the last block with the help of my shovel handle. Another 6 agent picked me up there, and after a circuitous route we arrived at a beach, where a Pemex helicopter from a platform wafted me to a Danish naval frigate on a goodwill visit to the Caribbean – or so I'm told; I had passed out on the beach – and I started my years of "recovery," for lack of a better term.

Of the eleven principal agents in my network, only two were caught – executed, of course – and I have some reason to believe that they had been blown to the Yanks already. But the punchline of my story is that Carol Unger in the CIA flesh, flowers in hand and training-manual smile on her overpainted lips, showed up six weeks later at my Chelsea bedside, and after the requisite concern and cooing, asked me where the rest of my agents might be found.

"I mean, we have their names, Max, it's just a question of saving us some trouble," she said, which I knew to be a lie; the names were in my head and had not left it.

I threw her bloody flowers, still in the vase, after her as she hurried out the door, missing by a centimeter. Damn. I would have enjoyed hitting her as much as hitting Rainmaker.

7
NOVEMBER 9 (TUESDAY)
With the solemnity of the Queen knighting one of her sub-jects, Rita gave Trudy her official Mad About Coffee polo shirt and baseball cap, tears in her eyes.

Trudy put on the magenta-colored garments and started her job-training. She wore a clip-on i.d. with "Helen" in fat capitals, and received some hairpins to keep her hair up, which was the company rule. She quickly learnt how to make the three most-ordered types of coffee – Cam the barista made the exotic ones – how to handle charge cards or cash, where to get more coffee beans. It was a relief to forget she was a fugitive, and she found herself trying to believe that the morning had never happened. "This is my new job, not Hallerbee – that's all," she said into the mirror, taking a break after the post-lunch rush.

Just before three, a man in a windbreaker came in, moving dis-tractedly towards the counter and eyeing the seated customers as if he were going to buy one. His head swung in alert jerks like a bird's. At the counter Trudy stood on a stout plastic pallet; it gave her an extra few inches of height. Cam was across the room, flirting as usu-al, this time with a couple of Japanese girls. Apparently speaking from experience, he had told her that foreign women on vacation were all looking for sex.

"Hi, how are you doing today, sir?" she chirped. Rita had been very firm about the idea that customers were to be greeted warm-ly: "We want to display right from our initial contact that we care about them as a human being," she had declared. Trudy resisted the temptation to make sure her hair was tucked up tight – she had been checking it every ten minutes – but did push her glasses back on her nose.

"Uh, fine…uh, thank you, ma'am," said the man, still looking at the customers. His gaze fixed on a tall, chunky blond woman who a minute earlier had ordered an XL café latté in an accent so heavy Trudy had asked her to repeat herself. A little ashamedly, he pulled back one side of his jacket, and Trudy spotted a police badge hooked on his belt. "It's real, y'know," the man added, though his blush said otherwise. He had military-short hair and a broad neck thick as a tree stump. He showed Trudy the picture of herself – without glass-es, her hair down – that had been taken during her Hallerbee job interview. "NYPD. We're looking for this woman. Had a possible i.d. a block away from here. Other cameras around here seem to be ITD'd. Pretty short – five-one, five-two. Long, blond hair. ETA was twelve-twenty-seven. You haven't seen her, have you, ma'am?"

Trudy brought her wet palms together. They knew she had been in the area. "Yeah, I think she ordered a latté and a cookie."

"And paid in cash, right?" asked the man.

Trudy thought of lowering her head in thought, bringing the visor down, but thought the better of it. "Ah. Yeah. Yeah, she paid in cash. Oh! And she bought a cap."

The man's head moved so sharply to her that Trudy nearly flinched.

"Like yours?"

"Yeah."

"Figures." He snatched out his cell phone. "Hey, that a back entrance?" he asked, jerking his head towards the hallway as he punched the screen.

"Yeah. Straight down that hallway past the restrooms. The last door." Trudy had already taken out a couple trash liners full of used coffee cups.

"Shit. *That's* why we don't have a viz. of her down the street," the man moaned. "Pardon my French, ma'am."

"That's okay."

But the man was already away, talking on his phone. "Yeah, I got a lead on her. She's wearing a pink-purple cap with a visor. Probable continue on… lemme get outta here…."

Trudy heard the clank of the heavy push-bar and edged out from behind the counter. Without any quick move that would alert people, she slipped down the hallway, past Rita's office and the restrooms, and punched in the code behind the false plant that stopped the door alarm from going off: it allowed just five seconds for this. Just before the door swung shut, she glimpsed the man talking on his phone and walking with jerky, crooked steps, nervous head jerking back and forth, checking one side and the other of the alleyway amidst the garbage cans and papers. He stumbled over an overturned baby carriage – "Shit!" – and gave it a savage kick that sent it cartwheeling down the alley.

8

AUGUST 30

Paul was looking for an opportunity, and it did not take long for one to present itself to that acute mind of his.

Something bureaucratically naughty.

The Monday morning after our Friday pub-pisser, Paul stopped at the entrance to the baleful black-windowed State Department Annex 3 Office Building, fifteen miles out of Washington in Virginia, which Paul said looked like "a place where an upstart shoe company rents space." It was already seven years "temporary" housing for nearly three hundred State staffers – and one floor of Veterans Affairs – most of them relegated to the drearier aspects of international relations, such as selling handheld grenade launchers to African generals, searching for errant husbands in Bora Bora, or ensuring the delivery of printer toner to embassies and consulates in Micronesia. A little crowd was staring far down the parking lot at a police line. Three members of an Afro-American gang had been gunned down by a Chinese one, and the scene was snowy from the packages of white powder the former group had been carrying.

Bureaucratically naughty, I'd told him. Paul took out his cell phone and called Parker Radow, the secretary of state's chief of staff. A quick stab in the back to his boss, Under Secretary of State for Political Affairs Trig Purtly, would certainly do the trick.

"Paul. *Hey.* How's it going?" Radow called in that pandering lapdog voice of his. "How you settling in over there? Goddammit, we've just got to get you in for some facetime one of these days." He had said that ever since the first day of the administration in January. Paul had tried three or four times to get meetings with Radow and only once managed to get one, but never with the secretary of state. Radow was the classic servant of power: bootlick or attack dog as the situation merited. Paul could imagine his thousand-watt smile jumping to attention and then fading.

"I'm good, Parker, thank you. Parker, just one quick thing. I heard on the grapevine that the secretary was complaining that Trig Purtly still hasn't written some essay for *Foreign Affairs* explaining the admin's new emphasis on diplomacy rather than war. I guess *FA* is kicking down his door because their publishing deadline is pressing."

"End of this week!" Radow exclaimed. "Which is the second deadline after the end of *last* week!"

"Well, I've been thinking that if the secretary wants, I have just the thing: a speech I wrote for the ambassador in Ecuador. If he'd like, I can retrofit it to make all the points of the new admin and have it in his mailbox this evening. For attribution to him, of course, not me."

"You're going to cut out your boss?" Radow gasped. Something about him always reminded Paul of a breathless teenage kid.

"I'm trying to serve the secretary. But if it teaches Trig a lesson about how to work in government, so much the better."

"Too true!" Paul knew that Radow, a Yale man who was very proud of being a Yale man, disdained Purtly as much as Paul did. Purtly was a vulgar oilman who had come to Washington as part of the president's Colorado Gang. Secretary of State Carlton Mason, though more Texan than Coloradan, had been given State over Purtly, and it was no secret that the department was too big for both of them.

"If he accepted the task, it should be executed on time."

"Copy that, copy that. Well! All right, Paul – I'm getting the idea here. Okay, I'll tell him. Now I can't guarantee he's going to say yes. I'm not *guaranteeing* that now."

Sighing, Paul looked heavenwards. That was another feature of Radow's: he couldn't *guarantee* anything. He would probably refuse to guarantee that he had ever driven a car.

"I understand, Parker. Just put the suggestion under the secretary's nose ASAP and let me know if it turns blue or pink."

Silence, then a giggle. "Oh yeah – like a prego test! Right! Turns blue or pink. I'll have to remember that one! Look, I'll see the secretary in about an hour between meetings, and I'll put it to him."

Paul had been thinking of a *litmus* test, but it didn't matter. He had a feeling he would get the green light from Secretary Mason.

9 **NOVEMBER 9 (TUESDAY)**
Trudy's shift at the coffee shop ended at five-thirty. Now she needed to go to a party, find a man and go to a hotel with him. She hated parties. She had no idea how to seduce a man. She looked so dismally at her timecard as Rita was showing her how to punch it that Rita asked, "Still thinkin' about that intimate physical harassment this mornin', huh? I *still* say you oughta make a complaint."

She had heard Cam talking on his phone to someone about going to a party and asked if she could go along. "Hey, sure, more the merrier." A wink. "My friend Tommy? He *will crawl all over you* – and there's nothing like the smell of coffee shop to bring out the native beast."

"Great," Trudy said without enthusiasm, then blurted, "Sure they won't mind?"

"Get lost! There'll be forty people there. What – you think they're gonna count?"

The party was to celebrate the success of one Tom Geske, who was some type of logistics manager just promoted in his company to inter-state or international or perhaps intergalactic level; Trudy heard conflicting stories among the vast number of guests, far more than forty. In another life, the building had been a warehouse, and the second-floor apartment looked like the studio set of a television sitcom, with walls that reached barely halfway to the distant ceiling. The dark living-dining room was lit by a single pink-colored bulb the size of a basketball. The only decoration was a huge black-and-white photograph of an arm: a dark-skinned arm, probably a woman's, from just beyond the shoulder to just before the wrist, stretching the length of the sofa it hung over. It gave Trudy the creeps. An open kitchen occupied the center of the floor, and a gap in one of its walls led back to a shadowy warren of rooms. People struggled in and out past each other like ants through their nest's opening. Somewhere a toilet flushed incessantly.

Cam had taken her only as far as the street door of the building, for by phone in the cab he had learnt that the Japanese women had accepted his invitation to a "real New Yorker's tour" of the city; Cam had neglected to tell them he had come from Maine two years earlier. She had expected to feel miserably self-conscious, but to her surprise, after a nervous day of dodging death and men carrying false badges, she felt oddly grateful to these people – she was just one more in the crowd – and with the help of some wine talked volubly to everyone. Hardly anyone mentioned the attack in Jersey City, which was good; her face had begun to show up on television. She gave out a false phone number to at least five men – they gallantly brought her drinks – and, more importantly, some of the sandwiches that overflowed the dining table. She had eaten nothing but cinnamon rolls all day. Half of the crowd were workmates and friends of this Tom – whom Trudy never met – and half of a contingent far older. This puzzled Trudy until she heard that Tom's father, who had opened the door to her, had invited his own friends as well from Columbia University.

After some forty-five minutes, a woman of about Trudy's age turned her back on a tiresome Humanities professor and said very quietly in some kind of East Coast accent, "Don't leave me, okay? Just talk to me and stay very close so no one else can get in between because this is really getting shitty. I'm Bettina."

"I'm, ah, Helen. Well, why don't you leave?"

"Because the dumbshit I came with, who in theory – *in theory* – is still supposed to be my BF, is playing poker in the back room and I can't get him out."

"*Really?* Playing poker? Texas Hold 'em?"

"Whatever it is, just talk to me because this is getting pretty ridiculous." She swung her glass at the room to indicate what "this" was.

"Gosh, why do you say that?" Trudy asked. "I'm having a pretty nice time." A head shorter, she had to tilt her head back to see her because Bettina was standing so close. All Trudy could see was a big nose with glasses as heavy as an oxen yoke sitting across it.

"Don't you see what's going on? Tom's father got this whole thing together so that he and his gray-haired friends could troll the younger people for sex. It's getting pretty outrageous."

Trudy nearly replied, "I thought they were just being nice," but managed to swallow it. Instead, she said, "I didn't think they were very serious."

"You didn't actually promise to go home with anyone, did you?" Bettina accused her.

Trudy had given promises to three men, but mainly in case one of the younger guys didn't work out, which in her life was usually the case. "No, or at least it was all kind of joking," she said lamely. "You don't think anyone took it seriously, do you?"

"Hah! Try getting your coat and walking to the door, and see how far you get," snapped Bettina.

"What – they wouldn't let me out?"

"Not without you choosing your cab partner." She pointed – rudely, in Trudy's book. "See that bald guy in the beard over there? He's a lit professor-cum-actor. He had a supporting role in some god-forsaken movie with Dustin Hoffman in the 90s, and he thinks that makes him God's gift."

Trudy had talked to him. He was from New Zealand and had promised Trudy free tickets to a play and said that after the party they could have a drink somewhere quiet. Trudy liked his accent. He pronounced "had" as "head."

"Yeah, I think his name's Peter. Someone introduced us."

"That all?" Bettina said suspiciously.

"Well, I'm pretty short, you know. Guys don't go for me much."

"To these geezers? Hah! They couldn't care less if you're a *midget*." Bettina looked more closely at her, and Trudy shrank. "You don't go to many parties, do you?"

"Not really, you know. I'm kind of new in town anyway."

Across the room, a woman shrieked, *"No!* Get it? Turn up your hearing aid, okay? I said no. No, as in 'You're old enough to be my fucking father.' Now lay the fuck off."

The crowd babble turned to whisper.

"Yeah, what is it around here?" said a young man's voice. "I'm like, hey, did I walk into the wrong apartment? I'm not into post-meno-pausals, okay? Does everybody get the message?"

Tom Sr. tried to calm the situation: "All right, I think a few people need to get their act back in perspective."

"Their 'acts,' Tom," said the English lit prof. "We are not perform-ing a collective act."

"Collective *or* private," barked another young woman.

Tom Sr. marshaled a false laugh, and the party was over.

"C'mon, help me get my BF – so I can break up with him," said Bettina, pulling Trudy across the room.

They went through the gap in the wall – between the sink and dishwasher – and the apartment seemed to wind for miles through narrow hallways against a tide of people, most of them trying to get their coats and leave, till they finally arrived at a quiet room with six men sitting around a card game: three younger, three older. It was indeed, Trudy recognized, Texas Hold 'em: two cards in the hand and three more face-up on the table. In the center of the table there was a small pile of money: ones, fives, tens and twenties.

Bettina walked around to a guy wearing a tie and grabbed him by it.

"Kevin, we're going. Party's fucked."

"I'm in the middle of a hand!"

Bettina jerked him up off the chair. "We are *going!*"

Kevin tried to grab back his money. "I got fifteen bucks in that pot!"

"I'll play for you," Trudy blurted, sitting down in his chair.

"See? Helen's going to play for you." She pulled the man away.

"Helen, if you win, ten bucks are mine, and you can keep five. Remember that! Bettina! For God's sake! *Ow!*"

The men at the table laughed. One of them snatched a ten-dollar bill from the pot and stuffed it in his pocket. "Go spend it on condoms with Caroline."

"Who's Caroline?" Bettina demanded.

"Too bad," said the guy on Trudy's left. "Guy was a total fish. Must've dropped fifty bucks already."

"I was going to order in a pizza on his money," said another.

"Helen – *Helen,* right? – you know how to play this?" said another.

"Yeah, I used to play all the time with my brothers." She was amazed at her own fluency – she had but one brother, long estranged from the family and last heard to be working on some kind of back-to-nature farm in Oregon. But a euphoria was sweeping over her. Here at last was something she controlled. And for another hour, at least, she could be inside and warm and off the street – and they even gave her food. Then: "Um, darn. Just one thing: I don't have much, ah, much cash on me," she said guiltily, digging in her pocket. She found fifteen dollars.

Some of the men pitched in a few bucks, joking that they would win it back soon enough.

Trudy looked at her cards: two fours. Kevin had bet fifteen dollars on *that?* It was the classic mistake of the poker amateur: to bet any time he had a pair in his hand. Well, for the moment, there was nothing to do but make them think she was as bad as the previous guy.

"Helen? Ten bucks if you want to call."

Trudy tossed in money. "Call."

She got down to her last five dollars before bluffing her way back up to twenty, but by that time she had settled on her strategy for the table: "the conservative maniac." She played barely one hand in five, making her seem conservative, and then bluffed recklessly whenever the pot started to build. Two hours later, to the shock of the table, she walked out with three-quarters of the money – nearly two hundred fifty dollars – and with Roger, who had contributed most to her fortune. He was twenty years older, but the younger guys hadn't paid her much attention and, she figured, were probably hoping for someone taller to hit on. Besides, an older man was likely to be more malleable. The thought gave her a pang of guilt.

10

SEPTEMBER 3

It was a week after our "pissy Friday down the pub." Paul nursed a glass of heavily-iced whiskey as he drifted through the Georgetown crowd, observing the local fauna. African diplomats murmured stock-market advice to each other, reporters nodded excitedly while coal-industry lobbyists planted stories with them, Saudi diplomats frowned into their mint tea as Algerians cheerfully guzzled French wine, and young interns pretty as sparks glided around looking for futures of all types.

Paul was in his element here. He was that rarest of men whose work met his needs for harsh, prolonged mental exercise. He tore into policy journals, devoured history books, picked his way through the State Department like an Indian through the forest; every Tweet and work assignment held a hidden message. Little wonder that this Kansas City native had drifted into diplomacy. Even now, scanning the room over the rim of his one lukewarm whiskey, he noted the French political attaché handing a drink to a low-level Russian communications director. The party host, the German ambassador, was muttering to his wife and with obvious anger pointing at the *Asian Times* bureau chief. The Chinese third cultural attaché, like a small stuffed exhibit in a museum, stood alone dully watching the room. A Malaysian diplomat – a woman with her hair hidden under a bright-green cloth, the second economic secretary of her embassy – said hello to him, added a comment, and received a nod in return. End of exchange; she walked away. What did that mean?

It was history in action, as Paul had observed to me from time to time: movers, shakers, sparkling cuff links and clacking strings of semi-precious stones. Meanwhile, barely a half-mile from them, society's losers bustled through Dickensian alleys of desperation: girls sold bits of their youth to tumescent marketing executives and brought home dinner to their brothers and sisters; immigrant women settled down to an evening of cleaning offices; poverty-stricken teenagers worked the 4-to-11 shift at supermarkets and restaurants, to stagger home past midnight for a few hours of sleep, which they would catch up on during English and Math classes the next morning.

In five thousand years only the clothes have changed, Paul observed to me once. *We diplomats just try to keep the bowling ball rumbling towards the pins without it falling into the gutter.*

He had scarcely crossed the room to refresh his scotch among the discreet Hondurans pouring steadily at the drinks table, when the women pounced; they always did. Here was the new Mysterious Beauty – "Margo," she called herself – doing a sophistication shtick; Jack Mirage, it seemed, was still trying to figure out his taste in women. The woman in the Helsinki hotel bar had been red-haired and slinky. Two weeks later at a post-conference cocktail in New York she was curvy and air-headed ("Once I start, I can't stop till dawn!"). The last, in a Parisian bar, had an insistent air of sadism about her; she pointed out twice how she liked male waiters and male hotel receptionists who "azzist to my needs." And she would not take no for an answer until Paul ditched her – and the bar check – by going outside to take a phone call and then walking away.

But Margo had been cast as The Unconquerable: the kind you see modeling expensive jewelry. Mid-twenties, brown-blond hair done in a tight bun like Alfred Hitchcock's cool heroines; long cheeks, eyes an overcast gray, make-up as if there were no make-up, an immaculate gray business suit with a draping, clinging dark-pink blouse. She worked as a sales rep for a political-campaign services company, but was doing her doctoral thesis on – by incredible co-incidence – Ecuadoran congressional politics. She'd heard that Paul had been no less than chief political officer there and begged him for "guidance" on her thesis, which she promised would not take but an hour of his time. He gave the lass some credit: she was an im-provement on the bald blatancy of the others. To her delight, Paul acquiesced, said he had to talk to a few other people, and would meet her down at the front gate at six-thirty sharp.

Then Juanita Ramirez, called "La Deseada" on the Senate floor, loomed up under her mushroom cloud of black hair, saying that if State wanted her boss's vote on aid for El Salvador, Paul would have to "go through me" to get it.

"And I mean *you personally,* Paul. You know, I am *so* tired of dealing with staffers. You just cannot *imagine*," she said in her whiny Puerto Rican Spanish with the muddy consonants.

"Well, I'll do what I can," replied Paul smoothly in the same language. "But they order us deputy assistant undersecretaries around as if we were cleaning ladies. Disgusting."

"I said *only you*. Like the song: 'Only you-u-u-u-u,'" Juanita sang in English. "Besides, my senator is willing to bargain, and he gave me carte blanche. Name your price."

Paul took a thoughtful sip of his scotch and replied, "Juana, we are both concerned about the well-being of Salvadorans, and neither of us wants more of their seven-year-olds stumbling a thousand miles across Mexico to reach our borders. Your senator understands the stakes involved in giving aid to Salvador, and no *prices* need be named." And because Paul was a gentleman, he tacked on the following with a knowing smile: "The senator's offer, of course, is a wonderfully generous one, and I know I speak for the entire State Department in acknowledging our gratitude."

Next up was not a woman and was not agreeable: Paul's boss, Under Secretary of State for Political Affairs Trig Purtly, who began the conversation with his usual pleasantries: "Well, if it ain't my favorite little bitch-boy," this pronounced in his thundering, slow Coloradan accent.

"All you guys use the same pick-up line," Paul complained. "You know, a girl likes to see a little originality from time to time."

"That's what I like about you, Klippen – maybe the only thing," Purtly chuckled, standing on tiptoe to watch Juanita sway over to the drinks table. "You never take it personal. Guy can call you a pansy, even a total motherfuckin' backstabber, and even if it's true you take it good."

"Life's too short to agonize over the little things."

Purtly's gray-blond haystack of hair never seemed to make it to a barber, catching on his shirt collar and billowing out on the sides in a 1970s style; this effect was worsened by the part in his hair, which was maybe a finger's width to the left of center. Paul occasionally wondered if it was a wig, and he itched to give it a tug to see if it would come off. The same with his thick blond paint-brush mustache worthy of a cartoon character: Paul wanted to jerk it. Purtly sat on the boards of three major corporations and an Ivy League school: this crude Coloradan, member of the Colorado Gang, of which the president was the sun and Secretary of State Carlton Mason its brightest moon.

But Purtly's network of contacts covered the planet, and his real work was to be the Coloradans' consigliere. When a quiet million dollars were needed to ensure a certain outcome in a Brazilian senate race, Purtly clawed the money out of a prince in Dubai and delivered the suitcase of cash himself in Manaus. If copper miners in Chile itched for a raise, Purtly calmed their leaders with the spectacle of three hundred English-speaking jackbooted thugs itching for a fight. When a British ambassador in Thailand exercised his homosexual tastes too extravagantly while his wife was shopping in Singapore, Purtly called the foreign minister in London and assured him that the scandal would be covered up, the local media paid off, and the wife could choose her gowns with untroubled glee.

Paul's writing the *Foreign Affairs* paper on the administration's movement towards diplomacy and away from armed intervention, however, had started a sore little scrap between Secretary Mason and Purtly. For not only had Paul cut Purtly out of the assignment, but the paper impressed the secretary so much – Paul had an elegant, if Spartan, hand with a pen – that he had personally called *Foreign Affairs* and told them to put Paul's name alongside his own.

The issue would not come out for another week, but Washington's gossip mill already had the story: Paul was a climber who had shrewdly boxed out his boss. Purtly, said the savants, had had a five-alarm argument with Mason and talked darkly to associates about how "two knives got stuck in my back because one wasn't enough fun."

Purtly now lowered himself to the floor. "If that girl doesn't have forty inches of ass, I'm a barnyard shithead," he said now. "Met her once, too. Hell was her name?"

"Juanita Ramirez."

Purtly rose on his tiptoes again, swaying so far Paul put out a hand. "That was it. Get into her panties?"

Paul hated Purtly and his shitkicker manners, hated them as he resented a bag of trash lying split open in the street. But it wasn't just an aesthetic hatred; he also feared Purtly for the predatory whiff of violence about him, and knew that he had to keep up a front of careless humor in order for Purtly not to sense his fear. A rumor said Purtly was pushing for a move to the White House, and Paul would be glad to see him go.

"If I hadn't told her to control herself," Paul replied, "she would've dragged me right upstairs to the ambassador's bedroom. What gets into them, Trig?" Paul said, shaking his head.

"Maybe it's that smell o' policy power you're startin' to give off. Now a paper, now chairin' a policy-review committee, now lunchin' some congressman who gets teary-eyed over starvin' Filipinos."

"Dirty job, someone's gotta do it."

Purtly continued, unfazed. "Don't use makeup, do ya?"

"Not with this suit, no. You?"

Purtly watched another lovely woman – the wife of the Canadian consul, blond and chic – wind herself onto a sofa like a cat and wait for the space beside her to fill up. "Must shame you like a whore, though, gettin' ahead by backstabbin'. And lately you're gettin' all the high-profile gigs too. Why the hell is *that?*"

The same thing had puzzled Paul over the last month: before the *Foreign Affairs* article, a leading role in the prestigious Inter-Agency European Affairs Policy Review Board, and three back-to-back heavyweight assignments in place of an higher-level official struck with appendicitis – one of the assignments had been in Helsinki, where Paul had met the redhead – mere substitutions, but plum jobs all the same, dealing directly with top people in Europe. Nobody in his lowly position – barely a State Department "official" at all – ever did that before.

"There's a good question, Trig: why? Maybe they're afraid I'll backstab them too."

"Doesn't shame you to be that kind of bastard, does it?"

Paul smiled. "What – you think drive, initiative, and hard work get you ahead these days? Trig, don't tell me you bought into *that* B.S.."

Purtly wore very expensive suits with excessive shoulder padding, which as he raised a hand to some acquaintance across the room, rucked up the material over the back of his collar. Paul thought he would look far more at home in soiled overalls and a chamois shirt. "Looks like we're gonna need a new ambassador to Niger, and I was thinkin' of *you* for the part."

"After Washington, it sounds restful," Paul answered. "Think the German ambassador there throws wing-dings like this one?"

"And you're this closet dove too – ev'body knows that. No balls. No balls for keeping the U.S. on top."

"That's completely wrong, Trig, and you know it. When I was still in Quito last year, I worked like hell to get the workers' movement crushed in Ecuador and a low new price set for their wages."

"Didn't work out, though."

"Because the CIA station chief messed up my op at the last minute – and that's on record too. You might consult –"

"Well, don't matter." Purtly suddenly chuckled into his drink. "I also heard you're gonna get your ass run through a shredder."

"Well, I've got some pretty dense skin. We'll see how it --"

"Probably shouldn't of told you that, but I just couldn't resist."

"In vino veritas."

"Yeah, I heard what's comin' up, and all I can say is get yourself a towel, boy. You're gonna need it to wipe the shit off your face. See ya 'round, bitch." He whacked Paul's shoulder, making his whiskey slosh stickily over his fingers.

Paul took out his handkerchief, dried the bottom of his glass, set down his drink on the coffee table, first taking care to use as a coaster a leaflet about saving the great white shark from extinction. He wondered what he was in for. He wondered if it was connected to the same thing I was seeing in Senator Crick's correspondence with Rainmaker. Somewhere, the gears of plots were turning, and he was in their teeth. *Niger really doesn't sound too bad,* he thought grimly.

Then he wandered upstairs to close the drapes of the window I was watching through binoculars, checked his watch, and went to get his coat. It was time to come to the rescue of the splendid Margo and her thesis on Ecuadoran congressional politics.

11 NOVEMBER 9 (TUESDAY)

Roger Terelski and Trudy went to a nearby apartment building that Roger had "heard a guy talk about once" where the rooms were rented by the hour. Terelski paid sixty dollars in cash. In the taxi, she had seen him slip off his wedding band and put it in his pants pocket. She hoped there was something of value in his scratched leather satchel other than his latest book, which he had shown her: *Darkness: Gothic Elements of Rhetoric in 19th Century*

New England Political Speech. He called it "589 pages of pure human thought."

She took a shower first, locking the door behind her, but leaving her purse and things out in the room so as to suggest trust; she had disposed of the stun gun after work. When she came out, she wore only a bra, panties and her blouse. Terelski had little in the way of romantic style. Wearing only underwear, he fairly leapt on her, picking her up and grinding his erection against her. Trudy bore this as long as she could before saying, "Roger, um, would you mind taking a shower first? I mean, it's not that you smell bad or anything, but...but everything's better after a shower, y'know."

And Roger, if no Don Juan, was at least a gentleman. "Sure. No problemo. Hey, I want *you* to have a good time too. I always say that if the girl doesn't ask you back, you haven't done your part by her." He gave her a playground punch in the shoulder. "And I'll let you in on a little secret, Helen. I never did this before, actually. I mean, like, pick up a girl at a party and go have sex with her."

It was a habit of Trudy's always to give a person positive encouragement, no matter the endeavor; perhaps this was part of her gymnastics background. She replied, "Really? I thought you were kind of an old pro."

"Me? Hah! Far from it!" Roger laughed. "Hey, lemme ask you: What was it that attracted you? I mean – besides my full head of hair," he said, running a hand over his egg-smooth dome.

"Oh, that isn't important, to me at least," Trudy said. "I think it was..." – now she had to invent – "I think it was the respect. I mean, you're interested in me as a *person*. We had a good talk after the game about poker strategies and, and a little about your book. All that before you got around to, y'know, doing this." She gestured at the room. "Oh, and you have great eyes." He didn't, but Trudy remembered saying this to the boy who'd taken her to the senior prom and it had evidently delighted him.

"The eyes, huh?" Roger said, and they misted up as if he might cry. "Hey, thanks, Helen. That's, y'know, that's really sweet of you." He bent down and gave her a peck on the cheek, then disappeared into the bathroom.

By the time he came out, Trudy was three blocks away in a yellow cab. In addition to Roger's fifty-five dollars, she had taken the handgun that she found in his satchel under *Darkness*. It had fairly begged to be taken along. She felt bad about tricking and robbing Roger. But as she walked the two blocks to a youth hostal, she muttered over and over, "You got in your little feel, though, didn't you? You creep!"

12

Margo was a simple young woman trying to sound like a sophisticated middle-aged one, and Paul had to stifle a smile more than once.

She had taken off her suit jacket before getting in Paul's car, and now with a few deft pulls of pins, her fine light-brown hair shot through with blond streaks fell to her shoulders. Her well-formed lips were not painted too brightly, a detail Paul appreciated. If there was one thing above another that he disliked, it was a look-at-me splotch in the middle of a woman's face. She had laid one slender leg across the other so that her skirt slid up her thigh, but she kept her hands folded over her waist.

Sophistication! She seemed to have been injected with a syringeful of it. She smiled but never grinned. She tossed up fancy terms like fireworks at the county fair. The situation with Palestine "concerned her deeply." She called a French diplomat at the party a "fromage-eating cretin." She considered the profanity of a Republican senator "inappropriate given that milieu." She observed in jest that Paul's compact car seemed "inconsistent for a top State Department official," and that a nice Lexus would be more "toward," which after some thought Paul figured was how she wished to express the opposite of "untoward."

She also made the requisite gestures regarding the finer things in life, saying that she had been looking at a computer screen all day and "hadn't had any exercise." She held forth with some passion on how rare it was to find someone who knew how to be "a gentleman and a guy too." She pulled down the sun visor, checked her perfect face in the mirror, and pronounced herself "a mess. You *must* forgive me, Paul." Oh, Sophistication, hear our prayer!

She understood as well that they were on their way to Margo's apartment, but had to take a quick detour first for Paul to buy a certain type of drain for his kitchen sink. *Did a top State Department official really do his own plumbing?* Margo wondered, heavenly gray eyes popping wide.

But at the shopping mall Paul parked well at the back and in the dark, away from other cars, didn't get out, and merely looked past Margo to where I pulled up so close to his car that Margo could not open the door more than a couple of inches. I had swung the sun visor to the side to keep my face out of sight. Now I pressed to the window a malignant-looking badge.

When Margo turned back to Paul, her lovely lips were parted. "So what the hell's all this?" she demanded.

"Well, Margo," Paul began, "the choices here are very simple. Either you answer my questions, or I turn you over to the CIA, who will ask you *their* questions."

"I don't have to answer anybody's goddamn questions!" The sophistication had vanished, leaving the pack-rat survivor.

Paul had held her bag while she took off her suit jacket, and run his hand through it. So he knew it held nothing more than a little bag for sexual "exercise" and a mobile phone and a wallet. He spoke gently.

"A little history first. You are the fourth in a series of beautiful women of mysterious origin who want to have an affair with me. Does Merill-Baker Private Investigations ring a bell?"

Margo said no, but her eyes said yes.

"They contract women to get in touch with me, apparently thinking I'm that open to a honey trap. So I talked to The Bureau of Intelligence and Research, which is the State Department's intel arm, and they discovered that I am being tailed by this Merill-Baker outfit." This was what I had learnt investigating Paul's shadow after our "pissy Friday down the pub."

"That has nothing to do with me, and you're telling that cocksucker to move his car or you're both up for a kidnapping-harassment charge, and believe you me, when I finish telling the jury my story, you're going to wish you were never born."

"So BIR tagged along to the cocktail party," Paul continued, "to see if another woman would try to get to know me, and here we are."

"This is boring, Paul."

Paul went on. "BIR figured that it would be best to haul you in, listen to your explanations and, depending on your candor or lack thereof, turn you over to the CIA. Now personally, I think you're a small fish doing the bidding of medium fish, who are paid by much larger ones. So: you can come clean with *me,* or you can spend a month in Guantánamo telling *them.*"

"Before or after the lawsuit?"

"Long before. From here, you're on a plane to Cuba, and you'll have your pick of the men, believe me."

Margo faltered, but to her credit, still tried to brazen it out. She started on a monologue, not worth your time, about how she really was a student at Brown and really was doing her thesis – but on Brazil, not Ecuador. She'd just wanted to meet Paul. When this met with his flat patience, she loosened a bit. Well, yes, she also worked for a high-class escort service. Very high class, it seemed: with just two jobs a month, she said, she could pay for her Master's in International Relations and had money left over for expensive clothing. And the work left her plenty of time for study.

This went on until Paul sighed and said, "Margo, your employers aren't coming for you, so you needn't stall for time."

Margo watched him.

"Look at your cell phone. C'mon, take it out and look at it."

Margo did. "What?" she murmured. "Shit. *Shit!*"

"No signal, is there?" said Paul. "The BIR man there" – Paul nodded my way – "has a signals jammer. It blacks out all radio signals in a radius of a hundred yards. It *has* blacked out everything for the last fifteen minutes that he's been following us."

"You were playing the radio," she challenged.

"That was recorded music. They told you they'd be nearby just in case, right?"

"Yeah, and they got a couple of guys in their car that are going to stick that badge up your friend's ass! All I have to do is…" A heavy swallow stopped this nonsense. "What are you going to do to me?" she whispered.

"Not a thing, dear, not a thing. I just want a little information. First, tell me about how you were selected."

She had been part of an elaborate casting call, it seemed. One of nearly ten girls, she had first sat in front of a photo camera, putting her hair up, trying on the three types of clothes she had been told to bring along. Then she had been brought back with three other girls – told to bring along evening clothes and jewelry – and by Skype auditioned for someone, a man; she couldn't see who on the blacked-out screen. He asked a few questions about her experience as an escort and watched while she changed from one outfit to the next: "I want to see if you know how to shift your clothes when someone is watching." He had a strong *Bah*-ston accent. She thought the man was the client; later the matter was explained to her. She was to get another man into bed and ask him for "rough sex. As rough as possible. If you wanted to tie me up, I had to let you." The session would be recorded – though never made public; that too was in the contract. And Margo would be sumptuously compensated if she brought it all off.

Jack Mirage, by the way, was from an old Boston family.

Paul listened to all of this and said, "All right, Margo, our other point of business is this: I just want you to give your people a message to send up the chain of command: Try this again, and they'll end up on the business end of a full State investigation. In fact, BIR wants to turn you around and blackmail you: act as if we're having an affair and try to find who's paying your employers, and haul every one of you up on a charge of attempting to extort money from me."

This sent poor Margo into full panic. "Hey, wait a minute here! I'm just supposed to sleep with you! I don't know anything about the agency's business!"

"My point exactly. I told them that no harm has been done, and most likely you are who you are: just one more girl trying to make it in a tough world."

"Yeah, that's for sure, yeah." And after this came a short squall of tears.

Paul drove Margo over to a nearby Burger King where she could wait for her handlers – and then came the cherry on top of the whole story.

She had calmed down somewhat, even thanked Paul for playing fair with her. But before getting out, she turned to him and said, "Hey, one thing. You live around here – in the Metro area?"

"Yes."

"Do you know of a killer dental surgeon? Someone who knows what he's doing and doesn't rip you off with extra charges? There's no way I'm going to one without a recommendation, and I need to have my wisdom teeth taken out. I just want to do all four and get it over with."

When Paul told me, I must have laughed for a full minute. That, in my view, is the most endearing characteristic of Americans: they may have conquered the world and created a monumental economy, but they remain at heart the same democratic people of garage sales, backyard barbecues, baseball games, do-it-yourselfers, nature hikers and P.T.A. meetings. Only in America would a honey-trap lass ask her target to recommend a good doctor.

13

NOVEMBER 9 (TUESDAY)

Trudy checked in for the night at The BBB&B Hostel, a down-at-heel fleabag in the Soho district. It was housed on two floors of a tired brick building with a fire escape zigzagging across its façade and fancy arches over the windows. The ground floor held a second-hand-clothing shop, the floor above that three Internet firms and a graphic designer, the next floor an experimental theater, and the top two floors comprised the hostel.

This place had better not be a front for a whorehouse, Trudy told herself nervously as she climbed the broad, uneven staircase: no elevator.

The BBB&B catered to young Europeans and Orientals with backpacks for luggage. The lounge was a sloppy room with the friendly smell of wet earth and coffee, full of college-aged youngsters slouched in mangy easy chairs, all of them engrossed in electronic screens of every size from credit-card to billboard, the latter showing a game of badminton in Singapore played not with rackets but the feet. A few Orientals – Japanese or Korean or Chinese, she could never tell – were squawking at the players. The rooms featured spindly bunk beds and battered lockers and tattered posters of the city; the bathrooms, yellowed with age, were shared.

She rented a bunk bed – the bent old woman requested no i.d. – the entire ceremony consisting of an exchange of money for a key, an armful of sheets, and a towel as rough as tree bark. She settled in a room with two Swedish girls, and one of them with Nordic egalitarianism lent her a tablet computer for Trudy to look at the Internet. "When you finish, just leave it on my bed, the overhead one," she said, pointing to the top bunk. Trudy settled in.

News reports of Charlesdrew played the important moments over and over on every TV network: Ellen Nguyen, head down, hands tied behind her back, trying to navigate the steps down from the porch, then getting shot; her long hair descending over her head like a shroud; then Steve Hallerbee, or whoever the poor fellow was, jerking down the steps till his forehead was blown forward off his face; lastly, the Charlesdrew house blowing up in a grand umbrella of dust that spread over the entire block. And it was a remiss newscaster indeed who failed to note that this could have happened on any American street, that terrorists might lurk on any American street, that people now lived in danger on any American street.

Other reports displayed images of body parts strewn over the area. On one channel a crying young woman described how her amazed little son had run in from the back yard carrying a foot and saying he'd found it in the sandbox. An elderly fellow talked of finding a torso, which reminded him of Vietnam. A dusty arm lay on the windshield of a parked car as if someone were trying to crawl out of the engine. A pair of jeans with the legs still in them hung from the branches of a leafless tree. The mayor of Jersey City proclaimed that this was terror that would go on for weeks and months as his fellow citizens came across decaying body parts. "It is just unacceptable that this can happen on any American street," he said with great conviction. He also asked citizens who owned dogs to keep the dogs away from body parts.

The FBI's frightening verdict on the unassembled terrorist bomb was also big news. First indications were correct: the three crates were meant to be put together as a bomb, its fuel being a bit of enriched uranium "the size and shape of a bullet" – the scientific team's phrase soon to be on all journalistic lips. The Bureau's director, Lee R. Shawn, took pains to point out that the degree of enrichment had not yet been determined, nor had the quality of the detonator. "This takes time. But we are moving forward with the focus that the objective was to detonate a small atomic weapon and topple the building. Depending on which way the Empire State Building would have fallen, it would have impacted between thirty and fifty different buildings. All New York – all America – owes an incredible debt of thanks to Officer Undershall Hicks."

No, the Empire State Building had not actually fallen, but that made no difference to newscasters. Every TV network carried splendid computer simulations of it toppling. One could watch the building falling to the north, south, east or west, see the damage estimate for each disaster building by building and business by business, as well as the number of wounded and dead; and the loss for New York City's economy. Experts gripped their coffee mugs and spoke gravely of "joules" of energy released; this word too spread like smoke across the land.

One anchorman summed up the mood: "All Manhattan is shuddering with fear tonight."

And the suspects? Syrians, of course, but especially those damn Iranians. That much had been established before the house had even blown up. The instructions for assembling the bomb had been written in both Farsi (the language of Iran) and Arabic; that was enough proof right there.

Both Iran and Syria flatly denied – shrilling, squealing, roaring, bellowing – involvement, though scarcely a soul believed scoundrels like those. The involvement of Russia was also floated, for neither Middle Eastern country, at least in theory, had bomb-grade uranium. Yet as to actual leads on the case, there were few. The Irvington, New Jersey, house that the terrorists had lived in before the attack had been found; investigators were still combing through it. Neighbors had seen a young woman with long blond hair sprinting down the back alley just a few minutes before the terrorists arrived. She had apparently gotten on a bus, but this aspect was "hazy"; the search for other bus riders was still on. The only possible suspect – Wanda Ricker in Hallerbee's New Business Department had *short* blond hair – was Gertrude Ingrid Schelling.

"We are still pending some sources," said Director Shawn. "She may be a mysterious blond woman that scanned through our radar off and on over the past eighteen months – mainly in Paris – though up to now we have never been able to identify her." He asked "responsible citizens" to call in any information on her whereabouts. "For the moment, if she *is* alive, we only wish to talk with Ms. Schelling – but she certainly has some explaining to do," he added sternly.

"So do you, you creep," Trudy snapped at the screen.

Then she watched pale-faced agents in FBI windbreakers walking out of her apartment building carrying enormous trash liners of her clothes and belongings – four of them. The camera recorded from across the street as the agents loaded them into their vans, the reporter pontificating for his anchorwoman about the ease with which terrorists "blend into the scene" and can hole up on "any American street."

And then with a shock of joy she spotted at the very top of the screen the orderly silhouettes of her three bonsai trees – a ficus retusa, a Chinese elm, and a serissa foetida – each more than twenty years old, on the sill of her living-room window. They were all right, surely the result of a prayer she had said to the Virgin Mary.

14

SEPTEMBER 10

Ever cautious, Paul took with a minute nod the news that he had been summoned to the Secretary of State's office.

He arrived there direct from Dakar, Senegal, where he had spent two days arguing with German and French diplomats at a conference about shipping protocols for non-dairy perishable pre-packaged foodstuffs. Must both U.S. and E.U. Food and Drug Agencies sign off on the packaging? Do they have to be labeled if derived from genetically-modified organisms? The French had raised hell on the latter point.

Ever glad to save the taxpayer some money, he got a lift back to Washington on a military transport from the American base in Rota, Spain, and as he sat strapped into a stingy, miserable L-shaped seat bolted to the side of the plane, shivering with cold and writing a summary memo of the meeting on his laptop, the co-pilot climbed down the ladder from the much-warmer cockpit and passed on a message from Parker Radow, the secretary of state's chief of staff, telling him to come by the secretary-of-state's office as soon as he touched down. No topic or reason for the late meeting was added.

So Paul had his defenses up as he walked into the reception room, and Radow's flash-grin didn't reassure him. His grin was some kind of tic, a splash of teeth and a slow fade like a spotlight going out – and all the more frequent when there was something big in the air. Paul wondered if Trig Purtly had managed to get him sent to Niger.

It was past eleven p.m., and the office – the building itself – was nearly deserted. He saw Secretary of State Carlton Mason sat slumped in his desk chair, tie dragged down, a stout little glass of whiskey clinched tight to his chest as he grunted at someone on the phone. He waggled the glass at Paul and sent him a tight smile. Paul followed Radow's bowling-pin body out the side door into the private office.

This room was a kind of British men's club. Windows were considered in poor taste, and thick floor-to-ceiling curtains concealed them. A group of overstuffed chairs stood hunched together as if in conference; facing away as if in a snit, a sofa stared at a coffee table with a vase of flowers on top. Beyond it, a huge lit cabinet with crystal and bottles stood like an ice queen. On a panel near the ceiling, a dozen black-and-white clocks, blank as zombies, showed the time around the world; one was labeled VILA, which after a moment's scrambling across the maps of memory, Paul remembered as the capital of the southern-Pacific island nation Vanuatu. Why did anyone need to know the hour in Vila?

Radow ushered Paul to one of the stuffed chairs and perched a buttock on the arm of another. It grunted in alarm, unsure that it could sustain him without breaking or tipping. Paul, too, had his doubts; though short, Radow had wide hips and a fleshy behind. He had a paper in his hand – with many annotations.

"Okedokee," said Radow, looking over the paper and swinging a foreleg in circles. "Paul, I'm going to have to ask about your wife,"

"My wife?" Paul exclaimed.

"Cindy, right?" The grin popped out and subsided as Paul concurred. "How are you guys about, say, someone coming to your house, photographing you and her, interviewing you, writing a story about you? I mean for a national magazine. Now I can't *guarantee* this, but…you up to that? Is *she* up to that?"

"Do you really think that would happen? People who write in *Foreign Affairs* are hardly celebrities."

"Just humor me. What if you and she showed up in, in *People Magazine*?"

Paul took a moment to digest this; it seemed that he wasn't being shipped out to Niger. As to the question itself, he wasn't at all sure he liked this kind of fame; to appear on Sunday-morning political talk shows and maybe, in later years, to publish an occasional op-ed in *The New York Times* – those were the heights of his public ambition. He disliked the idea of appearing in a supermarket magazine with smirking movie stars and alcoholic pop singers staggering sheepishly into rehab.

Radow was waiting for an answer.

"Well, Cindy's already accompanied me to State dinners and the like. I don't think she'd have a problem."

"Her long struggle to walk – is she ready and willing to expand on that?" asked Radow. The smile jumped and subsided. "You see, that kind of thing might play really well as background for an article."

"Background? To what exactly?"

Radow's smile burst and faded. "What we're thinking, Paul – though I can't guarantee it – is to send you on a little outreach tour of the country. Drill down into the bedrock. Raise awareness for the administration's pivot to diplomacy and away from military intervention as a means of conflict resolution."

"Which was basically what the *Foreign Affairs* article was about."

"Right. Because we're already dealing with a lot of pushback in Congress and the right-wing media. So…Cindy?"

A dozen questions flew through Paul's mind, but with that superb mental discipline of his he corralled them and focused on Radow. "Cindy. Well, sure, she's made great progress, and the doctor's prognosis is that she'll go on to recover much of her original, pre-accident ability. How much remains to be seen."

"I saw in a profile brief that for years you've put out for growth-hormone shots. Must take a big chunk out of a dip's salary."

"The insurance people refused to cover it. They said it was too experimental."

Radow's grin again jumped. "Bet they're not saying that anymore!"

"Oh no, they are: you know insurance companies. They tell us that Cindy's progress is due to her P.T. program and her hard work – which they do pay for – but not the shots. We reply that hardly one patient in a hundred makes the recovery she's making. But nobody can actually *prove* anything until they do a lot of clinical trials, so no deal."

Radow thought about this, looking around the ceiling as if tasting a new ice cream. The armchair gave a dire squeak beneath him, and Paul wished he would sit down properly. "Right: an insurance conflict. You know, that could cog right into what we're looking at too – stroke the right demographics."

Paul nearly laughed, but said, "Parker, I can hardly believe that Americans are a hard sell on diplomacy versus more war. I mean, the country has been at war since 2001. And though the president never really came out in the campaign and said that peace was his policy, I think that was mainly so as not to lose the military vote."

"Americans aren't a hard sell on this, Paul, but the tectonics are shifting beneath our feet: now, besides the military, millions of Americans are plugged into direct or indirect employment re: security agencies. And the Pentagon will go to the mat with us on this pivot thing every step of the way."

Paul nodded, reflecting on how the Pentagon might go to the mat and still keep up every step of the way; but only a fool doubted its versatility.

"Peace and diplomacy go against a lot of grains out there," Radow continued. "But every interview you do on some talk show is going to defeat five articles planted by the Company in the *Times*." Another flash grin, like a rattan shade jerked up by its string and let fall again.

"'On some talk show,'" Paul repeated. What on earth did that refer to? "Well, it's certainly a worthy cause, Parker. If Secretary Mason is for it, I'll go make all the appearances he wants."

"Great. Now we come to the good part," Radow went on. "We can't exactly have our spokesman introduced as the *deputy assistant under secretary* of state for political affairs. That wouldn't sound any good at all. Hell, Barney Fife in Mayberry was a *deputy*." Another sudden grin. "So whaddaya say we make you a plain old 'under secretary'? For political affairs, that is."

It took Paul a moment to realize he was being promoted: under secretary of state for political affairs was the third-ranking position in the department, behind the secretary and the two deputy secretaries. Still, he waited, wondering if Radow would add that he couldn't guarantee the change, but this did not come.

"Well…well, that would be wonderful – if Trig Purtly doesn't mind," he added carefully. "He's under secretary, and I can just hear him now screaming about how I'm taking his job. I can do without the –"

"Oh, don't worry about Trig. He's still a little crispy about that paper you wrote with Carlton." Another grin as he rolled his eyes to the ceiling. "Among other things. He's moving over to the White House: chief counsel or something. Wants to be tighter with the president. Besides" – another flash – "Secretary Mason test-drove this one with him first. He clenched up a bit, but at the end....." Another grin.

"Well, I'm glad to hear it because I wouldn't like to be on Trig's –"

Secretary of State Carlton Mason – lanky, baggy-eyed, red-tied, a boardroom veteran who had a reputation for telling billionaire CEOs to go to hell – slouched through the door, whiskey in one hand, a bottle held by the neck in the other. To shake Paul's, he slid the bottle under his left arm.

"Lookin' for great things from ya, Paul," he said, the full Texan sheriff, which he once was, entering his voice as it never did in public. Up to that moment Paul had never spoken to him when not in a meeting with another dozen people around. "We're gonna turn you loose. Make our case. Can't tell you how important your role's gonna be." If he wasn't drunk, he wasn't far from it.

"I'm honored by your confidence, Mr. Secretary."

"*Carl*, for Chrissakes. We're pretty informal once the G-14 midgets all traipse off back to the 'burbs for the night. And if you need to call me a dumb fuckass piece o' shit, just let fly – not made of glass. Might talk some sense into me. And speakin' o' shitheads: Parker! Get the hell over here! How come I see this guy without a drink?" he growled with real anger. "Paul, what you sippin' these days? You're gonna try this scotch with me, right?"

"My pleasure. Little bit of ice, Parker," he called after Radow, who was running to the drinks cabinet.

"God-*damn*, my ass hurts," Mason added and tumbled into a chair. With a groan, he keeled forward as if shot – Paul nearly made to catch him – and set the bottle between his feet. Paul was reminded of a jazz singer in Kansas City, brilliant but nearly always reeling drunk on stage, always about to fall apart – which he sometimes did.

Mason sipped his drink silently till Radow brought Paul his whiskey with a single fat ice cube clinking around inside. "Parker, you wanna go count the pixels on my screen, make sure none's missin'?"

"Right, chief." He pointed to the paper he'd left on another chair. "There's the questionnaire. Hundred percent." Radow flashed a smile and left.

Mason snatched it up with a big hand, looked at it with unfocused eyes, and muttered something about "make-work bullshit." Then he tossed it aside – it fell off the chair onto the floor – and picked up the bottle. With lucid accuracy, he poured two fingers into Paul's glass and two more into his own.

"Here's to your promo, Paul. Hope ya make a good run of it."

Paul drank and felt the burn all the way to his stomach. "Wow! That's rich."

"Damn right – stays in your mouth, don't it? Thick." Mason nodded at his glass approvingly. "Now, business. Look, Paul, I just gotta warn you 'bout this appointment."

"*Warn* me?"

"'Cause it wasn't my idea, see." He wagged up a tired hand. "No problem with it: good man, all that. Thing is, though, I got the word from the Oval: Trig transfers over, and you – you in p'ticular – get moved up. They want to sell diplomacy over military intervention, and they're lookin' at *you* to do it."

"Why not do it yourself? I know you've generally been hawkish, but the signs have been clear enough since the election that you want to, ah, go a little more moderate."

"Naw, makes sense," Mason said sheepishly. "Thing is, Paul, the president and me, you know, back in Congress, voted for and/or supported war on Af-Pak, Iraq, Libya, Syria, Yemen, Somalia, the fuckin' Islamic State – you name it. And maybe we did it a little too publicly. Shoulda straddled a little more – or just plain shut the hell up. I start makin' the case for diplomacy, and all I'm gonna get is a lot o' folks sayin', 'Yeah, you big Texan dumbshit, tell me another,' and remindin' me o' what we were sayin' *before* we made the White House. Catch? What we need for this thing is a new voice. Someone fresh, cred shinin' out his ass."

"Right. I see."

"Also better if it's someone young and attractive. POTUS has some demographics that didn't like him much in the election. West Coast, mainly."

"It *is* a democracy," Paul said with a smile.

"Democracy elected that pissant Hitler."

"Point taken. So what's the, ah, the warning?"

"Good question – not sure I got a good answer for ya." Mason swallowed a gulp that made Paul's spine tingle. "Damn, how 'bout this scotch, huh? Double-malt, older 'n' Adam. Foreign Minister Andy Ricewood gave it to me, and he's a Scot, so he oughta know."

"Best I've ever tasted. I'll have to make friends with some Scots."

"Five centuries of whiskey knowledge right there in your hand, boy." Mason drank more and with a grimace adjusted his sitting position. "Don't know – can't put a finger on it. Maybe the way POTUS told me 'bout the change, maybe the way Trig looked like he already had the news. That son-of-a-bitch always seems to know more than he should, funny thing. Or maybe…maybe it's just some wigglin' around behind the curtain, Deep State bullshit, who knows? Thought I had a handle on that stuff, but when we were settin' up the new admin', I got told that now and then there'd be policy as I just hadda open up and swallow, and ask POTUS if it ain't so. So I did, and he just looks at me, not a word, and makes like he's givin' a blowjob."

Paul sipped the scotch. "I think I see what you're saying. You know, a while back I was talking to a man writing a history of Obama foreign policy and he was thinking of giving up. He couldn't get to the bottom of anything. He said flat out, 'Nobody will ever give a true account of this era in American history.'"

Mason nodded. "That's on target…Thing is, with you gettin' moved up and all….this is lookin' like all the other times I saw some well-meanin' s.o.b. gettin' set up to be the scapegoat. They brought you outta Ecuador, no friends on the Hill, nobody to catch you if you fall, and of course once you're out on the stump, the whole neocon gang is gonna be slingin' mud at you till their arms drop off. Dumb fucks, the whole bunch. I oughta know: used to be one m'self."

Paul nodded. He was remembering Trig Purtly: *You're gonna get your ass run through a shredder.*

"Another thing, a clue: I told Parker to run your nomination by Dottie Crick – at Senate Foreign Affairs? – see if she could get it done before the next ice age? Came right back, said she'd fast-track your confirmation hearing! Fast-track it! When was the last time that old bitch fast-tracked anything for anybody who didn't stuff her campaign with a half-million bucks?"

"Well, that was nice of her," Paul said lamely.

"Nice shmice. An old war-monger like Dottie Crick, who takes money from half the arms makers in America, wants *you* out there selling the pivot to diplomacy? And do it as the number three man at State?"

"I see."

He looked at Paul with his baggy eyes. "See what I mean? Somethin's goin' on, and I can see you don't have a clue either."

"No."

To Paul, the very silence of the room seemed to rear up, menacing like a cobra.

Mason took another sip, staring floorwards, one arm braced on the chair, which seemed to be all that kept him from keeling over completely. Paul was wondering if he'd fallen asleep when he put down the glass, reached over and patted Paul's arm.

"Well, just watch your ass, son – all *I* can say. Good man: State hasn't turned you into a robot yet. If I can pick up your pieces – if you got any left to get picked up – I'll stick you out in some damn consulate in Trinidad-Tobago: sit on the beach, put yourself back together."

15

NOVEMBER 10 (WEDNESDAY)

By the next morning, Trudy had been turned into a terrorist.

The two Swedish girls yakked at each other like honking geese until past midnight, when Trudy finally mustered her nerve and asked them to go to sleep or go out to the lounge.

After they had left in the morning, stuffing thick backpacks worthy of climbers attempting Mount Everest, Trudy sat on the edge of her bed and held Roger's gun flat in her hands and slightly away from her as if it were a snake.

"'Glock,'" she read on the barrel just over the trigger. "Who would call their product 'Glock'?"

She had seen guns in movies all her life but had never touched one. The hole at the end – she looked at it from the side, head tilted back – was too small even for her pinky, and it was hard to believe that a bullet was spat out of it at supersonic speed.

"So *now* what are you going to do?" she muttered to herself. "Shoot someone? Jeepers, why did I take this stupid thing? It probably cost Roger a good fifty bucks…Well, I suppose I had to."

Tears began to peek out, but she wiped them away. "Now don't go feeling sorry for yourself."

After some thinking, she decided to make sure it wasn't loaded till she could get rid of it. To take the bullet magazine out of the gun butt required some prodding, but after a minute of probing and squeezing, it slid out neatly as a train on its track. Then she remembered that "the bullet chamber" – a TV term – sometimes contained a bullet.

She fiddled more till she could pull back the slide on top of the gun just enough to look into the chamber. There lay a coppery-silver bullet just as snug as baby in its carriage.

Trudy groaned.

She turned the gun upside down and gently shook it, but the bullet didn't fall out. It took her some minutes of experimenting, and finally she had to place herself upside down on the bed, braced on the three points of her head and her feet, aim the gun between her legs at the wall, and jiggle the gun and pull the slide back harder and farther. Suddenly the bullet popped out sideways, hit the wall, and rolled under the bed. Another minute of probing among the dustballs and a cockroach far braver than she was, and she had it.

"Now what? Throw everything in a wastebasket?"

She loaded it all into her knapsack instead and waited as long as she could in the hostel. With her glasses and Yankees cap on, she ate a pancake breakfast in a coffee shop and watched the news on its TV. The headline was she had gone to a hotel with "an unnamed man" and stolen his gun. A fingerprint analysis of the hotel room quickly confirmed his story.

And now the news programs were all talking about her, for the CIA had leaked a brief, a true work of art as those things go, and Trudy watched with rising astonishment as her life was reinvented for her.

She had worked in Paris for three years and been "indoctrinated as a terrorist" there. Work colleagues remembered her as "reserved and secretive." One woman that Trudy had never met in her life was introduced as her "closest workmate" in Paris and said that Trudy "never talked about herself, as like she have a secret or somesing." Neighbors in her building outside Paris agreed that she rarely spoke to anyone; but to Trudy's disgust the reporter neglected to mention that they were nearly all Arab, and that "bonjour" to an Arab fellow – even to his sister or mother – inevitably resulted in five annoying minutes of convincing the bloody fool that "bonjour" was not an invitation to her bed. Her "friends" in America were also asked for their opinions, and all agreed that Trudy was shifty. Only Perry Howard, the handsome instructor at her gym in Newark, stuck up for her: "Oh yeah, Trudy's totally fabulous, one of my best students. Really comes in here ready to sweat. She was a top gymnast in college, you know. Yeah: Monday, Wednesday, Friday – regular as clockwork. Don't know where she is this morning." He looked around the gym. "Must be busy with this terrorism thing."

But no sooner had Perry said this than some terrorism expert in a business suit was explaining to a nodding anchorwoman how terrorists "whipped themselves into top shape" for even small roles in missions. "And as we're realizing at this point in time, of course, Gertrude Ingrid Schelling was Plan B – the fallback hangout in case the Empire State Building job went sideways. Which is a new twist in terrorist planning that we're already gaming into our scenarios."

In France, the CIA brief said, Trudy was "lonely and friendless" – just the kind of person that terrorist groups preyed on. They pulled her in and secretly indoctrinated her in the ways of Islam. Trudy was the "mysterious blond" who had troubled French and American intelligence over the past eighteen months. A grainy video showed a blond woman – who could have been Trudy or Marilyn Monroe – walking arm in arm in a sunny Parisian park with Raschid al-Bousapha, the 11/9 mastermind. A grainy photo had Trudy sitting on his lap in a bar, wearing a mini-skirt. (Trudy scowled; it was a garment she loathed.) And here was a security-cam photo of her pulling her suitcase alongside Ashnani al-Haq, another of the identified 11/9 terrorists, in Madrid's high-speed-train terminal.

"We even had a code name for her: 'Sally Brown,'" one anonymous CIA source said from behind a panel, his voice distorted. "As in, Charlie Brown's little sister? Short and blond?" But the information was never followed up: "She was just a terrorist comfort girl," said the source. "We've seen them before."

A joint press conference with the assistant directors of both the CIA and FBI, who coincidentally were twin brothers, was held live, and in response to media outrage – *"Isn't this yet another intelligence failure?" "How could this happen again?"* – the usual excuses came out one after another like the various courses of a gourmet meal. The signals were "painfully clear in retrospect," "a half-inch under the radar," "never quite actionable." And that old standard: "Nobody connected the dots." You can't believe the blizzard of information we work with, the assistant directors complained. The sheer volume. The lack of budget to scale. The constitutional guarantees they were duty-bound to respect. The clamor of emergencies far shriller and needing immediate attention.

"Creeps – every single one of them," Trudy muttered, getting to her feet and picking up her knapsack. She missed Perry and her early-Wednesday workout, she thought in the bathroom, buttoning her Yankees baseball cap in the back so that her pony tail hung out the hole, as tennis players do. From the start she'd thought he was pretty great – always upbeat and patient, especially with the older women who didn't have the flexibility. One of the other women in her class, however, had whispered to her that he was gay – a great disappointment.

16 NOVEMBER 10 (WEDNESDAY)

Trudy mooned around the discount department store, examined women's blouses and cheap athletic socks ten for the price of six. She gradually ascended floor by floor through women's wear and camping equipment, and found herself around noon on the top floor, wandering amidst dishwashers and plastic plants and bathroom fixtures.

The store was part of a big chain that she had seen before, a stacked-up version of the ones in suburban strip-malls. The rest was the same: primary colors, music dribbling from the ceiling, lazy shopping carts drifting around like grazing cows, and everywhere signs confidently proclaiming the ultimate doormat, the ultimate towel, the ultimate shower curtain that could not be bought anywhere else on the planet. Trudy stopped to look at the latter for a whole minute, trying to figure out what made it unique, turning it this way and that, which gave her a chance to check her watch: 11:55.

In the towel section, she saw an employee walk out an emergency door onto the roof; two other employees were out there smoking and enjoying the sunshine. They kept it propped open a few inches with a plowed-up pile of black gravel, a few grains of which had spilled into the store.

Trudy drifted over by the huge floor rugs that were hanging on swinging racks, like posters for sale, and thus kept herself out of sight of passers-by. From here she could see the appliances section, where a largish woman wearing a green raincoat and gray headscarf was examining washing machines and driers. After a few minutes, the lady raised the lid of a washing machine and looked inside from one side to the other, as if considering living in it rather than washing anything.

Trudy left the rugs and strolled to the towels again, slinging her knapsack off and hooking it with her index finger by the little center strap. They were folded and stacked, pastel colors arranged like the rainbow from red to violet. An employee, finished smoking, passed behind her in a stinking aura of tobacco. An old Michael Jackson tune, "One Day in your Life," was playing through the speakers. Trudy had always liked its melancholy sweetness. Then:

Pounding steps on the escalator. "Comin' through, please. Comin' through! Comin'—"

"Ouch! Hey, you watch where yah goin', eh, sonny?" screeched a mighty female Bronx accent. Trudy looked up. The woman in the green coat had got tangled up with a spare, simian-faced fellow whose looks were not improved by his black jacket with zippers all over it like scars. He looked wildly around as he scraped the woman off, and his eyes met Trudy's.

Trudy snatched off her glasses and stuffed them in her pocket, made a little ballerina hop, took a step back, looked around, saw the exit, and ran to it, stiff-arming the door. She found herself on a plain of stubbly gravel and puddled tar, with the entire Manhattan skyline looking down at her.

17 SEPTEMBER 22

Paul's confirmation hearing for his new job – "All this for a shorter job title," as he modestly told the Senate committee – had been scheduled with celerity and held with brevity. Word was out that Paul was rising fast at State, and the senators wanted to be on his good side. Except one: Nate Flangle of New Hampshire. "I read your report, thoroughly appalled," he told Paul about the classified summary of his operation in Ecuador. "You clearly have no gut feeling for the plight of working people, in view of your work last year against Ecuadorean field workers. For about two seconds, I had a good mind to send your report to Wikileaks. And if your dastardly scheme had turned out successful and the workers had gotten just a minimal raise in wages, I think I would have done just that, I don't mind saying."

"One thing is gut feeling, Senator, another is a wage so high that it makes our food bill in America go through the roof," Paul replied, amazed at the senator's faux pas. Didn't he know that every senator and staff member on this committee was checked constantly for any sympathy with leaks? Having merely mentioned Wikileaks, Flangle would soon be set apart from any truly vital security intel.

He waited while Flangle complained more.

"The wage ended up too high," Paul continued. "Workers strikes have developed in other countries, and you can see what's happening with our food bills for yourself. There are already different options being discussed on how to undercut the momentum of the unions, and I second these wholeheartedly." This was his standard lie, but he knew that in the present atmosphere of America-Firstism, it was career suicide to say otherwise.

"Well, I don't!" Flangle snapped. He sifted through a mess of papers in front of himself till he found what he wanted. "According to the Congressional Budget Office, the increase in hemispheric produce non-dairy, excluding eggs, means that an average American family of four spends seven dollars more per month on their food bill. I think that's affordable. I'm *glad* the Latinos got their raise!"

Paul had his answer ready. "That also means seven dollars more for a family already on a food-assistance program." It was a stupid dodge, and he hated it, but he had to keep his credibility intact. "I have nothing against a good living wage for Ecuadoran workers, Senator. Quite the contrary: I'm very much in favor. But the present wage should have been reached in stages over a period of –"

"Yeah, yeah: over a period of years. Decades, if *you* guys had anything to do with it. I heard you give that same fanatical little speech to that Commerce-Ag joint subcommittee last year when you came to inform us of the deal you were putting together in order to keep workers at a subsistence wage. I am shocked and dismayed that you are being named to such a high position at State – but not surprised. No sir, I'm not surprised at all. Guys like you always get ahead. No more questions, Madam Chairwoman."

His was the only dissenting vote.

Madam Chairwoman, Senator Dorothy Crick from Connecticut, in her third term as senator, not only gave him her vote but popped up at a cocktail party some days later, in the middle of Paul's arms-v.-dip media crusade. She was a thin, silver-haired aristocratic woman in her sixties, all elbows and knees and pearls, left arm perennially crooked as if to hold an invisible purse, the hand hanging backward as if wilted. Her right did the work of handshaking – a perfunctory gesture that she got out of the way in order to move along to whatever was on her festering mind.

It had been an irritating party up to then. He had needed to talk with a British diplomat, and whenever the man was unoccupied, someone else buttonholed him before Paul could get there. A TV producer he had dodged for some weeks caught up with him, nagged him to go on a national cooking show and make pasta while he talked about foreign policy: "But it'll be great for getting out the administration's message, Paul! Cooking shows – I've been producing them for twelve years. That's where the people live! And *anybody* can make spaghetti!" Paul said he would think about it and put the card in a suit-jacket pocket that he was sure never to look at.

And no sooner had he shuffled away than "Reid, a congressional assistant," held him for several minutes by asking him a series of questions about State and State Department careers – until Senator Crick showed up and dismissed him in mid-question with a "Thank you, Reid." The young man disappeared, and before Paul could say a word, she said, "Follow me, Mr. Under Secretary," and marched through the crowd – "Make way, please!" – to an uninhabited area behind the grand piano.

"You're going to be invited to Doers," she announced, swinging around to face him, her limp hand swishing through the air like a streamer on the end of a wand. Her small mouth was turned down in its usual frown; it was not a mouth that kissed babies, that was for sure. *How did a sourpuss like this ever get elected in American politics?* Paul wondered. "Are you sure you're up to it?" she asked.

"Hello, Senator. Thank you for your vote on the committee. I will try to live up to your confidence," Paul replied. This was received with an impatient base stare; Crick was the same spoiled brat as sixty years before. "As to the Doers, I can't really say."

"Purtly's told you nothing? He said he gave you an inkling."

"Trig? He told me that I was going to get my ass run through a lawnmower – no, a 'shredder' – so if this has to do with 'Doers,' as you say, it sounds like a bad career move."

"Don't be a fool. It's where the work gets done. It's where the path ahead gets cleared. An invitation to Doers is an invitation to the trunk of the tree."

Though his heart was pounding, Paul took a long sip of his drink and watched the burning black eyes of the senator. "And what about the shredder?"

Crick's wagging hand waved that away. "Oh that: Old West big talk. Come with us and you'll be Secretary of State in ten years. *If* we invite you, that is. First, though, I want to know a few things. You have no trouble with working a back channel of influence?"

"No trouble at all," Paul said, feeling he was better off playing along. "Remember the operation that Senator Flangle took exception to in the –"

"That man is a fool," snarled Crick. She had a reformed smoker's undergrowl to her voice. "He's up for re-election next year, and he won't make it past the primaries, I can assure you."

"Thank goodness," Paul said. "To set up my operation in Quito last year required nearly two hundred *normal-channel* meetings. After that experience, a back channel that runs through well-connected people sounds like bureaucratic paradise."

"What if I told you that we authorize dirty-but-necessary operations?"

"I worked in embassies for ten years, Senator. Politics is a rough business." Paul was going to say more, but he left it there.

Crick was searching his eyes now. "Is it true you drove deep into some sticky jungle for a health clinic?"

Paul was surprised, but hid this behind another thick sip of whiskey. "In Cameroon, yes. The clinic we sponsored had used up more supplies than expected and the next supply got delayed because of a truckers strike. So I borrowed an SUV and took them enough supplies to keep going for – I don't remember – a week, ten days."

Crick snorted.

"And the rest was simple math," Paul went on. "If all those village women had carried their children all those jungle miles to a clinic that didn't work, well, the clinic's credibility would have been in ruins, hence the embassy's, hence my own: the whole project had been dumped in my lap a few weeks before. Why do you ask?"

"Ah, so that might have repercussed on *you* – I get it, yes," said Crick softly, black eyes still searching his, her lips pursing to one side, then the other. "You see, Paul, someone who isn't out for himself is wobbly, he's unreliable. You tip your barber big. Why?"

Dear God, even my barber, Paul thought. He gave half the truth, the other half being that poor Harry had to take care of an aging mother who was entering dementia. "Well, I've found that if you want your hair cut so that it doesn't look like it's *just* been cut, you've got to impress the barber with the importance of this concept."

"Yes, that lovely dark hair," murmured Crick, black eyes flicking up that way; she seemed to judge its trustworthiness as well. "You're not wealthy, are you, Paul?" she accused. "You're strictly middle-class. All your life. Kansas City, for God's sake. You spend so much money on growth hormone that you're just barely getting by. Yet you don't take loans, you don't do graft, and you don't steal."

"Senator, why do I get the feeling I'm being judged?"

"Because you are. You see, I haven't made up my mind about you, and you seem too nice – too damn scrupulous," Crick retorted, jabbing his jacket lapel with her right hand. "That's why I wanted to feel your bones for myself. Because you seemed too nice a person in that committee hearing: too Midwestern, not interested enough in money, a little too inclined to respect the Constitution, which has some fine ideals, of course, but was written by men who never saw an electric light bulb. But then I re-read that detailed report of your derring-do last year to keep Ecuadoran workers in their hovels where they belong so that we, the civilized people, can go to a piano concert in peace; and I was relieved. It reads like poetry. It's why you're even in this town."

"I still tell anyone – with clearance – who'll listen that if the CIA station chief in Quito hadn't intervened, my plan would've worked. I made *that* clear in my report too."

"Yes. Yes, there is a refreshing current of bureaucratic revenge in you – like snatching away that *Foreign Affairs* assignment from Trig Purtly." Her laugh was a single rasping squeak. "Oh, he was livid, the poor bastard. But it renewed the faith in you, that's for sure. Except Jack Mirage. He doesn't trust a man who's faithful to his wife."

Paul painted surprise on his face. "Jack Mirage the financier – he's in this?"

"Do you know of another? Then you put the fear of God into that last floozy he sent you – *yes,* she was from him – and that, well, at least it *mollified* him a bit. He still doesn't trust you. But my god, anyone could see a honey trap like that coming a mile off. Of course, most men just don't want to see it – that speaks well for you."

Paul smiled. "He was a fool to try beautiful women in obvious settings. It's the girl in blue jeans at the photocopier who can keep a secret."

Another long stare, in which the inverted U of her lips pulled even deeper. "So what does this have to do with this Doers thing?" Paul inquired finally.

"We will soon vote on whether or not to accept you, and everyone else is so enthralled with your handsome face and manners – because of our next operation – that I felt that someone had to be an adult and check you over properly. The fact that you worked so hard against the workers is of course a plus. But by itself it's not good enough."

"So they need me for an operation?"

"Humph! *Operation!*" Crick's mobile mouth turned jagged. "I call it 'The Three Stooges rob a bank.' They need you to take part – an *active* part. Actually, they've already started on you. Haven't you noticed?"

Paul couldn't find an answer in his mouth. "Noticed…noticed what exactly?"

"That you're getting into the most important meetings in Washington! That you're making a PR blitz for the new foreign policy. Who do you think has arranged to give you that kind of national exposure? The tooth fairy?"

"Right – all that. Well, Secretary Mason said that the administration wanted me out in front on the diplomacy issue."

"Carl does what he's told." Crick's dry lips worked busily for some time. "Well, what's done is done, I suppose," she said to herself. "But, goddammit, new members usually go through a probationary period when they join – all right, not always, but the few who don't are old Washington hands and don't need real vetting. You *do*."

Paul shrugged.

"It's just that whenever I see a stampede, my instinct is to look ahead and see if there's a cliff." She nodded at the cocktail crowd. "The Gadarene swine, you know – that's humanity on any day of the week."

"Well, I'm glad that someone --"

"Though what the hell The Rainmaker and those other mastersof-the-universe think they're doing *I* certainly don't know. Always so goddamn careful: security, security, security. Encrypt everything. Be careful what you say and where and to whom – heavens! And then they pull *you* in on the strength of one operation – in one little dot in the Andes, of all places – and even *that* didn't turn out as planned, though I believe you about Station Chief Kruger. What a holy fool *he* was! Last week I sat down the assistant DCIA, Mitch Harmon, in a secure room at Langley and grilled him about your op till he screamed like a little girl." She grunted with disgust. "But my god, to pull someone like you in for an op *before* you've even been vetted. Oh, you would be on a very, very short leash if *I* had anything to do with it. But since the bin Laden kill raid in Abbottabad, you would think he owns Doers."

"Who? The assistant DCIA?"

"No! The Rainmaker, that old fool – though you didn't hear that name from me. Another of his useless security rules. Half the intel world must have heard of him by now, in one connection or another. He's practically a Cold War *legend*." Her eyes clenched up, and her naturally down-turned mouth rose to level: Paul realized this was a smile. "But I know his name – his *real* name. Don't ask me how, but I found it. One time at a Doer's meeting I took him aside and said it to his face. And sure enough, he nearly fainted. You would have thought I'd shown him photos of him molesting a child!"

"He must have pretty high clearance."

"He's clearanced above POTUS – loves to brag about it. He was in a car accident a few years ago, and his staff had to disburse three hundred thousand dollars to keep his name out of it. Personally, I wonder if the taxpayer got his/her money's worth."

"Spoken like a true senator," Paul said.

"Though if you *do* come on board, Paul…." She moved closer and slightly to one side, a conniver's hunch curving her thin old frame.

"If I do come on board?" asked Paul.

"If you *do* come on board, what I'd really like to do is *take over* Doers," Crick said more quietly. "On the *civilian* side, for once. And shove out or shove aside The Rainmaker and the ex-veep Ted Greene and those military-security bumpkins like Chet Nicely – law to themselves, those ungodly bastards."

"*General* Chet Nicely?"

"Retired. Actually he represents the oil interests in Doers. But with the two of us working together and talking to Jack from the financial side, we might pull Doers back from its more extravagant operations – like this one."

"Which is what?"

Crick ignored him, looking away for a moment. Then she turned and jabbed him with a finger again. "That's what Doers really is, you see," she said on a sudden inspiration. "It's the few key people who can keep this country from plunging over the cliffs. And someone has got to do it, by God. In the next few years, the food shortages will begin, the water shortages. My god, what we're doing to the aquifers! Rising temperatures, rising seas. By 2030 the situation will be critical. By then, we have *got* to have control of this planet. We have got to be the ones who, all alone, cut the pie, and cut it in our favor: ours, the Europeans', and to some extent the Latin Americans', who aren't all that rational, but they have good fertile lands and water that's still drinkable. The Australians and New Zealanders will always get along, they don't concern me. And nobody gives a damn about Africa – including Africans. But the Asians and Russians – those people must be *brought to heel.* I suppose you don't agree with this?" she asked suddenly.

"'Agree' – that isn't quite the word here, Senator," Paul said. "I think that it would be more accurate to say that I don't normally think in such broad terms." He paused, feeling her burning eyes on him. "But clearly it's time that I did. And you make a good point: the deadline is coming, and the time to do something is now, not then. And the people to do it are us, not them."

"Good," said Crick. She stepped back and gave him a mannish swat on the arm. "Good for you. That's exactly the right take. You know, when I was twelve years old, I went to protest marches with my flower-power parents?"

"Senator, you are full of surprises."

"Yes: the hair, the love beads, the pot. And then the Vietnam War ended, and in six months, it all vanished. My parents were disgusted beyond belief. They were in it for a proper use of the earth's resources, against all this materialistic hedonism. They said, 'from now on, to hell with collective answers.' My father cut his hair, went into real estate, made twenty million dollars in five years and two hundred million in the next fifteen. Spent it? Certainly he spent it. He bought half the state of Connecticut and began planting trees: oaks and maples and the like, trees that take a hundred years to grow ten feet high. Do you understand why I'm telling you all this?"

"So that I'll understand how you've come to your point of view."

"Excellent, Mr. Under Secretary. I've been in the forefront of every environmental fight in the Senate since Al Gore was in diapers. And that's what Doers requires" – she raised a bony fist and knocked on Paul's chest with each word – *"people with fight."*

Paul could hardly think of a reply. "Well, if Doers will have me, tell them I'll be glad to step up."

"And steer it the right way with me. I'm on my last years with them, and I intend to leave them in good young hands, with The Rainmaker either bound and chained or preferably pensioned off to some air base in the Arizona desert where he can say Mass on Sundays and sleep the rest of the week."

"Say Mass? What – is he some kind of priest?"

But again the senator wasn't listening. "He did the bin Laden raid, you know, he and the CIA – pre-Mitch Harmon, that is – Ted organizing helicopters and the like. Chet a bit. I didn't like it at all: they had to lose twenty good Seals, and there were better options. But history had to record that bin Laden died at the end of an American rifle, not that he crawled off to die of kidney disease in the mountains of Pakistan."

"You mean he *didn't* die at the end of an American rifle?"

Crick squinted at him angrily. "Oh, don't tell me you're *that* kind of fool. Even the White House doorman knows it was a put-up job."

"Well, I've heard rumors, of course, but I never really –"

"Since then, the swagger has become so thick around Doers that you can practically taste it. Hence the present wacko operation. It's necessary? Yes, fine, yes. Something *like it* is necessary; *I* co-sponsored the initiative! But wait till they tell you, Paul. God in heaven – the *Ladies Aid* could have planned something with fewer chances for disaster."

"Well, I'll be curious to –"

"I'm glad we had this little chat, Paul. I feel better about you now. See you at Doers."

And with a swing of her hanging wrist, she was gone through the crowd. Paul discovered that a stripe of sweat lay down the center of his back like a cold snake.

"Bin Laden," he muttered in wonder.

18 NOVEMBER 10 (WEDNESDAY)

A department store employee-smoker squawked as Trudy slammed out the door and turned right, heading for the next, contiguous building. With a discus-thrower's whirl, she heaved her knapsack ahead of her. This startled a conference of pigeons, which burst up from the low parapet. Trudy hurdled the parapet at the point where a rusty old coffee can leaned against it.

She flew with her legs forward like a long-jumper, then turned sideways so that her good shoulder would take the pressure. Down and down – it was only one floor of difference, but it seemed like five till she hit in a splash of gravel and rolled sideways – then backwards – staggered up, regained her stride, swerved, bent low, and snatched her knapsack on the run. Gravel clinging to her beaten pony tail rained over her shoulders.

Her goal was the triangular cement structure with the stern metal door – like the entrance to an underground bomb shelter – which stood wide open some twenty yards ahead. Behind her, she heard a panicked "Shit!" And then a thump and a cry of pain because her pursuer, rather than hurdling the low parapet, had slipped on the copious gravel spread atop it the day before, which started his leap very much on the wrong foot. He landed badly and broke something, but he still had enough intact limbs to pull out a silenced handgun and squeeze off a shot in Trudy's direction. By then, however, she was well down the stairway, and the cinder blocks of the roof entrance spat fragments in vain over the metal steps. A twisted poem of profanity followed this, and then I was closing the interior door to the roof entrance behind Trudy: two bolts thick as table legs made jovial clanks as they slid into place at the top and bottom of the door

I leaned down and hugged her vigorously; I couldn't help myself. "Trudy, old love, marvelous! Well done you! Bravo!" I said, brushing off the gravel, though most likely Trudy could barely hear me over the noise of ventilators and other rooftop machines. "You're all right then? Shoulder still intact? All extremities present and accounted for? Lovely to see you again, by the way."

"Yeah, I think I'm okay. Can you hold my bag? I gotta shake out my hair." Her pony tail had become undone, and she undid the rest and combed out the gravel with her fingers.

"Yes, but let's get going, shall we?" I said, pulling her along, and we traversed a dim River Styx of ventilator fans big as jet engines, gloomy metal grills, faceless electrical cabinets and greasy riveted beams thick with furry coats of dust. Yellow signs warning of one danger and another loomed and passed like level crossings beside a speeding train, and finally we passed through a no-nonsense security door – I threw the lock on this as well – and trotted down a flight of echoing iron stairs to a final door of honest oak. Open and shut, and suddenly we stood in a civilized hallway lined with office doors, "Jarks and Hezelstein, Attorneys-at-Law," read the plaque in front of us. A few steps down, I pressed the elevator button, and it opened instantly, for I had called it less than a minute before. From the janitor's closet I took a new student's knapsack with Spiderman swinging across it.

"In we go, old love. Now then, a quick checklist," I said, punching the second-floor button. "We kept our lovely head down until we heard Irene yell?"

"Yeah."

"Excellent. And Rolanda in the hostal took no note of you?"

"No – just took the money and gave me sheets and stuff."

"And how did we spend the lax hours yesterday? Goodness, I was worried."

She told me about the donut shop.

"Brilliant – bravo. Yes, I thought a temp job was the best bet. And poor Roger. We couldn't find a more, ah, *lissome* victim than him, could we?"

"Max, c'mon. I just went to a hotel and walked out on him," she said sourly.

"Quite right, old love. Cheers."

Meanwhile, I had told her to pile her hair up on top of her head again as best she could, and rammed a dark-gray wool cap down on her head. It had a needless little visor on it.

"Now then, off with that jacket." I handed her a teenager's red jacket with patches all over it and a hood. Trudy slipped it on as the elevator doors opened.

I led her out across the hall and into an ugly emergency stairway.

"And now the pants, if you'd be so kind, old fruit," I said. They were athletic pants, at the time very fashionable with youngsters, had an elastic waistband, and slipped on quickly over her other pants.

While she was putting them on, I opened the Spiderman knapsack and swallowed hers into it. "In the pocket you'll find a pair of sunglasses – put them on when we get outside. I did what I could for, ah, matters of style, but my apologies all the same. And you'll find a new pair of reading glasses – of the same type – in the pocket; don't know if yours have survived the fall. But don't put them on till tonight. They now have a description of you with glasses on."

Trudy tied the pants tight. "Okay. Ready."

"There! You are a typical New York teenager. Even with a second look it will be hard to spot you. Now then, follow me till we get out through the street entrance."

We walked down the last flight of stairs and into the lobby, a typical one as those things go in New York: a minimalist echoing mausoleum of gray-veined white marble that displayed a gray-veined white marble reception desk, which was empty. There was nobody on duty at the desk – nobody anywhere. Then I made out both the petite receptionist and chubby security guard standing just beyond the glass doors, staring along with others at the mass of police cars, cherry lights uselessly turning, in front of the department store Trudy had just left. Word of Trudy had gone around fast.

"Max! There are cameras here!" Trudy hissed, pointing at the ceiling.

"Burglary defense, old fruit. They don't begin recording until six in the evening. One or two of these law offices, I gather, are mafia outfits that would rather not have a record of who is going in and out. But just for the security guard's benefit, you go out first. Turn left. I'll follow you down the sidewalk and we'll meet down a ways."

I pulled on a floppy hat, counted to ten, and walked out head down.

"There! Done! Good fun, wasn't it?" I said, catching up to Trudy.

"Yeah, I guess it was okay. Hey, look."

A couple of hard fellows in jeans sprinted into the office building we had just left. The security guard whirled and chased after them, moving his 250 pounds as best he could. The men shouted at him to lock down the building, and like security men all over the world, the guard was not going to be told what to do on his own turf. A lovely argument ensued.

"Who are those guys, anyway?" asked Trudy.

"The men trying to get there before the police. Also known as 'henchman': the enablers of the people we are trying to defeat. Let's start walking, shall we?"

"They sure got here fast."

"Indeed. Faster than I'd expected. Well, old love, our debriefing will have to wait till tonight, but there's one thing I must ask you about: you had a little chat with the priest who came out of the house on Charlesdrew. What was *that* about?"

Trudy told me, ending, "Isn't that a funny name for a priest – John *Paper*?"

"It's funnier still that he told you his name," I said, and made a mental note to look him up by name – that could be damned useful. "Though on the other hand, he certainly never expected you to tell anyone."

"Yeah. The last thing he told me was that the Lord would take good care of me," she added with a shiver. "I had a nightmare about that last night."

"You're not the first of my agents to have them, I can assure you. We'll have time to talk later this evening. Now then…" I looked around. "It seems that we'll need to change our plans due to the police force's quick response. We obviously can't go that way, so we'll go the other." We crossed at the corner and I pointed down Chambers Street. "Here's the plan then, old fruit: keep walking straight, same side of the street, till a taxi picks you up a few blocks down. His name is Joe – just good old Joe with a fine Belfast brogue. I left my phone in my car – no use leaving an electronic trace in the office building here. So it will take me a few minutes to contact Joe and get him started in the right direction. But don't worry; he'll be there."

"Okay – just walk straight."

"He will take you to his house in Newark, where you can take a hot bath and enjoy Irene's fine Irish stew this evening. You'll recognize Irene: she was the lady spotting for you in the department store."

"Wow, Irish stew and a bath sound great," said Trudy.

"Now then, I've made sure through my computer friend Ian that no security cameras were pointing our way at the office building, but just in case there's an iPhone trained on us somewhere, give me a daughterly kiss on the cheek and wander off, the classic picture of a divorced father taking his daughter in to have her braces adjusted by an overpaid dentist."

"Okay, Max, see you, uh, soon, I hope," she said, standing on tip-toe to kiss me. "Say hi to Paul for me."

"Will do. I'll look in on you tonight. Off you go now."

With that odd sawing swing of her arm, she strode off down Chambers, which by the oddest trick of destiny would turn out to be significant. I stayed around long enough to make sure she got away undetected, then dashed – as much as my limp allowed – a few blocks to a parking ramp and got my phone. I called Joe to tell him of the change in plan; Joe, by the way, was a former MI6 street artist turned New York cabbie. He said he would have to swing around a few blocks because the police were rerouting all the traffic, but if Trudy just kept walking down the same street, he would catch up with her in about twenty minutes. *Rightee-oh, Max; always did love a little improvisation in an op. Piece o' cake. Chasin' a blond bird down the street – remind me of my youth, that will.*

And yet.

"Into every op a little rain must fall," as an old MI6 "Operation Histories" instructor used to sing, adding a maddening "tra-la-la." Well, it was about to pour an icy shower on mine.

19 SEPTEMBER-OCTOBER

And now Paul was everywhere defending the administration's turn towards diplomacy: speeches, articles in the *Times* and the *Journal*; interviews, debates on C-SPAN, testimony in front of jowly congressional panels. It was work he could believe in. To put international dialog and diplomacy again at the center of policy was the only means to counter those like Senator Crick who wanted America to "cut the pie," which as Paul and I had discussed very much in private, was a fantasy entertained by American elites: Russia and China would never accept such back-seat status; and America no longer had the political stability or economic dominance to make the rules by itself. Nor would the planet's environment remain patient. With a bit of luck, he thought, he might really make up for some lost time in American foreign policy, which since 9/11 had swung disastrously to military intervention, which was like using surgery to cure the common cold.

Paul, of course, took his lumps in the cause. A red-faced interviewer accused him flatly of being a "Chamberlain-style appeaser."

Conservative columnists said he was making up policy that flew in the face of the president's ideas. Others were openly skeptical that the president and Carlton "Never-met-a-war-he-didn't-like" Mason were going to return to diplomacy, observe international law, and make negotiation the center of policy. On Mason's suggestion, Paul even dangled America's possible entry into the International Criminal Court at the Hague – "folks think we already are a member, and it's time we give 'em a wake-up call" – causing both the president and the secretary to demur publicly, the latter sourly implying that Under Secretary of State Klippen was getting too big for his britches. But Mason and Paul had another fine whiskey bash that same night and laughed till they were too tipsy to remember the joke, a meeting that the president's press secretary called "getting taken behind the woodshed." Mason told Paul, "POTUS figured out real quick that I'd put you up to it. Called me up and said I'm a connivin' dumbshit. Then he said that was shrewd work. Remind folks we're the ones in charge. Asked me when he can get some o' this whiskey. I told him to fuck off."

About halfway through this campaign was his appearance on the top Sunday-morning show, *Meet the Nation*, with Marlene Hanneker.

"Awright, *Pwal*," she began, "let's say that Al Qaeda seeded a ma-juh footbwall stadium with bombs and killed three thousand people at a swipe. Are you saying that the United States would have *no* military respwonse? That renewed diplomacy is always the ansuh?"

I won't insist anymore on her plangent Brooklyn accent; you get the idea.

"Well, first, let's remember that diplomacy is not surrender. Diplomacy can mean quite the opposite. Second, as always, one reserves the right to make a judgment on each case of terror, which is –"

"Especially in the case of this president, a.k.a. *your boss*. He *used to* come down in favor of carrying the war to everyone else's backyard. I mean, that's another issue: Can we really believe that *this president* is in favor of diplomatic responses to crises?" This with a dramatic lean forward to emphasize her round bosom.

"Well, let me get to the first question first. A terrorist organization is not a country. And it is not always clear what country supported the guilty party. Organizational meetings for 9/11 were held in Berlin, but did anyone think to retaliate against Germany? On the other hand, America retaliated against Afghanistan for hosting Osama bin Laden, though neither the government nor any Afghans took part in 9/11. Did that get them a --"

"So what are you saying? That we should just try to feel the pain of these monsters who attack us? Like they were inner-city kids who never had a break? C'mon, what do you do in the case of a major attack?"

A smile of patience. "Well, the *first* thing I do, Marlene, is ask to be able to explain myself without any interruptions...."

A nervous laugh, hands held up in apology, though it was easy to see that she resented the comment: Hanneker's program was about Hanneker. The camera loved her big, brown eyes and torrent of black hair that sat upon her well-padded shoulder like a pirate's cockatoo. She was unhappy about being sent *Under* Secretary of State Klippen when she had asked for Secretary of State Mason. She was determined to chew Paul up and spit him out.

"What I'm trying to say, Marlene, is that going to war against a group is not like going to war against another country. Terrorist support and financing usually has many roots, particularly in the oil and heroine markets. Should we bomb the banks? If you want to weaken the conditions in which terrorists are born, you're far better off sending in the Red Cross than the U.S. Air Force. Now as to your second question --"

But Hanneker's dam was already bursting: "Then why do we have a military we spend a trillion dollars a year on?" she cried.

"This administration, Marlene, is saying that from now on, our armed forces are to prepare for war against another major power – period. Against terrorist groups, your best bet is what it always has been: ruthless intelligence work and infiltration."

Hanneker flung her hair off one shoulder and scooped it onto the other. "What about sending drones? Don't these people deserve to get their organizational meeting broken up with a great big bunker-buster?"

"They may well deserve it. The trouble is that your bunker-buster will take out half the neighborhood with it, and then law-abiding people who the day before abhorred terrorism start to see it in a kinder light."

A sigh, as if she could not make him see reason. "A lot of people would dispute that because the meeting is developing a plan to drop its own bunker-buster on Time Square. Okay, Paul, we've got to stop for a break." To the camera, skeptically: "Well, don't go away. We'll be right back for our customary Last Word with Under Secretary of State Paul Klippen."

The Last Word was *Hanneker's* last word, her summary – that is, her opinion – of what she had heard during the program. The guest was allowed a rebuttal, normally truncated by the time limit of the show. Paul braced himself: that last comment of hers, "a lot of people would dispute that," meant that she had both barrels prepared for Paul. Her last syndicated opinion column had argued that the real problem with fighting terrorist groups was that America always did it with only half the necessary boots on the ground.

The commercials were running. Hanneker now walked off the set and had a scrabbling, whispering, hissing, rasping argument with the director, just behind the cameras. Paul could not see them beyond the studio lights, but they sounded like two cats locked in a blood duel in an alley. This went on and on. The last commercial was ending, and Paul wondered if he was going to be on camera alone to finish the program. Finally, with the floor manager pleading, "Marlene, five seconds. *Please!*", Hanneker leapt into her chair just in time for the man's trembling finger to swing to her.

"Welcome back, everyone. Time for the Last Word. And for, ah, for a change, Paul, I'd like to ask you a more general question. We're always so wrapped up in politics on the show that I don't often get a chance to, you know, ask a guest to step back and take the long view, the overview, but…you, Paul Klippen, new Under Secretary of State for Political Affairs, you are a veteran diplomat with several postings under your belt…"

"Well, three at least, Marlene."

"What for you is the fascination of international relations? To most of us it's a pretty dry, academic subject: history, economics, politics. You obviously enjoy it; otherwise you could easily have moved into the private sector. Why? What makes it so interesting?"

At this, Hanneker sat back and crossed her arms like a child who refuses to eat her greens, this to let everyone know that she had asked this question against her will.

Paul had not prepared for the question, but his naturally philosophical mind and lovely concision rose to the challenge.

"I suppose, really, that it's…the spectacle of it, actually, Marlene. International relations are the battleships of history. A diplomat stands there watching them on a collision path. When he can, he tries to ward them off or alter their direction or at least minimize the impact when they smack up against each other. There's great poetry to this work, and often real drama and tension – because the result of bad diplomacy can be war, but more often it's the loss of jobs, distorted trade relations, bad blood between neighbors, the further degradation of the environment – in short, innocent people getting crushed between the ships of history. International relations is the center of the world – everything else, well, everything else is just the result."

Paul knew that this had come off well – if only because Hanneker quickly closed the show and stormed off the set without another word to him. But to his amazement, his fine bit of oratory ended up on network news programs and dozens of Internet websites. And then everyone wanted a piece of him: news shows, magazines, networks. A women's talk show in San Francisco pined for him – yes, cooking spaghetti with the host, an offer which, you remember, Paul had declined. But the producer went straight to Carlton Mason, showed him his college fraternity ring, and talked turkey. "Oh, just go and stir a little pasta 'round the goddamn pot, would ya, Paul? I still kinda owe this old dumbshit that wrote my compositions for English 101," Mason told him on the phone from Mexico. Such is politics.

But everyone's favorite, for which he took no end of ribbing, was Paul's picture on the cover of one of those overwrought magazines with a day-glow masthead that tracks the love lives of movie stars, complete with the headline, *Is This Our Sexiest Diplomat?* And Paul did look sexy – effortlessly photogenic, with that lovely dark-brown hair combed high above his forehead – jauntily sitting on the corner of his desk, jacketless, trim waist, tie left to hang. My wife, who brought the magazine home from the supermarket, asked me if I'd mind if she had an affair with him. "After all, we're both American," she added a propos of nothing.

20

I later called it "Sod's Law," which Paul calls "Murphy's Law." If things could go wrong, they would; and indeed they did.

Joe started out after Trudy. But you know how things go in places like New York, Bangkok, or Calcutta. The immense police blockade of the department store – you had to wonder how many hulking police officers were required to arrest one tiny woman – stifled nearly all traffic in a radius of a quarter mile. Two-way streets turned into one-ways or no-ways-at-all, and the traffic lights let through only enough cars to produce further gridlock. When Joe finally turned onto Chambers and glimpsed Trudy walking along just a block ahead, he found himself before an apoplectic policeman fanning him to the right. He decided to park the taxi and run after Trudy, but couldn't find a place to park, even illegally, and he ended up jamming the car into a service alley near Rockefeller Plaza and taking a subway to Police Plaza. It was an hour before he could even get back to the place where he had last seen her.

Trudy, meanwhile, followed directions as only a statistical analyst could, and continued straight. She walked all the way down Chambers, across Police Plaza probably fifteen minutes before Joe, and stopped for a long moment at the upslope to the Brooklyn Bridge Promenade. Well, Max *had* said straight. Probably Joe would be waiting on the other side. So up she walked, and walked and walked, embraced by a peaceful November sun; it was the lovely kind of autumn day that makes you forgiving of global warming. Her legs were overly warm in the double pair of pants, but the exercise felt wonderful, and her tension drained away amidst the commingling of sky and Gothic arches and geometrical cables. She kept a steady pace all the way across to Brooklyn Heights, along with a friendly seagull, which would fly ahead of her, wait, and then fly on.

She reached the Heights in late afternoon and found no Irishman waiting for her, and now she began to worry. I'd never given her an emergency contact number: the interview with "Hallerbee," surely recorded, would allow the technologists to find her by voice print over the phone lines; indeed, I had specifically warned Trudy to stay off the phone once she was on the run. Dusk was setting in, with monstrous shadows painting the narrow streets, and if Trudy hated one thing above another, it was darkness. So a steady panic, like water rising through floor after floor of the *Titanic*, was spreading through her.

A police siren blared behind her, and she walked right off the promenade. She turned a corner, walked a ways, and turned another: Pineapple Street. Trudy had to control her feet in order not to break into a run.

"No, no, no. I am not doing this anymore. Thanks a bunch, Joe – and Max too," she griped quietly as she walked – always swiftly, as if she had some place to go; I had taught her that lesson, among several others, to survive her first twenty-four hours on the street. "A hot bath and Irish stew, right? You creeps. I am getting off the street, and I am doing it *right now*."

She was walking down a line of apartment blocks, many with sub-level apartments whose occupants seemed to be standing in trenches. Ahead of her, a woman came out a gate wedged between two tall apartment buildings. Trudy pushed it open and went in.

She walked through the car-wide canyon and emerged into a small twilit courtyard where some half-dozen girls – African, Chinese, and Latino – were jumping rope. Trudy had loved to jump rope as a kid, and she had an urge to join them. The kids had two ropes going at the same time, like egg beaters. The girl in the middle kept up, feet chopping like a cook dicing celery, the other girls counting. When they reached "26 times," she jumped out as easily as jumping off a bus.

"I wanna see you do dat, SuLyn!" squealed the jumper.

The two ropes turned in unison now. A Chinese girl leapt in. The others chanted:

On East Forty-Fourth Street a lady kicked a cat.
She slipped on a peel and her ass went splat.
Along came a cop and he helped her to her feet,
But he touched her boobs and she kicked him in his meat.
Once, twice, three times four times five times six times....

With the "times," the ropes began to work alternately, so that the jumper had to hop from foot to foot to keep up. They reached "twenty-three times" before SuLyn missed, and the ropes went awry. The girls all yelled and screamed at each other. The girls turning the ropes changed.

"Wow! You guys are really good!" Trudy blurted, "Can I try it?"

The girls stared.

"You sure, lady? I mean, like, it's not normal," said a handsome Latino girl.

But they let her in.

It took her two tries to get going, but on the second she went all the way through the rhyme and reached "15 times" before missing. The girls congratulated her, reaching up to pat her shoulders. It was odd for Trudy; for once she was actually taller than other people.

"Wow! I never seen no a-dult do dat b'fore."

"Nobody. That was pre'y incre'ble."

"Hey, lady, you live around here?"

"No, I'm just visiting…a friend. She lives there." Trudy pointed at one of the buildings. "It's kind of a surprise. I'm just…I was just kind of in the area. I don't even know if she's home."

She walked over toward the doorway and made as if pressing a button on the intercom.

"That thing's bustet sometimes. Jussa sec," called one of the girls, running over. She pulled a cell phone out of the back pocket of her pants.

Please get me inside, Trudy pleaded silently. *I can sleep on the roof, I don't care.*

The girl punched some buttons on the intercom, and a moment later, her cell phone made a beep. She looked at the number on the screen, punched that in, and the door buzzed open.

"Thanks," said Trudy.

"Be careful with the el'vator," the girl warned. "If you get stuck, just bang on the doors till someone comes out. They gotta call the janitor."

"Okay. Thanks." Trudy headed for the stairs.

The stairway had a fresh coat of paint, the top half of the wall in maroon, the bottom half in light blue; the wooden handrail beckoned upwards. She walked up all ten flights of stairs, and would happily have walked ten more. Finally, she sat down on the top step, out of breath. She took off her exterior pants: her legs were baking under two layers.

"Now what?" she muttered, stuffing them in the Spiderman knapsack. "Now I'm just going to sit her and think and take it easy."

The other floors had three apartment doors each, but this one had just two and no elevator. A service door occupied the space of the third apartment. And from the hum and vibration, she guessed that there was elevator machinery behind it.

She looked hopefully at the other two doors, one marked A, from which a warble of music struggled out, and the other B, which offered the plosive honk of a television. Maybe if she just knocked politely on the door and explained the situation…

But that was stupid, she reasoned: this was New York City; they would take her for a serial killer and kick her straight out of the building. Like most Midwesterners who had little experience of New York, Trudy believed that it was populated by curmudgeons who would rather see a fellow dismembered on the street than help him.

"Well, what else can I do?" she whispered. "I can't just walk back out. Max, you are the biggest creep in the world! Why didn't you get me picked up? You creep!" Then she remembered herself and said three Hail Maries. Then another three, asking the Virgin for help.

Her panic rose higher. It was getting late. Two floors below, a woman walked out of her apartment and took the elevator. Trudy remembered Roger's gun and jerked it out of the knapsack. That was it, she thought wildly: just get inside and hold someone hostage. Maybe with a little luck, she thought, she would find some nice, fat, elderly Jewish lady with a refrigerator full of kosher food who would probably love to have company for the evening.

I know! I'll make her a pumpkin bread or a bacon quiche – whatever she's got.

She was trying to decide on door A or B, as if it were a TV game show, when A opened. Trudy rushed the door. She shoved it open, knocking the person back in.

Who turned out to be neither female, nor fat, nor old, nor Jewish. He was a lean fellow, mid-thirties, with frizzy brown hair, dressed in a light suede jacket. What she noticed most, as she pointed the gun at him, was his big lower jaw, which was a straight square robotic overbite.

"Hands up," she ordered, for lack of anything better to say, closing the door behind her.

The man backed straight across the room to the line of windows there. "Okay okay okay, just don't fire the gun, okay? Just *don't* fire the gun. You can have anything you want, no problem. Money, booze, shirt off my back. Help yourself."

He hadn't really raised his hands, but kept them well away from his sides. Then he turned around to the ledge full of plants by the windows and leaned on it. "I'm just going to hang a while over here by the plants – haven't talked to them today, anyway, and you know plants: they're worse than girlfriends."

"Um, I think you better close the window," Trudy said. She could hear the girls still chanting below: *On East Forty-Fourth Street a lady kicked a cat.....*

The man cranked it shut. "Sorry. I like to open up after I take a shower. I just got up, you know – work nights. By the way, I really haven't seen you, so I can't i.d. you. Just take what you want. Wallet's in the back pocket here. All yours." A pause. "Just leave my Actors Guild card, okay? Just out on the stairs, that'll be fine. Guild folks get pissed when people start asking for replacements."

He spoke so fast that Trudy could hardly follow him. Now what? "Just stay there," she ordered.

The apartment was a one-room studio the size of a single-car garage, clean though poorly furnished – college-freshman quality. The armchair's upholstery was threadbare. The round three-legged table beside it had been scratched by a dog and carved on by a five-year old. Beside the door to the steamy bathroom, the kitchen was immaculate: a few dishes set to dry in a plastic rack, two pots and two pans hanging by a three-foot length of copper piping that hung from the ceiling on two thick electrical wires. Under the windows, two shelves full of used paperback books and DVDs ran the length of the room. She glanced down at the table beside her and saw a notebook full of scribbled sentences written as if for a theater play. Beside one dialog there was an underlined note: *Not too hard!*

"Don't hear you stuffing things in a bag," the man said over his shoulder. "If you need one, they're under the sink, bottom left over there. Sorry I don't have much to offer. Best thing in the place are these African violets. Northern window, you know – grow like crazy. But they're yours if you want 'em."

A cluster of violets lined the sill. Amidst the clumsy, bottle-green leaves, the flowers fairly sang with color: purple, magenta, a majestic dark-blue.

"I actually didn't come for flowers," Trudy replied as toughly as she could. She glanced at her watch. "Let's see, it's almost five."

"You came for the time," the man said.

"Don't you have a TV?"

"I just use the PC." With his head the man indicated a laptop at the far end of the shelf, where the plants ended. "This is actually a low-budget outfit – even if it doesn't look it."

"Well, turn it on and –" She wrinkled her nose. "You don't sound like you're from New York."

"I'm from Milwaukee. You aren't exactly The Bronx yourself."

This confused Trudy. "Um, just put on the news."

He did, fiddling with an external mouse for a moment, and put the set on the table. A sports report was on. "You came to watch the news then?"

"Just be quiet and sit on that thing," Trudy said, pointing to an ancient ottoman.

The man did, setting his elbows on his knees, curiosity growing in his eyes. He had rather bad skin but it fit well with his frizzy hair. And that stupendous jaw was magnificent. His light-blue shirt sat well on him, and his jacket over that, zipped halfway up. "Got pota-to chips if you want 'em. No Coke. That was one of the things I was just about to run out and get."

"That's okay. Wait. I'm starving – get out the potato chips. And don't forget I have a gun," she said.

The man got a bag of potato chips and set it on the table beside her. She couldn't open the bag with one hand, so the man did it for her. Then he sat down again on the ottoman, gathered his hands to-gether, his long legs angled up. He looked at her thoughtfully. "You don't hold it right, you know. Your wrist's crooked. They teach you that in acting class. You have to hold your forearm in line with the gun. Fire it like that, and you punch yourself in the gut."

By habit, Trudy took this advice and changed her posture; but this only made her look worse.

The man looked her over, mirth growing like a flame in his face, and his jaw reaching steadily forward. "Let's see, you're not an opi-um junkie that needs a fix, you're not a thief, you're not a sex ma-niac. You're dressed in nice clothes and a new backpack like, ah, 'Barbie goes to an outdoor concert with Ken.' Except for the rapper's cap – the hell is *that* about? Let's see…what else? No makeup – I admire that, not so much as a line under the eyes. And the jacket's zipped up so high it practically shouts, 'I don't do it on the first date, so keep your hands where I can see them.'"

Trudy was trying to find news about herself. "Can't you be quiet, please?"

"Please? *Please?*" With his index fingers, he played a drum roll on his cheeks. "I can't quite figure out the hat, but for the rest, I'd say you're in big trouble, like you just got foreclosed on and your boyfriend's throwing it all on you – or maybe you shot him, but hey, the bastard had it coming. *Now* you're down to muscling your way into some poor stiff's apartment or spending another night on the street. That ballpark?"

"Okay, yeah, it's something like that," Trudy growled.

"Sorry. Just that whenever people hold guns on me, I get nervous. And when I get nervous, I blab."

She waved the gun. "But don't think I'm going to walk out of here now that I've gotten in. I just need to stay here a few hours. Then you can go."

"Okay, but lose the piece, would you? You're in good hands here. You want to stay for dinner? You're welcome. Hell, it's a relief to meet someone who's a worse actor than me."

Again that word. "You're an actor?"

A big, dawning overbite grin. "Now and then. Mainly I do stand-up in the Village. Well, *mainly,* I do freelance translation – Russian-English. But the standup is going all right lately. I don't have to give blowjobs to get a gig anymore."

"You're a comedian?"

A despairing grimace. "You haven't noticed? Babe, I've just given you two minutes of new material here."

"What's your name?"

A corny bow. "On stage, Jerry Stretch. Not quite a household ring to that, but I'm workin' on it."

She repeated the name blankly.

"But if you need your business plan translated to Russian, then call Jerry Strajenska. *Ta-da-a-a.*" He drummed on his cheeks again.

Trudy looked at him, indecisive.

"Look, just put the gun down, okay? Gives me the willies, and that's only to start with. Bruises, warts and zits quickly follow. I'm not going to jump you. Promise. Just put down the piece, tell Uncle Jerry your problems, and we'll get something worked out, deal? You're one of these decent, upstanding types – Stevie Wonder could see that. Whatever you've done –" He had slowly ducked his head, staring at the gun and now stifled a laugh. "You, ah, forgot to put the clip in."

Trudy sighed. "Yeah – yeah, that's right." She put the gun back in the backpack, and Jerry huffed with relief; he really had been frightened.

"Good move. Good move, babe. The future of American comedy thanks you."

Trudy felt guilty. "Sorry. I'm just, y'know, I'm really in kind of a mess." She leaned forward on her knees, head in hands, and began to weep, and Jerry jumped up, which gave her a bad moment, but only to grab a box of tissues for her from the bathroom.

"That's all right, babe. Just let it out. Lotta pressure in there. How about a cup of tea? Cures half the evils of the world – learnt that when I was working London for a summer."

"Yeah, thanks," Trudy croaked.

"Hey, and you can stay the night, and you don't even have to worry about me jumping you because I'm on at eight-thirty at Crazy Mabel's in the Village, so lately I'm not getting home till two or three. Four eight-minuters, you know, and in between I help shake drinks."

Trudy looked at the computer and fiddled with it again, without success. "But I'm not crazy, okay? I'm just, I'm just going through something."

"Yeah, I picked that up."

"I'm, ah, my name is Trudy Schelling."

Her name meant nothing to Jerry. From the kitchen end, he set his palms together and made a Chinese bow. "Trudy Schelling, welcome. As they say in Spanish, my-a house-a is your-a house-a." He bent down to the small refrigerator and began to take what he needed for the tea. "Gotta keep everything in here. Otherwise Charlie Cockroach comes a-callin'. If you have anything to eat in that pack, out it comes right now."

"No – I just have some clothes." Trudy grabbed the bag of potato chips. "God, I'm starving."

"Well, why didn't you say so? Here at 32-and-a-half Pineapple, we're all hospitality. Bet a sandwich would slip down nice too, huh? Let's see: cheese, tuna…I got salami, all three?"

"Anything – whatever you have would be just great."

Jerry dropped tea bags in two cups and turned around, leaning back against the counter, and crossed his arms and long legs. "So what's the problem, babe? Give it your best shot."

"Well, okay." She sighed. "Oh, Jerry, I'm so glad I can talk to someone! You know that terrorist attack over in Jersey City yesterday?"

"Ick! News, information, politics – *big* mistake. Babe, in this house, we take pride in ignorance. Cultivate it like a garden. Now I did hear there was a big boom over there in Jersey City yesterday, but if you live in Jersey, it's your own fault."

Trudy giggled. "Jerry, you're too much, really. You must be a great comedian."

"Hey, I actually did politics once. I did a standup for the Occupy Wall Street folks. You know: lift troop morale, all that?" He winked. "Also a nice bit of free publicity for Jerry Stretch. Come to think of it, they're doing an Occupy this week at Madison Park. I should go over. I had a great crowd: around two-three hundred people. You get good at counting crowds in my business. Like this one." He looked around. "All right, light box-office tonight, but what the hell: wherever two or three are gathered together, my motto. Give yourself a big hand, folks."

Trudy laughed.

"Um, just one thing – *Trudy*, was it? Lose, ah, lose the hat, huh? You kinda look like, y'know, Frankenstein's lesbian daughter doing open-mike rap."

"Yeah, it's awful. And hot." Trudy jerked it off and stuffed it away in her sack, then ran her fingers through her hair till it was at least straight. When she turned back, Jerry was looking at her, jaw jutting forward. His light, almost powdery, eyebrows were knitted up. He might have caught her taking his money.

"What's the matter?"

Jerry raised a hand to an inflated cheek and tapped on it twice: *bop-bop.* "Babe, please: hair like that? And I'm thinking that's your color, right?"

"Yeah, sure." She blushed. "I put in highlights, a little."

"A little, huh?" Jerry laughed. "Well, if the armed-assault gig doesn't work out for you – and frankly it looks bad – maybe I can set you up with a photographer friend of mine for some head shots. There's, y'know, there's good money to be made there: shampoo commercials, hair-dye packaging, whatever."

Trudy felt herself blushing. "Thanks."

He shook his head. "God damn: right in out of the stairway… Okay, so let 'er rip on your troubles, and I'll put together a sandwich for you. One gut-buster comin' up."

21

MID-OCTOBER

Paul had a notion that he would soon be summoned to his first Doers meeting. I met him at a Virginia strip-mall salad bar and told him that he had cleared the last hurdles. "Jack Mirage still thinks you're crazy for turning down women for security reasons, but he seems to be the only one, and Senator Crick has given you the thumbs up – much to the relief of everyone else. They'll clear a spot in your agenda 'by accident' and call you on the spur of the moment." When Paul asked why on the spur of the moment, I answered, "Because they don't trust you completely. They don't want you to come prepared."

And indeed he wasn't.

The Doers meeting was gathered a week after Paul's chat with Senator Crick, still in the midst of his media campaign for a peaceful turn in the administration's foreign policy.

It was Friday, and Paul was finishing a three-day swing through the western and southern states, making speeches every day at both lunches and dinners, being interviewed on radio, on local television, and doing a taping for a Sunday morning local-politics show in Tampa, Florida. It was all paying off. Polls showed people heavily in favor of the policy, and that Paul himself was well-known and his opinion held weight. Still, conservatives abhorred him.

He was still in Tampa, heading for the airport to catch a flight back to Washington, when Parker Radow phoned to tell him that reservations had been made for him to take a flight not to Washington but to JFK, where he would be helicoptered to "an essential top-secret meeting," which would actually start on Saturday morning.

"Oh, and dress is casual," he added. "Venue's some sort of hunting lodge."

Paul snapped off his phone with a growl. For three days packed with speeches, Rotary luncheons, and interviews, he traveled with nothing even distantly casual.

But he hated to be improperly dressed for an occasion. In the airport parking lot, he lightened his carry-on bag and stuffed what he could into his big suitcase. This he foisted on one of his two assistants and kept only his briefcase and carry-on. Before flying to New York, he bought a flannel shirt, a sweater, a T-shirt, loose slacks, and a pair of canvas shoes, biting his tongue over the horrendous airport prices. But he had great respect for first impressions, and even more so in Washington, where success or failure often depended on the snap judgments people made as they ran from meeting to meeting.

When he arrived in New York, a driver showed him his security clearance and drove him to a nearby heliport, where Paul got into a fragile-looking helicopter – just a glass bubble with a propeller on top – for the ride into a darkening upstate New York sky, his shopping bags crackling on his lap, for he hadn't had time to pack his purchases into his carry-on.

With the last evening light, the helicopter descended over solid forest, found a clearing in it, and left him on the front lawn of a baleful Gothic-looking stone building, the sort of thing supposed to look vaguely Teutonic and invincible. Ultimately, though, it had turned out ridiculous. The front door under its arch seemed no bigger than a cartoon mousehole. Alongside it, the windows were far too large. The roof was a zombie army of small chimneys that seemed to be on the march. Lashed incongruously to them, three antennae dishes peered into different parts of the heavens. Only corduroy furrows of light behind shutters in two of the upstairs dormer windows hinted at habitation. Now a light went on over the front door, a single eye-shattering beam that razed the entire front lawn.

Paul gripped his shopping bags with his briefcase in one hand and pulled his carry-on with the other; his entrance would have little grace. Against the roaring glare of the front-door light, he felt his way around a long hedge and trudged, squinting, toward it. His hands full, he couldn't shade his eyes, and ended up turning his back to it and walking backwards. Finally at the door, without the light in his eyes, he could see that there was a break in the hedge that allowed direct access there from the heliport. Well.

When he turned around, the door was open, and inside stood a slender man with a cement-gray crewcut, body tilted a fraction to one side as if one leg were longer than the other. Deep-set peasant eyes, no chin at all, an unloved face whose yellowish pallor carried the memory of interagency meetings and tall stacks of manila files. And he was dressed in black and wore a priest's dog collar.

"Under Secretary Klippen, a pleasure to finally meet you. I'm The Rainmaker," he said in a purring, ashy voice. He took Paul's hand softly, as if it might break, his fingers reaching forward searchingly to his wrist.

"Oh! The Rainmaker," Paul exclaimed, and silently shouted, "Max, I found him!"

"You've heard about me?" said The Rainmaker with alarm.

"Ah, just, just tangentially. Senator Crick gave me a quick run-down on –"

"On Doers? On me? Where? When?" The Rainmaker had an ugly little lipless mouth that writhed as Paul told him. "At a cocktail party," he fumed. "Behind a piano! God help us. Dottie Crick thinks this is all a boys' game: rules, protocols, security – that's just nonsense to her."

Paul's first instinct was to assure The Rainmaker that no one had overheard the conversation, but he checked it. "So that was all very much classified information."

"Of course it was! Nobody is to know about me. That damn woman – I've given her one lecture and another about security, to absolutely no good." A jagged little volcano boiled inside this man.

He led Paul inside and stepped around to a small lectern, raising a sternly rectangular pair of glasses to his face from the cord they hung on. He whacked something with a fingernail, and a computer screen lit his face.

The place was roomy and dim and smelled of a recently-eaten dinner and, behind that, lemon wood polish. A distant table lamp spread a cautious light in the living room to their left, and the lowest bulb in the dining room chandelier glowed to their right. And the place definitely was, just as Radow had said, a hunting lodge: animal horns, oak paneling, carved sideboards, paintings of defiant mountains, black fireplaces – only from there he could see four – with three pristine logs of exactly the same length stacked in each one.

"I didn't expect to be greeted by a priest," said Paul, to change the subject. "Are you actually a priest?"

"Baptized babies in Communist Poland, held Mass on Trident submarines, taken confession from some of the highest-placed humint sources this country's ever had. Security clearance higher than the president's." It was a set piece, like a general explaining his medals.

"Higher than the president's? I never thought that was possible."

"I've heard there aren't a half-dozen of us in the whole USG." The Rainmaker was past seventy but had the spartan body of a fitness enthusiast. His neck and chinless face rose out of the dog collar like a single thick peg, and his shoulders were well-defined. Only the slight listing to one side belied age. Perhaps one of his hips was failing.

"So did you join the army as a chaplain?" said Paul. "If you don't mind my asking."

Again the pride spurted out. "Said my first Mass in a field hospital south of Da Nang in '71."

"Right in the thick of Vietnam."

"A noble cause, by the way." He laid an index finger on his cheek, head bent, a jutting hip cocked: a posture that reminded Paul vividly of his mother. The house was quiet, though with that restless silence that indicates inhabitance. Now he heard a scrap of laughter somewhere – shared laughter.

Paul said something neutral.

"Yup: sending the boys home in wheelchairs to be booed and insulted by longhairs on the street," he said, tapping more on the screen. "I never forgot that. I forgave – to be sure, I forgave; our Lord says we must." He moved something on the screen and frowned, reading something; Paul wondered what. "But I learnt right then and there that our fellow citizens have no idea of our national security needs. No appreciation of the sacrifices. What-so-ever." He spoke in a plaintive dusty baritone more apt for burying persons than wedding them.

"It's one reason I prefer diplomacy: the level of conversation is better."

The Rainmaker scarcely heard and went on with black bitterness. "Oh, if Doers had only been around back in the Nam days! We would have red-dogged those damn longhairs back under the rocks where they belonged." His thick fingernail banged more on the computer screen. "That's one reason Doers was activated, you know. With that off-the-farm press discrediting our ongoing efforts against communism and all the rock-throwing in the streets, some of us got together and said, 'Never again.'"

"So Doers came out of the Nixon administration."

"Nixon and Ford, mainly, a bit of Reagan – during the Iran-hostage crisis – though naturally the torch has been passed along. We made sure that fool Carter wasn't going to win re-election."

"So the rumors are true about secret negotiations with Iranians; and they kept the hostages there until after the election."

Not looking up, The Rainmaker smiled – a wrinkled collision of his thin lips. "Talk about previous ops is not encouraged in Doers."

"Good policy."

"We keep the ship of state headed in the right direction despite changing fads and soft administrations. Oh, where *are* these people?" he griped, searching the screen for answers.

"Are you expecting more arrivals?"

"At least two. By the rules, all Doers should be on-site the evening before a meeting. We allow some exceptions, like Jack Mirage, but…."

The Rainmaker banged more on the computer. "And slowly we've evolved into the force we are today. We've done as many as one major and two minor ops in a year."

"I thought that was the CIA's business. Or the Bureau's."

"As I like to say, they're a bird rifle; we're a sniper rifle with a twenty-power scope on it." He shook his head and slipped off his glasses as the screen went dark on his face. "These damn machines. You would think those fools at Microsoft could make icons big enough for an *adult* finger. Let me take you to your room, Mr. Under Secretary."

"'Paul' would be fine. And you must be one of the only original members," Paul replied carefully, picking up his things.

"Yes, though Ted Greene chairs now," he said, crossing the foyer to a staircase. "And we've done some important work – world-changing work. I'm very proud of Doers. America was turning into a fat, slow-footed second-rate, you know. Look how fast that happened to Britain and France. If America is still the only superpower, it's because Doers has been on the job."

Was this astonishing arrogance or astonishing fact? Paul scarcely knew what to think. "So I take it that I'm being asked to step up to an important position."

On the first step, The Rainmaker turned around to him. "Some people write books, some write articles, some make policy recommendations, others read them and critique them and argue about them. We're doers and we *do*, Mr. Under Secretary: nine eminent personages from key points of American life, plus yours truly; I manage a highly competent staff that researches our initiatives. You are replacing Bill Reichow – counsel to the last three secretaries of state? Our first order of business tomorrow will be to vote on your induction."

Paul followed him up the stairway – the banister was a single carven piece with two turns in it – and down a long corridor of bedrooms, some open, dark and empty and smelling of antiques. In fact, the whole place needed a good airing-out. It was easily a hundred years old, probably turn-of-the-century, to judge by the oaken wainscoting and doorknobs of white-and-blue-striped porcelain, which Paul had only seen in some of the oldest houses in Kansas City. The hinges were serious cast-iron artifacts that supported solid doors. Paul could hear someone talking on a phone behind one door and a television going behind another.

"This room's the one where the radiator's AWOL and it's a bit warm, so just prop the window open with a brick. There's some sandwich material in the mini-bar fridge. Dinner was over an hour ago. I believe Ted Greene is playing pool in the billiards room with Chet Nicely. Breakfast begins tomorrow at seven-thirty. I say a brief Mass with communion at nine." He looked at Paul with a priest's blunt invitation.

"Right."

A gray-black cat flowed out of the room on the other side of the hall and rubbed against The Rainmaker's leg.

"You seem to have a friend," said Paul.

The cat leapt up into his arms. "This is Prayers. Prayers, say hello to Paul Klippen! He's the new under secretary of state for political affairs – a big man at State! Isn't that wonderful?" he explained, taking one of the cat's legs and waving it at Paul. "Now don't you mess with my glasses, you dummy!" he scolded as the cat flailed at them hanging on their string. He swept them around behind him. "You'd think they were catnip."

Paul kept a straight face.

"Well, I've got some damn paperwork to get done before lights-out. So I'll see you…Oh! And one last thing. Would you mind meeting me downstairs in the study at eight-thirty? Bureaucracy, you know."

"Bureaucracy?"

"Oaths, signatures – non-disclosure business." A huff. "The same one that did little good as per Dottie Crick. Here at Doers we call it your hazing."

"Eight-thirty it is, then," said Paul.

The Rainmaker suddenly yawned, covering his mouth with the

back of his hand; the gesture had a distinct feminine flutter to it. "Well! Big day tomorrow – new inductee, green-light the new op," he declared exuberantly to Prayers. And head down in the cat's fur and murmuring endearments that Paul couldn't hear, he crossed the hall and closed the door behind him.

22

NOVEMBER 10 (WEDNESDAY)

Trudy ate a tuna sandwich while Jerry went out and bought something for dinner.

"I'm glad you didn't bring the police with you," Trudy said quietly when he returned, for she had given Jerry a quick idea of her problem.

"Ick! Cops. Nothing against 'em, but I always get the impression that those guys love trouble. Just itch for it."

"I meant thanks for not turning me in."

"Got that, babe. No prob." He hung up his jacket and began putting everything in the refrigerator. "Will that be Coke, wine, or are we moving on directly to Jack Daniels?"

"Did you get wine? That'd be great! I really started to like wine when I was living in France."

Jerry fried a couple of small steaks and made a salad while Trudy kept reading news reports.

"Pre-show meal, you know. Whenever I'm making money, I blow a little on a decent dinner."

"Yeah, and this wine is pretty good. I never had Chileno wine before. And holy moley, do I ever need something to pick me up. I'm all over the news. That building where I had to jump off the roof? They –"

"You jumped off a roof?"

"Well, only right onto another one. They evacuated the whole building, and they're *still* looking for me there, like in the air-conditioner pipes and stuff. They said they're expecting 'developments' any minute. And the news people are calling me a 'terrorist' now. This morning I was just an *'alleged* terrorist.'"

"Well, they want to give the story some flow," Jerry said as he set the table.

"They're all creeps."

"See what I mean, babe? *Never* trust the news. Ignore it completely." He surveyed the table, then sat down, swinging a leg over the back of his chair and dropping onto it. "All right – that will do. Dig in!"

"Thanks, Jerry. Really. Um, just a sec." She bowed her head a moment and said a silent prayer. Jerry waited. "There," she said, blushing as she looked up at him.

They worked their way through dinner, largely in silence. Jerry said that he wouldn't ruin a good steak with bomb problems. When they finished, Jerry immediately washed the dishes and took out the scraps. Returning, he sat back in his chair with his glass of wine and said, "All right then, let's hear the whole story, Trudy Schelling – and that's 'miss,' right? As in 'Miss Trudy Schelling who broke up with her last guy over who had to sleep on the wet spot and hasn't had a good roll in the blankets for months,' right?"

Trudy laughed.

"Now you just lay it down to Uncle Jerry and hold nothing back. You were talking terrorist attack. Truth be told, I did hear something gnarly like that. Iranian dudes, I think it was – south-of-the-border types anyway. Bastards can't just come, have lunch in The Russian Tea Room, and go home like everybody else." He smiled broadly with that enormous overbite, watching her laugh. "You're right: this wine *is* nice. Get it from Kook-shin's around the corner; he has a very decent little wine section behind the curtain. Trusted customers only."

Trudy drank more. "Yeah, it's yummy. Okay. That house in Jersey City? That was actually a business. That's where I was going to start working yesterday."

Jerry sat up. "Oh God, I'm sorry, Trudy," he said. "Did you know people there?"

"Only one, and he was a creep too." Trudy told him everything that had happened, from the time Paul and I had come to visit her. Jerry said nothing. He just sat drinking wine and chewing steadily on his upper lip, which his great overbite swallowed easily. "And now they're trying to say I was part of the gang," she finished.

"So it's our own people behind this," Jerry said quietly.

"Yeah, I was pretty shocked when they told me."

"God…you know, you hear rumors, you hear people convinced that man never walked on the moon, all that. But you never give them…y'know, you never give them the time of day." He shrugged. "And then to get this, y'know, straight from the source: makes you

think. Like the man said, 'Just when I figured nothing could surprise me anymore, I realize I haven't heard the half of it.'" He looked
away, remembering. "Paul Klippen – I saw him on some program
once. Seemed like a pretty decent guy for a State Department type."

"Yeah, I just met him real quick, at the beginning, so I'd know
everything was on the up-and-up. He and Max figured they'd lump
me in with the terrorists. I didn't really believe it till now. "

Jerry chuckled. "You: a terrorist. Jesus! You're the girl who gets tied
to the train tracks. Those guys can sure spin one when they need to."

"Yeah, they're really creeps."

"Hey, let's watch that strong language in my house, huh, babe?"
Jerry said with a grin. "Just one thing here. Paul and Max – you can
trust these guys? They didn't hang you out to dry?"

"No – that's why Paul wanted to meet me. He said it was unfair to
stay in the dark. He told me if I got caught to name him directly and
let him carry the blame. But if I didn't have to, I wasn't supposed to
name Max – just steer right around him."

"And you don't have any way to get in touch with either one?"

"Well, Paul works in the State Department, there's that – but he
said he has to be super careful."

Jerry tipped his head to each side. "Yeah, the bad guys'll kill him
ten times over if they find out about him. We'll keep that as Plan C
or D. How come Max's friend didn't pick you up – after the escape
gig in Manhattan?"

Trudy had to wipe her eyes. "I don't really know. Something must
have gotten messed up. Maybe I should have just waited around in
that…in that park or whatever it was before going across the bridge.
That was probably pretty stupid, but I was so nervous and scared
and I just needed to keep moving…"

Jerry refilled her glass while Trudy got back under control.

"There was this big mess of police cars and traffic outside the
building when I walked out with Max: maybe that had something
to do with it."

"Manhattan traffic. One more good reason not to have a car."

"So I really don't know what to do or where to go."

Jerry spread his arms wide. "Babe. Please. This is very deep doo-
doo and there's no safer place than 32-and-a-half Pineapple. Happy
to help out. And if those power maniacs are shitting bricks looking
for you, fantastic."

"Gosh, Jerry, just, just thanks so much." She wiped her eyes again.

"Did anyone see you come in here?"

"Just the girls skipping rope downstairs."

"Nobody on the stairs? Not Mrs. Gelling across the landing?"

"No, just the girls."

"They aren't newshounds. So this will do for the time being. Just chill, do some Internet, let things play out – that's Uncle Jerry's take. And I'm serious about the bed situation too: I'm not going to come collecting carnal rent on you or anything like that."

"Thanks – really."

Jerry drank more, remembering something. "My sister – in Madison? She works at UW, runs the library system. She's told me stories about the strong-arm stuff guys do around there, especially the athletes. Pretty shitty stuff. So believe me, you're safe here."

"Well, that'd be really so nice, Jerry – really."

"Babe: least I can do for a comrade – that's my Russian side, you know. Just don't leave anything sitting around for Charlie Cockroach, and everything'll be fine. Me and Mrs. Gelling across the way? We're always saying this is the only floor in The Apple where Charlie crawls away disappointed." Jerry looked at his watch and got up. "Well, I'm on in about an hour, so I'd better get rolling. Gotta do my mee-maw-moos before I go on. Locution, you know. Sounds dumb, but it's what separates the men from the boys once you put a mic in front of your mug."

Trudy suddenly jumped out of her chair and hugged him. "I'm sorry, Jerry, it's just that it's, I'm, it's been kind of a long day."

23 MID-OCTOBER

The next morning, Paul came down for breakfast in his stiff new leisure clothes, a sweater tied over his shoulders. He had debated tucking in his shirt or not, but once he reached the dining room, he was glad of his decision: this was a tucked-in group. He recognized from photos nearly everyone eating there, including former Vice President Ted Greene, who was across the small square table from the former chief of the U.S. Air Force, General Chester Nicely. Near them were Mitch and Mark Harmon, twins who though in their early forties were still identical, their wet hair parted on the left, necks as thick as pylons, biceps like balloons, each with a series of facial moles like connect-the-dots games for kids. They sat in T-shirts tucked into jeans, just in from the showers after their morning jog. Each was an assistant director, Mitch of the CIA and Mark of the FBI. They had knocked on Paul's door the night before and introduced themselves. Now they each raised a hand and uttered rough hellos as if welcoming him to a pick-up game of basketball.

Raising his fork – his mouth was full – was Randy Jannik, a boyish slip of a man in his sixties. He sat with the brothers before a single slice of melon, furiously thumbing a cell phone. Paul had met him at a cocktail party a month before. At the time, Paul had had the weird feeling that Jannik, a TV and Hollywood producer, was checking him out as if for a role in one of his movies. Now he knew why.

Trig Purtly, shaggy as a mutt and dressed in jeans, boots and a sweat shirt – which sat on him far more naturally than a suit – wandered out of the kitchen with a stack of pancakes on a plate. He smacked Paul on the shoulder. "Bitch-boy! Good to see ya."

"Trig! So you really *are* in this?"

Purtly just laughed and sat down with the Harmons and Jannik.

Humming loudly in the kitchen, The Rainmaker himself was at the stove, glowing happily as a mother with her newborn. He wore an apron over his priest's habit and insisted on filling Paul's tray with a full breakfast: eggs, bacon, pancakes. "You'll find orange juice, coffee and tea out in the dining room. Syrup on the table. Breakfast is the most important meal of the day, you know, Paul. *Never* skimp on it," he said sternly.

"Paul! Hey, come on over here and sit with some real men," called Ted Greene. He jerked a thumb over his shoulder. "All those faggots talk about is new cell-phone apps."

He was sitting before a bowl of fruit – pieces of melon and bananas, grapes, slices of peach. Across from him sat the rock-hewn form of General Nicely.

"You should give cell phones a try, Ted, they're really great," said one of the Harmon brothers. "Of course, it means you have to memorize a new phone number, and it's pretty long, but you can always just write it down and keep it in your hatband."

"Tell him, bro'!" laughed his brother, and the two exchanged a high-five.

"Shove it, Mitch."

"Mark."

"Whatever." Greene stood and shook Paul's hand. "Pleasure to have you on board, Paul."

"Mr. Vice President, it's an honor."

"'Ted' will do. Don't know if you've met Chet Nicely."

Nicely's grip might have crushed his hand, but Paul had learnt from painful experience with military men that he had to get in deep and fast and tensed-up. But otherwise Nicely too was kind and welcoming.

"Proud to know you, Paul, heard a lot about you, make y'self at home," he said in a Southern singsong. "And that's just 'Chet' to you – 'nless you're thinkin' of enlistin'."

Paul said what was appropriate and sat down numbly. *I'm having breakfast with "Ted," the vice president, and "Chet," who had the U.S. Air Force at his command!*

"I was tellin' Ted 'bout this dumbshit in charge of an FOL out by Fiji. Anyway, long story short, Ted, I got up at 4 a.m. to snag a ferry and flew all the way *back* just to derecognize the son-of-a-bitch," said Nicely. He wore a plaid sports shirt and a watch as wide as his wrist and full of dials. His military haircut was combed over, huge flat ears on display like mushrooms. Paul reflected again on how a military man inevitably looked awkward if not wearing some type of uniform.

"Incompetence," answered Greene with a shake of his head. "You can't eliminate it; you ringfence it till it dries out and falls off the vine. Enough said. Paul: your opinion. A moment ago Chet and I were talking about Russia. What's to be done about that bastard Putin? Do we have him taken down? Where do you come out?"

"Multiple fallout, see," said Nicely. "Spans over into lots of areas: internal politics, barrel prices, Silk Road stuff." He took a slender bit of bacon in his thick hand and bit it in half with a crisp snap. Paul was reminded of King Kong with the girl in his hand. "Hell, I'd still love to intervene-and-assume those oil fields down towards Kazakhstan. My people say they aren't half as exploited as they oughta be."

"Chet reps the oil interests on Doers," Greene told Paul.

"My brother's president of Brigg Oil," Nicely added.

"The Harmon brothers, of course, are with the police-slash-se-curity milieu, Trig takes care of the White House – well, a little of everything, end of the day: Wall Street, the banks, informatics and tech. Randy reps the media and Israel."

"*Israel* has a place at the Doers' table?"

"Israel has a place at *everyone's* table," said Ted Greene with the hard smile of one enduring his son's loud music.

"Sometimes I'd say Israel *is* the table," Chet Nicely grumbled in a low voice.

"And what about you, Ted?"

"The Pentagon, mainly. I also meet with a certain…committee; call it a sort of international Doers. That's almost purely strategic, though; Doers is more tactical and, by and large, more domestic."

"*By and large,*" giggled Chet Nicely into a forkful of eggs.

"An international Doers – that must be interesting," Paul said. He remembered that Greene had also been CEO of a military-aerospace company in his years before getting into politics.

"It is, it is. Some big hitters there. Stay with us, Paul, and I'll nominate you up to them when I leave. Doers likes to have a man with a foot in both."

"So what about the Poot-man, Paul?" Nicely asked. "How do we fix his wagon?"

"Well! Geopolitics before my morning coffee, this is a little –"

"That's all *we* do – mornin', noon and night," said Nicely with another adolescent giggle. "Ain't it, Ted?"

"With a little insider trading to keep domestic staff paid," Greene answered with a smile. He had a warm baritone voice and the watery gray eyes of an accountant or surgeon, a man who could deal with numbers or bodies with equanimity. His good head of hair was as smoothly combed as ever, though thinned and gone white since his time in office several years earlier. At State, Paul had heard complaints that he was still talking to world leaders, especially in Central Europe, as if his title had never expired, and was received with salutes and smiles at the Pentagon.

"I was tellin' Ted, first we replace the Poot-man with someone with a decent mindset, someone who knows how to gauge a metric, just someone that *correlates* a little – hell, I'm not picky. And then we take the rest o' the cogs outta the Russian network – the stans, Armenia and the like – and we do it *now* before there are so many roads and railroads and pipelines runnin' through it that our own interests get jammed up in the spokes. That's why we gotta do Iran:

that's gonna be our bridgehead. Along with Af-Pak." He scooped up the last of his scrambled eggs and with one movement slid them into his mouth. Paul noticed that he held his fork by the sides between three fingers and thumb.

"So what do you say, Paul?" Greene insisted. "Do you want to give Putin a handshake with one of those poisonous rings on your finger?"

"Me, I say poison's the way to go," Nicely explained through his eggs.

"Tough one. Tough one." Paul took off his glasses and gave them a polish with his napkin. He needed a moment to adjust. "I mean, you kill Putin, and then what? Dmitry Medvedev? He's not a shoo-in, remember, and what happens if you get a hard-liner in the Kremlin, maybe someone not so patient with the, ah, the *vicissitudes* of our politics?" He shrugged. "I mean, say what you like about Putin: he's no hot-head."

"Let's say we could guarantee Medvedev would be the next president," said Greene.

"These pancakes are terrific – I'll have to tell The Rainmaker," Paul said. He knew that he was being tested, and as so often at State, he knew he'd better go along. "Yes, I pretty much got the impression from Senator Crick that people in Doers think big."

"We think big," Greene admitted. "Sometimes we *do* big."

"Sometimes *bigger* than big," Nicely giggled, lunging at his jellied toast.

"So?" Greene said challengingly.

"Thinking out loud?" said Paul. "Assassination's certainly an option. But it would have to be airtight, you'd have to implicate the Chechens, maybe the Uzbekis, the Ukranians. And it would have to be fast, sudden. If Putin suspected he was being poisoned, whether it was with a month or an hour to die, he would nominate a hard-liner in his place, just out of spite. Or worse." Paul pressed an invisible button on the table.

"Uh-huh. Scans feasible," said Nicely through his toast.

Greene nodded thoughtfully. "The suggestion was wafted out in Doers some months ago, and The Rainmaker's study group hasn't turned in a recommendation yet."

Nicely: "Rainmaker let you see the futures book yet?"

Paul looked at him.

"He hasn't been hazed yet, Chet. The 'futures book,' Paul, is a summary of recommendations-slash-proposals for future ops. Someone makes a proposal, we hash it around in Doers first, and then if it's green-lighted it goes in for a feasibility study with The Rainmaker's people. That begins the process."

"He keeps a little 'gistics outfit in Fort Meade," added Nicely. "Great people."

"The best," added Ted Greene. "Staff I'd kill to have."

"The Rainmaker said you're – we're – making a final decision today on an op. How long has that been under study?"

Greene squinted searchingly across the room. "How long, Chet? Dottie Crick, Mitch and I were sponsors. Eighteen months?"

"Longer. With the election last year."

"That's right: we were waiting to see which way the shoe was going to drop. A year is unusual, but this is a big initiative. Dottie has insisted on sending it back for tweaking twice now."

"And she's still not gonna be happy – bet you anything," grumbled Nicely. "But we gotta move on this and get it –"

"Happiness is for the little people, Chet. Good morning, gentlemen." Senator Dorothy Crick walked up, looking as usual sleek and silvery. Her only bow to the "casual" atmosphere was that she wore a pantsuit: silver with a white blouse. Paul found it hard to imagine her in a pair of jeans planting trees with her father. "May I?" she said, setting her coffee mug on the table.

Paul quickly stood up and pulled her chair back for her, though the other two men only rumbled a vague, unhappy assent, as if she were an older sister who corrected their table manners.

"I trust you haven't been raking this young man over the coals for shouting his progressive views on diplomacy to the four winds, Ted," she said, reaching for the sugar bowl in the center of the table.

Greene's answer amazed Paul: "Actually, I think he's done a great job of shouting, Dottie." To Paul: "Most of our present op was my brainchild."

"Chet, you've put on weight," said Senator Crick. "Hasn't Renée been taking care of you?"

"*My* body – I take full responsibility."

"Well, let's see if The Rainmaker has improved on the coffee since June." She sipped and put down her cup on its saucer. "No."

"Dottie, we were just asking Paul his opinion on taking down Vladimir Putin," said Greene.

"Yes, Putin – he *is* a problem." Senator Crick pushed away her cup and saucer. "He refuses to be a Yeltsin, doesn't he? Though every effort has been made to show him the error of his ways."

"Maybe that's why Yeltsin appointed Putin his successor," Paul put in. "Yeltsin was drunk most of the time, but even he couldn't have been blind to his country getting taken to the cleaners by the West."

"You have some problem with that, Paul?" Ted Greene asked pointedly.

Paul could not mistake the danger in his eyes and remembered that he needed to play along. "None at all. But if we'd been a little more patient, a little more subtle, a little less brazen, we might have gotten *another* nice jolly half-drunk Yeltsin: Yeltsin II rather than Putin, and by now we would have had a Russia that throws it arms around our investors and begs for Hollywood blockbusters." He gave the table a thumbs-up. "Great job there, guys. You know, I had a college prof who was a Russia expert, and *six months before Putin arrived on the scene,* he wrote a paper on what was going to happen. Nailed it: a stern new leader, the return to a proud Russia – everything."

General Nicely jumped in. "I still say we take down his plane."

"After the bungled first try?" said Greene skeptically. "Too suspicious."

Paul started – he couldn't help it. "What – that Dutch flight bound for Malaysia?" He was referring to a commercial airliner shot down over the Ukraine during the Obama Administration. The guilty party – Russian-backed eastern Ukrainians or the army from Kiev – had never been determined.

Nicely nodded his rock-like head. "Putin's plane had the optic – exactly the same – but it was eighteen minutes OH."

"OH?" Paul asked.

"Over horizon."

"What it took to muddy up *that* trail!" Senator Crick said and scowled again at her coffee. "And even then it hasn't really gone cold. The families won't let it go."

"My point exactly in the present case, Dottie. Remember?" said Ted Greene. He tapped the table three times: *"Never use regulars.*

Yes, I know: they drive the drama and actors add risk. But mothers and fathers of regulars come baying for blood and they won't take a buyout."

"How many regulars in this op?" asked Nicely around his gravelly chewing.

"The Rainmaker told me he's whittled it down to three – just to throw reporters a bone. One has a full c.v. but comes without family – just some spaced-out brother on a commune in Oregon. The two others will be homeless people, one Chinese. They're already spotted."

With a napkin Nicely wiped his mouth roughly as if trying to erase it from his face. "Well, all's I can say is, if we don't plug Putin's piehole now, we're lookin' at another fifteen-to-twenty o' that asshole flyin' up the ointment."

"Such a way with words, General," Crick murmured, forking one of Ted Greene's pieces of fruit.

"But I think this young man's got a point, Chet," said Ted Greene, nodding at Paul. "We should be talking fast and surgical, or nothing."

"See? This *young man* is no fool," declared Senator Crick. "And *old* fools would do well to listen to him."

"Take it down, Dottie," said Greene with irritation. "Just take it down a notch."

Paul finished his breakfast, and when he looked up, The Rainmaker was standing in the doorway of the kitchen, his apron off. "Well, I've got to talk to The Rainmaker," he said. "My 'hazing.'"

Greene smiled sympathetically. "Don't take it hard, Paul. As you're certainly aware by now, you've been vetted pretty thoroughly. We just like to make sure you're clear on the rules and regulations. This isn't exactly a college debating forum, you know. We *do* things here, we don't write papers and split hairs."

"You wanna do that, go sit in a damn think tank and die o' mildew," Nicely giggled.

Paul took his plate and glass to the kitchen, and as he left the dining room, the ex-general and the ex-vice president, their heads together, were talking quietly, Dottie Crick watching them with her black eyes.

24 **MID-OCTOBER**
The study was large and dark, a place for seventeenth-century philosophers to mull whether or not the earth was flat and the planets balanced on teacups. A tentative light, like a child's hand groping in a rabbit hole, entered from a window at the far end, and Paul saw a swingset standing in the backyard with clownish prominence. The Rainmaker came in smelling of wet cotton, humid deodorant and fried bacon; Paul figured he must have had a workout that morning. Along with the priest's habit, he was now wearing both a crucifix and glasses around his neck.

"Breakfast good?"

"Yes, great pancakes – those pieces of apple in them really make a difference," said Paul. "And you can't beat having breakfast with a former vice president."

The Rainmaker tried to stifle a pleased smile. "My mom's recipe, actually. And long years of practice. I keep it to one day a week – have to watch the beltline, you know."

"Don't we all?"

"*Yours* seems to be in good shape," The Rainmaker said, and Paul caught a heavy admiration hanging in his tone.

They sat on opposite sides of a timeless oaken desk; again the sneaky tang of lemon wood polish in the air. Behind The Rainmaker, the entire wall was a library, and many of the books were in series; Paul spotted an encyclopedia, legal volumes, and several decades of *Who's Who*. One shelf, a flurry of color, held a menagerie of popular novels, the authors's names far larger than the titles, another shelf featured books in a variety of languages, including Arabic, Portuguese, Russian, Chinese, and Japanese. A distant section held stacks and stacks of DVD movies. Of course: it was a safe house, Paul realized now. It was a cooling-off or debriefing facility for spies or defectors and their families; hence the backyard swingset.

The Rainmaker had pulled on his glasses and was stroking the screen of a laptop computer. "All right: that is that," he was murmuring to himself. "Now let's just get a few things lined up here…" From nowhere, his cat Prayers jumped up onto his lap and, rather than sitting down, paced around, its back arched. The Rainmaker absently stroked it from behind the ears to the end of its tail.

"Yeah, such a *good* cat," he murmured as he worked. "Such a good *baby!*" It was clear who his best friend was. "Oh, where is that other damn file?" To Paul with apology: "I only pull it out every few years."

"Rainmaker, just so that I have things clear: Doers *does* have official sanction, right?"

"Official? *Officially*, we don't exist," he said with a smirk, not taking his eyes from the screen. "We have no *official* budget; Jack Mirage takes care of that. Officially, Ted Greene is in retirement in Arizona. Officially, Mitch Harmon is a CIA AD on two-day leave. Officially, his brother Mark is at a conference. *Officially*, I died in a helicopter crash in Vietnam. Now and then, for a lark, I take a walk past the memorial wall and look at my name."

"But...are we going off the farm, then?"

"The farm would have much more to worry about if it went off *us*," The Rainmaker replied with a chuckle.

"C'mon, seriously."

The Rainmaker sighed, as if he'd explained this a hundred times. "Sanctioned, yes, official, no. Doers clears the path ahead, and the administration walks down it. We enjoy the backing of the Pentagon, NSA, FBI and CIA, among others – that is essential because, at different times in different ways, they provide logistical support, but blindly."

"Blindly?"

The Rainmaker was watching the screen, tapping his fingers on the desk either side of the keyboard. "Oh, hurry up, damn you. For example, the present op. Navy Intel is given money and told to purchase two houses in such-and-such an area, but through third parties. They don't know why; they just hand me the keys and the deeds. An NSA unit is told to steal three police cars in different cities – disconnecting the GPS, of course – and deliver them to such-and-such an FBI parking lot. An FBI unit repaints them to our specifications; neither unit knows why. A CIA unit contracts a company to provide unknown actors to cry in front of the cameras after a massacre, another quietly gathers cadavers from morgues, another is told to kidnap anonymous street people of specific ethnic types on a certain date and deliver them to a certain place. A Special Ops unit holds them in custody, feeds them, keeps them quiet, and delivers them to a certain place at a certain time. No single group has need-to-know status."

"Right. Blind."

"It's what I like to call" – opening a lipless smile, The Rainmaker opened his arms wide like God blessing the earth – "making it rain."

Paul wondered what kind of man he was sitting in front of: a priest with pretensions to real divinity. "If you don't mind my asking, how did you make the jump from, ah, the work of God to the work of American intel?"

"They're not so different, end of the day. CIA boys used to let me sit in on planning sessions in 'Nam. They saw I had talent, and pretty soon I was slipping into the North to visit the healthier POW camps with my dog collar and cross, which had a radio transmitter directing our bombers. Later on, when some prominent Americans were forming Doers to give some much-needed direction to our foreign policy, they asked me to come aboard, organize the…." He beat the screen repeatedly, one big finger stomping as if he were playing Chopsticks on a piano. "These damn things….There! Finally!"

"I pity the guy who finds you on the other side of a confession box."

For this light comment, Paul got another set piece. "Oh, I've taken confession – from our highest intel agents, a few generals, even government assassins filled with guilt. They need a man of the cloth to talk them down off the ledge. They know they can unzip to me. In fact, I'm probably the only one they can unzip *to*, given *my* clearance."

"Higher than the president's."

"That's right," breezed The Rainmaker. "A few years back I had a little fender-bender in Washington – my own damn fault. But we – my staff – had to spend nearly a half-million dollars to keep my name out of it. I'm too important – it's that simple. Me and my work." He gave a jerk. "Prayersie! Careful with those claws!"

His bald hubris shocked Paul, but for The Rainmaker everything he said was a fact of life, as simple as gravity. "Which is what exactly? You work, I mean."

"Making it rain," he repeated, gently dropping the cat to the floor. "In Doers we decide where the rain should fall, how much, sometimes when. And I gather the clouds."

"Don't other government agencies object?"

The Rainmaker found this idea laughable. "Object? Dear Lord, no! To the rest of government, we're just a legend, and anyone who seriously talks about the possibility of our existence is a conspiracy nut."

"Not Congress?"

"Oh yes, that's a rule: we always have one elected member – for the moment Dottie I-hate-security Crick – and someone either from the administration or close to the president. In this case, Trig Purtly, who straddles the last one and this one." The Rainmaker again brought his hands wide as if blessing the congregation: "Our resources are unlimited."

"Well, it looks like I've found the right place. What kind of op are we looking at today?"

The Rainmaker gave the screen a last tap. "Okay…ready. It's a big project, or at least bigger than normal, involving two venues *and* is a public psy-op."

"Is that unusual?"

"Not really. Most are domestic, some foreign."

"For example?"

A patient smile. "Doer rules frown on discussing past projects unless it's absolutely necessary."

"Oh, that's right."

"Suffice it to say that Randy Jannik, who directs perception management for us, will weigh in heavily on this one."

"The Hollywood guy."

"The producer, yes. This op will be on page one, the lead of every newscast from here to Tokyo, for two weeks," said The Rainmaker. "And *you* play a part in it."

"*I* play a part?"

"A leading role, in fact. That's why there was such a rush to vet you: you're perfect for the role. However" – he scowled at the screen as if at a bad smell – "you might be tempted to go off-message, and it was thought that a little insurance never hurts. So…"

The Rainmaker turned the laptop around on the desk and glanced at his watch. "Dammit, we're running a bit late. Too much chitchat. And I still have to arrange chapel. This video runs about three minutes, and then just tap on the other icon…this one here."

He came around the desk and, one hand on Paul's shoulder, tapped the space bar; the computer screen sprang into life. Ted Greene, ten years younger-looking, appeared on it. He was dressed in his informal golf clothes and reading from a paper on his desk.

"Hello. You have been invited to Doers, and in order for everyone to have the exact same directions and for there to be no accusations of partiality, we've decided to prepare a video that every new candidate sees. These are the rules of Doers…"

But Paul was more aware of the hand that lingered on his shoulder, the fingers reaching down to his chest. Finally, like a spurned lover, it swept away.

25

NOVEMBER 12 (FRIDAY)

Friday night, Jerry's apartment empty, the shades down. Trudy did a little tidying up to earn her keep – though there was little to do, Jerry was so neat – so she separated his clothes for the laundry. A cockroach fell out of a bunch of socks, and though Trudy normally feared cockroaches, she knew how Jerry hated them, and she went after this one like a madwoman. Having moved around a bunch of sports equipment – a basketball, a baseball bat and glove – she swatted it with a shoe heel before it could squeeze under the skirting board of the closet. Proud of her victory over Charlie Cockroach, she sat down to watch the latest news about her.

The various shows held a true cornucopia of information, disinformation, and every shade in between.

The terrorist attack on Charlesdrew Street having been fully dissected, the victims were now taken one by one from the Hallerbee website and profiled, their families interviewed. Steve Hallerbee was a brave entrepreneur from Gary, Indiana, who had come east and pulled himself up by the bootstraps. His wife showed photos of him – clean-shaven and not at all the man Trudy had met – and their two children ages three and six, and talked about his hobby running marathons. "It's just so symbolic!" she simpered. "Steve died *running!*" Ellen Nguyen's life was less colorful, but her Vietnamese parents' story – escape from Saigon, weeks at sea, their meeting in a Malaysian refugee camp, their new life in America – was celebrated over several interviews with the couple as a true American success. Ellen was cast as a loyal Asian daughter who served her parents.

The narrative on Gertrude Ingrid Schelling – the name now rolled off the newscasting tongue as easily as John Fitzgerald Kennedy – was now far richer for the three days of research.

She had been a brilliant gymnast with Olympic prospects ("I

wish!" Trudy murmured.) who became "embittered" and "disillusioned with society" after her shoulder injury. Marsha, a teammate from her gymnastics team that she had never liked, lied straight-faced to a reporter that Trudy had been depressed and disillusioned for the rest of her two years at Cornell, and that she had alternated between suing the college and "out-and-out committing suicide." Trudy looked for the countervailing testimony of her coach at Cornell, Danni Yard, who had fought hard and ultimately prevailed in getting Trudy's scholarship extended on a partial basis for the balance of her college career. But Danni, who mothered Trudy through her three horrible shoulder operations, appeared nowhere.

Discovering that her parents were no long alive, one news network went to the extreme of finding her brother. Trudy remembered him as an unhappy, glowering youth, five years older than her. He was still living at that Oregon commune, it seemed. The footage, however, consisted of shaky images of a snarling hairy ogre chasing the reporter away and swatting at the camera with a heavy stick. "Whew!" gasped the reporter, leaning against their news truck. "Well, now we know Gertrude comes by her unmanaged anger honestly!"

The FBI reported finding emails on Trudy's home computer to the effect that she had picked up the terrorist team in Montana and, according to traffic cameras, driven them to the New York City area, this in late October. The terrorists had entered the United States from Canada at a border crossing in the very middle of Montana called Sweetgrass, population 150 – "where border security is about at the level of a junior-high locker," griped a Border Patrol spokesman. "Count on terrorists to exploit our weak points," he added.

Here by the simple expedient of sticking to the sidestreets in the village of Coutts, on the Canadian side, and slipping through a gap used by teenagers in the chain-link fence, one could sidestep the tiresome border guards at the customs control on U.S. Highway 15. In Coutts, the terrorists foolishly had left behind an Arab-English dictionary and a Koran in the car they had rented in Calgary, where they had arrived one by one from various destinations.

Then came the bombshell in *The New York Times*, which won a Pulitzer Prize for the investigative reporter that dropped it: the CIA had actually attempted to *recruit* Schelling in France in order to steal information from the French pharmaceutical laboratory where she worked. But only attempted: Schelling had refused the offer. (The French government later called in the American ambassador to lodge a protest.)

Which was all true, as I knew myself, but not all the truth: Trudy had indeed been approached by the CIA and had indeed refused. The reporter, however, neglected to mention that the offer scandalized her so deeply that Trudy sat down that same evening and wrote a letter to the French Foreign Ministry and another to the American ambassador recounting the entire event: *You mean the U.S. Government goes around spying on foreign companies and stealing their business secrets? And they go and try to get normal people to spy on their own company? That seems pretty dirty pool to me, and I really don't think that my taxes ought to be spent that way. If you see any CIA people in your embassy, I think you'd better sit them down and have a little talk with them.*

"An attempted recruitment by the CIA? Schelling must have laughed till her sides split," said one commentator. Another made the telling point that her refusal to cooperate was itself a clear sign that she was rotten, for "What American abroad would say no when his or her government asked for a helping hand?"

The answer was clear: it was at the same time that Gertrude was being "recruited," "trained," "turned," "indoctrinated," "brainwashed" – reporters exhausted the participles – to be sent back to America to await orders.

And to gather funds. "To the fullest extent of the law," an FBI spokesman was quoted ad nauseum, "Ms. Schelling exploited her gambling abilities to fund their unlawful activities."

Ah, "gambling" – what a lascivious ring that word had as it strutted across newscasts, along with the term "lady gambler," which every panel of experts in the land employed with a tinge of righteousness. Trudy's winnings, averaging five hundred dollars a month, both in America and France, were leaked promiscuously and discussed exhaustively. "And let's not forget 'the rake,'" said an online poker expert consulted by a network. "That's the tiny percentage the casino gives players for each hand they participate in. And this little lady reportedly played four tables at a time, meaning even at the relatively low stakes she was playing – five to ten dollars a pot – the rake alone probably netted her easily an extra hundred dollars a month."

It all added up to a pretty story as neat as a model-train-hobby-ist's display with trees and level-crossings. Some alert citizens, however, refused to take it at face value. For by now 11/9 Truthers had websites up and running, and they were prickly, contentious ones indeed.

One of their biggest features dealt with the shooter in the Charlesdrew brownstone's bay window. A photo of him had surfaced, taken with a telephoto lens from a tree on the next block, but directly in front of 126; some intrepid freelancer, it seemed, had slipped past police lines. Though grainy, it showed a whitish beefy neck and a whitish beefy arm, these two extremities separated by a dark T-shirt, the man firing not a handgun, but an enormous rifle, out the bay window at Ellen Nguyen; her buckling legs were visible at the extreme side of the photo. This bulky fellow resembled none of the terrorists, Truthers pointed out. And even if he did, the police video of them running into Hallerbee reveals no rifle in anyone's hands. Where did that come from? (The FBI soon replied that Gertrude Ingrid Schelling had surely prepared the house in the days before the event. And when Truthers pointed out that experts estimated that the explosion of the house had required between 120 and 140 pounds of C-4, the Bureau had the same explanation: Gertrude the Sleeper Agent.)

Other controversies dealt with the evidence against Trudy. She and al-Bousapha on the park video, Truthers pointed out, cast no shadow on the ground, though trees behind them did. The woman sitting on his lap in the discotheque had legs that nearly reached the floor; she was clearly his height, if not taller; though in the park image Gertrude was a head shorter. An NSA photo of her with Ashnani al-Haq could not have been taken in Madrid's high-speed station because the train just pulling out on the other wide of the platform did not have a sleek, dolphin-nosed lead car, but the boxy type found on commuter trains. And the symbol on its front was that of *Stockholm* commuter trains. Furthermore, the police cars that had chased the terrorists' van to Charlesdrew were not the same model as the Jersey City Police used.

The story of her attempted recruitment by the CIA was also suspect, they said. Were she really an Islamist agent, she would have gladly accepted the CIA job. The job would have given her credibility with the CIA, and perhaps in time allowed her to become a double agent for jihadists.

Truthers ridiculed as well the issue of her picking up six terrorists in Montana. Their rented car found in Coutts, on the Canadian side, was a six-seat mini-van. Gertrude Ingrid Schelling, it had been reported in the first hours of 11/9, had a Nissan Micra, and indeed this was the car, right down to its license plate, that the FBI produced in a photo. The trouble was that the aptly-named Micra comfortably seats four, uncomfortably five, and impossibly seven: that is, six terrorists plus the driver. They also pointed out that from the east coast to Montana was at the very least a four-thousand-mile round trip; and Schelling had bought the car new after coming back from France. Did the car really have that many miles on it? What did the car's odometer read?

Most likely, they concluded, Gertrude Ingrid Schelling was a victim, one who managed to get out of the house as al-Bousapha and his crew ran inside, which is why she ran out the back way, scaled the wall – it had no door – and ran down the alley. If she had wished to slip out discreetly before their arrival, she would simply have made her excuses and walked out the front door.

Lastly came the matter of the bus Trudy had boarded. Interviewed passengers stated flatly that the time was some fifteen minutes *before* the arrival of al-Bousapha's gang on Charledrew Street. Truthers – and even a local newscast – cited the testimony of Greta Marie Tick, already well-known as an animal-rights activist from Newark. She said that Schelling had jumped on board practically in tears and said that she had gone to her place of work that morning and found everyone dead, "laid out in the living room," and one fellow being carried upstairs. Ms. Tick pointed out a police station, and Schelling had got off the bus at that stop. "I should of gone with her," she concluded with shame during a radio interview. "I should of realized my possibilities." The police, however, had no record of Ms. Schelling.

The issue of the city bus *was* unclear, an FBI spokesman admitted awkwardly, as if reluctant to speak badly of the dead. The Bureau hoped that more citizens would come forward. The Micra odometer, however, was considered part of an ongoing investigation and its mileage could not be disclosed.

The larger point – and the more conservative the news outlet, the larger it became – was that Gertrude Ingrid Schelling, having cleaned up at poker and stolen Roger Terelski's gun, was now "armed and dangerous, and willing to take risks." As one anchorman summed up, "Raschid al-Bousapaha and Gertrude Ingrid Schelling have proven to be a mortal pair: one woman, one man; one dark-haired, one blonde; one a martyr to his cause, the other an expert gambler with money in her hands now free to roam and commit further mayhem. On any American street."

26

MID-OCTOBER
The Doers existed, a slightly younger Ted Greene was explaining on the video, in order to effect operations necessary to further the interests of the United States of America, but at the same time avoid bureaucratic snarls and turf battles – "which hobbled us so much in, for example, Vietnam, Central America, and Africa." Doers also provided deniability to government agencies, "but more important, I believe, we provide 'surprisibility.' It is crucial that both the military-security bureaucracy *and* our leaders be shocked by events. This galvanizes their response and silences skeptics. Our leaders need to be able to credibly state before the camera that events took them by surprise.

"Which is why Doers exists only as a very small group of leading Americans, both from the public and private sectors. We use the services of both public and private agencies, though they never have the big picture on any given operation; and all written or electronic record of an operation is expunged and destroyed the moment the operation ends. We are not cowboys; I want to emphasize this. Our decision-making follows a rational, careful, step-by-step method governed by strict procedures."

Which he then described. Any Doer could suggest an operation, and if a simple majority voted in favor, it would be referred to The Rainmaker's staff for a Plan Feasibility and Budgetary Assessment and a Human/Material Requirements Survey. (Not even Doers escaped moribund bureaucratic terminology.) Once presented, a majority of the nine Doers had to approve the next stage of planning; The Rainmaker, being in charge of research, had no vote on anything except new members. Drafts of plans continued until one was accepted for actual execution, for which seven of nine votes were the standard. Voting was by raised hands; if a Doer could not be present, he could vote by phone. The only vote by secret paper ballots was for the admittance of new members.

Doers had two main rules. The first was that, although "vigorous debate was encouraged," once a project had been approved, any Doer needed to carry it out a part of it was obligated to do so, without exception, even if the Doer had voted against. The second was that Doers could not even mention the group, much less speak about its operations, outside a secure area; any documents had to be viewed in a Doer-cleared secure room and not removed from it; and talk of previous operations was discouraged. "Security must be airtight," Greene finished.

The video ended. Paul tapped on the other icon, marked *Klippen*. Greene continued, but now wearing other clothes, and looking his present age.

"Lastly, a message for you in particular, Paul. Please understand that this is nothing against you personally, but because you're a new member and have been brought on – as you'll see – in somewhat extraordinary circumstances, we have to take some security precautions. Frankly, it's blackmail and it's distasteful to all of us. Please bear with me. We warn you that we have three young women – two of them State employees – ready to publicly charge you with sexual harassment over the last six months should you attempt to disclose our existence or operations to any third party whatsoever. I don't need to mention what this would do to your reputation and career. Again, we dislike this option and are sure that it is unnecessary. You've been chosen after long consideration and study, Paul, and we're convinced you're going to be a great and long-term member of Doers. Welcome aboard."

The screen went black.

"'Extraordinary circumstances.' What the hell?" Paul murmured, sitting back in the chair. Maybe they really did want him to murder Putin.

27

NOVEMBER 13 (SATURDAY)
I should report to you on the state of international affairs at this point, for events were becoming steadily more serious.

The American media was beating the war drums against Iran. The proof of Iran's involvement in the attacks of 11/9 being still ambiguous, they focused on the humiliating 14-month standoff in 1979-80, when Iranian youngsters had stormed the American Embassy in Tehran and took dozens of American diplomats hostage. Now gray and retired, many of them were interviewed, recalling the long days of fear and boredom. Air Force pilots with foggy voices talked about the disastrous American rescue attempt. The re-heated memory of those days, plus the discovery of a nuclear weapon sent to the Empire State Building itself, sufficed to rile Americans.

Under Secretary of State Paul Klippen appeared before hostile interviewers who accused him of appeasement: "Isn't it true that your love-and-peace offensive left us open to just this kind of attack?" Paul replied stiffly that this was an exaggeration and that, like the administration, he now "reluctantly leaned towards a declaration of war because this kind of thing cannot be tolerated."

American U.N. Ambassador Lori Fischler herself made a presentation to the Security Council, complete with 3D graphics (borrowed from one of the networks) of the Empire State Building falling over three blocks of Manhattan. She declared that Iran had chosen Raschid al-Bousapha from the Revolutionary Guard – "which just does whatever it wants, completely out of control of their own government!" – trained him in handling and assembling the nuclear bomb, and infiltrated him and his henchmen into Canada. She ended with what was now a national cry, "And if it hadn't been for Officer Undershall Hicks – may God rest his soul – who martyred himself upon our Republic, the beating heart of Manhattan would have been extinguished!"

She called for the United Nations to declare Iran and Syria – the latter pulled into the matter because of the nationality of two of the Charlesdrew terrorists – "aggressive criminal states" so that the United States could invoke the right of self-defense in attacking them.

Russia and Iran and Syria all dismissed this account of events. Al-Bousapha's body had recently been identified by local forensics, and they wanted an independent expert from the European Union to confirm this. Russia and Iran also demanded to examine the "bullet" of enriched uranium that American authorities said they had found. Fischler tartly replied, "My government's honesty is not in question, sir, but we will soon make a sample available to the International Atomic Energy Agency for their inspection."

"A sample? Of a bullet-sized piece of uranium?" retorted the Russian delegate. "Why not the entire bullet? Why not the entire contraption of three crates? Our scientists are highly interested in examining an atomic bomb that could be delivered in three parts to be lifted through a window onto the fourth floor of a building."

As to Raschid al-Bousapha, the Iranian ambassador confirmed that, yes, he had belonged to the Revolutionary Guards – but had been drummed out of the unit five years earlier for stealing office supplies and selling them on the black market. Later on, he was arrested for smuggling Africans from the beaches of Libya to Lampedusa, Italy, and ended up in Abu Salim Prison in Tripoli.

"He disappeared from this facility six months ago," the ambassador went on. "He escaped from a maximum-security prison built by Muammar el Gaddafi to torture all who resisted his rule! Would the American ambassador please ask her nation's intelligence services if they know anything about that?" Ambassador Fischler did not react to this for some seconds, busy tapping on her mobile phone. A high-up camera in the chamber saw why. She had been playing Candy Crunch the whole time – and she was a real ace.

28 MID-OCTOBER

"Congratulations, Paul, you are officially elected to Doers. Stand up and take a bow," said Ted Greene as the other members of the Doers applauded. The only one who didn't applaud was Trig Purtly, who pointedly walked into the dining room, where the cell phones lay on the table, and checked his messages.

Paul made a comic bow as the others around the circle applauded.

"America's sexiest diplomat," hooted Mitch from the CIA.

Ted Greene threw the paper ballots – little slips of paper that The Rainmaker had cut from a sheet of photocopy paper – into the fireplace. Then he took Paul's phone and transferred to it all the codes and phone numbers of the Doers.

At this point, Paul half-expected to be led to an elevator that dropped twenty floors under the house to some kind of sound-proof, bomb-proof situation room surrounded by wall-sized maps and Marine guards. But no – this was where the Doers, with proud simplicity, made the decisions that moved history: in the hunting lodge's broad, luminous, nineteenth-century living room with its heavy furniture and moose horns, fragrant with three pine logs burning in the hearth. The nine Doers plus The Rainmaker sat in an improvised oval on some stuffed chairs, the sofa and four straight-back chairs brought in from the dining room. Paul admired this. Doers had to rely on their wits. No one could consult papers, briefcases, computers, or cell phones. At the peak of the oval stood a whiteboard that had four markers – red, green, blue, and black – on its tray, and a fat magnetic eraser stuck to it like a snail on the side of an aquarium.

The dining chairs were used by Ted Greene, Paul and the Harmon brothers. Mitch (CIA) had jerked Mark's (FBI) chair away as he sat down. "Bastard does it about once a year," Mark explained to Paul with an angry grin, getting to his feet.

"*That* bastard falls for it every time," laughed Mitch.

Trig Purtly, who did not sit but stood leaning against the doorframe to the front foyer, laughed so hard his mop of gray-blond hair flopped around his face. "Every fuckin' time!"

Mark sat down, still grinning, and swatted his brother in the face – a single lightning-like open-handed straight-arm to his side that knocked Mitch off his chair.

"I don't do *that* every year, but it's about time I started, don't you think, Paul?"

"Better late than never," he said – but he was amazed at the rangy teenagers hiding just beneath the surface of these men, still playing locker-room jokes as if waiting for the coach's pre-game pep talk.

Mark: "I always say, 'Ya gotta show resolve.'"

Mitch retook his seat, rubbing his face. "That leaves a mark, I'm gonna kick your ass," he muttered.

"Try it. Just don't tell Mom."

Parse it as he would, Paul couldn't tell if this remark was serious or not.

Senator Crick sat at one end of the sofa, morose and impatient, gently kicking one leg in the air like a commuter whose train is late. The other end was occupied by Randy Jannik, sixty-something years young, whose flecked parchment-like skin was stretched so tight over his cheeks and jaw that Paul wondered if he had some wasting disease. But he was also tanned and magnificently groomed. His stiff high wave of hair rose hand-width over his forehead. Though jacket-less, he wore a brown shirt and an electric-blue tie as far down as his crotch, where a lump as big as a dog bone nestled beneath his tight blue jeans. He was very pleasant, however, with that sort of institutional warmth that Hollywood stars had: *Paul, hey! Great to see you again!* What he most remembered was Jannik's constant repetition of the phrase "in today's society": "In today's society, people need to eliminate doubt as quickly and fully as it comes in." "In today's society, a politician has to be able to talk in four dialects: street, me-too-women, elder-statesman, and macho-man-sheriff."

Lastly there was financier Jack Mirage, a chic and very serious man in a dark-red turtleneck sweater and dark-gray leisure suit. With his graying hair oiled and combed straight back, he looked more like an opera director in a chill-out lounge. He sat on one of the thick armchairs near Senator Crick, hands flat on the arms like a reigning pasha, relaxed with one leg folded over the other as if listening to music. Only Dorothy Crick had greeted him warmly. They were clearly allies in the room and Crick was looking to Paul to join them. General Chet Nicely had murmured to Paul with an odd quiver in his voice that Mirage had arrived in his private helicopter with his girlfriend, "and she's a real looker."

Before the vote on Paul, Mirage had grilled him:

"Excuse me, Ted," he said. He spoke in the clipped monotone that reminded Paul of President Kennedy. "I arrived a little late – my apologies – took headwinds getting out of the *Bah*-ston area. Paul *has* been hazed, correct? Apprised of everything going forward?"

"First thing this morning, Jack," said The Rainmaker. "He is on board."

"Good. Good. Just checking. Very glad to have you, Paul. I understand we'll be voting on you this morning. Can I just ask you a few questions before we get going on that?"

"Fire away."

"You have a mortgaged house and no assets except a little stock you inherited from grandparents. Why?"

"Diplomacy doesn't pay badly, but I've had a lot of medical bills to pay for my wife."

Mirage sat forward tense as a pointer dog. "So why didn't you go private sector?" he griped, as if only fool would not do that. "Y'see, Paul, no offense, but I don't trust a man who has less than ten million in assets – or is at least working on it. Less than that, they can go either way when the heat's on. Depends on which side of you gets the hammerlock on the other. What kind of power did you accumulate in your last posting? Power isn't a bad substitute if that's your thing, but *Ecuador?*"

"Actually, as power goes, I was the point man of the entire embassy. The ambassador was just a campaign contributor for the president, his chief of staff was… well, 'hopeless' is the most charitable term. By the end of my first year there, anything that got done got done either through me or by me. Which is why, when the ambassador needed someone to put down a national fruit-workers strike, he turned to me."

"Not CIA?" asked Mitch.

"Actually, he wanted the CIA kept out of it. He wanted subtlety."

"So you're saying we can't be subtle?"

"With all respect, Mitch, your man in Quito, Harry Kruger, was as subtle as a pile driver. He took over my op and quickly turned it into a –"

"Yeah, he messed it up. I've heard that story," said Mirage, raising a hand to silence Mitch. "All right, people are what people are: you're poor and at best you've had a taste of power. I'll tell you now, Paul: no offense personally, but I don't like you. Not for Doers." He sat back. "All right, let's get on with it, Ted."

The vote had turned out 7 to 2 in Paul's favor. Clearly, Mirage and Purtly had voted against.

"We've got a lot of ground to cover this morning," Greene said, standing up now. "Before I turn operational explanations over to The Rainmaker, let's sum over the goals of Operation AnyStreet one last time. We're looking for an event, a narrative, in which…" He hooked one finger in the other and went on in that reasonable voice.

"One: involves a nuclear element and strongly implicates Russia as the source of such element.

"Two: Iran, as both a people and a government, is implicated in a major terrorist attack upon the United States – but with limited casualties, ten-to-fifteen tops – thus provoking a nationwide reaction among everyday Americans and preparing them for military action against Iran."

"And making barrel prices go through the roof," Chet Nicely giggled.

"Three: puts pressure on Canada to ramp up domestic security, thus obligating them to merge their security systems with our own, allowing us to dominate these systems."

"Why don't we just make them the fifty-first state and get it over with?" called Mark, and his brother gave him a high-five. Paul mustered a tight smile for them; he knew that others in the room were watching him, as if he were not quite in Doers yet. It was strange.

"Which brings us to the fourth and last," Greene went on cuttingly – he didn't like to be interrupted – "which is that the continuing terrorist threat from abroad compels a complete reversal of administration policy such that it discards diplomacy and returns to military strength as the salient element of policy. That's where you come in, Paul. We've established you as a household name in foreign policy and a big advocate of diplomacy. So now that we need war, you will have the cred to make the case publicly."

Just barely, and only from long practice through years of diplomacy, Paul kept a grip on himself. "That's…that's a smart plan, Ted."

"You can see the logic of it, right?"

"Because the president and secretary of state, being old hawks, wouldn't have the, ah, the cred."

"Right."

Paul fought for another anodyne comment and found none in his repertoire. The logs mumbled in the fire.

"So when your moment comes to say that an about-face is necessary, Americans will listen to you," Ted Greene added.

"You've got killer name recognition, Paul. In today's society? An aspiring pop star would give his guitar strings for what you've got," added Randy Jannik.

"I can see that," Paul said. By now, the whole ghastly joke had opened in his mind. This was why he had been brought from Ecuador, why his good looks were so important, why he had been promoted and publicized. Trig Purtly, leaning in the doorway, was smirking delightedly under his fat mustache.

You're gonna get your ass run through a shredder, boy.

"You'll be a star, man!" said Mark.

"I can see that," Paul repeated. "So that's what all this build-up of me has been about. I thought that was *the administration's* doing."

"That and we also have great faith in you, Paul," said Greene with simple sincerity. "Bringing you here from Ecuador and promoting you was largely Randy's brainchild."

"Much more yours, Ted. I just jacked up our boy in the media, that's all. No need for applause, ladies and gentlemen," said Jannik, raising his wrinkled hands; they alone showed his age. "All in a day's work."

At the other end of the sofa, Dorothy Crick scratched her hanging wrist slowly, watching him.

"So you're still on board, Paul?" said Mirage, the financial man, and it was clear that the possibility that Paul would *not* be on board had been discussed, probably debated quite thoroughly.

"Of course he's on board," said Mitch.

"Who wouldn't be?" added Mark. "This is Doers, Paul. This is where decisions get turned into action – *your* decisions."

Paul knew his silence was running too long and signaled disapproval. He could feel the temperature rising in the room.

"Well, what is there to say, Ted," he asked without any question in his voice, and let a bemused little laugh get out. "This has all been pretty…pretty damn clever. I hope you're all going to be honest enough to recognize that this is also a pretty dirty trick." And waited as long as necessary for an answer.

"It's unusual," Greene said finally.

"But Doers *is* unusual," The Rainmaker added.

"True enough," Paul observed. He took off his glasses and polished them on the arm of the sweater that he wore tied over his shoulders. He was formulating a plan.

"Doers clears the path ahead, and the administration walks down it," The Rainmaker repeated, and others around the circle nodded. "It's always been that way."

The financial man was as still as a lizard.

"You'll be compensated in time, Paul," Greene said evenly.

"POTUS is the one gonna be takin' the serious pies in the face, boy, not you," said Trig Purtly carelessly. "He can take a few lumps for once."

"POTUS has never shied away from war," added Mitch the CIA man.

"Point taken," Paul said reasonably. Another pause. "The difference is, Trig, *he'll* change direction in a stately speech before cadets at Annapolis; *I* will do it before Marlene Hanneker and her pointed questions. Not to mention interviews, ridicule around State and Georgetown, floods of messages on every social network ever invented, and hate mail from liberals calling me a turncoat. Conservatives who have been frying my butt for weeks will laugh themselves silly." He was stalling for time, looking for a theme.

Dorothy Crick provided it. She cut in now, and her voice was motherly: "They're going to owe you big-time, though, Paul. *We're* going to owe you big-time."

"Paul, it's part of being in *Doers*," said Greene simply. "You're in, you're one of us, for Christ's sake. You're looking at National Security Advisor before you're fifty. You'll be on the next president's short list for SecState. You aren't going to throw that away for a hiccup like this, are you?"

Paul let the anger build up in him a moment before letting it out. He knew what his play was now, but to pull it off he had to convince them that he could be bought. *"A hiccup?* Ted, when anyone looks up my name on Wikipedia, long after I've retired and am living peacefully in Florida, this episode will feature prominently. None of *you* have to deal with that."

"Paul, Paul, Paul, you're looking at this the wrong way," said Jannik the media man soothingly. "In today's society, people *love* it when someone admits they were wrong. It all depends on how you write the narrative. You just gotta go all Abraham-Lincolny about it: 'I was wrong. I never anticipated a catastrophic event. Diplomacy has to wait, but not forever.' What will people say? 'Here's a man who can admit when he's made a mistake. Here's a man of integrity.' It's classic. What happened to JFK after the Bay of Pigs? He took full responsibility and his poll numbers went to the moon."

By a reflex of politeness, Paul pulled a grin for him and let silence gather again. *Go all the way,* he told himself. These were not people who understood, or even respected, half-measures. But they respected ambition – big ambition.

A huff. A slap of the knees.

"All right. All right, I'll go along." As a cheer started, he raised a monitory hand. "But hold on. You – all of you – remember Dorothy's two little words: 'big time,' as in 'Paul, we owe you big-time.' So let's define our terms. What does 'big time' mean?" He looked around and selected The Rainmaker's chinless face for his stare. "It means the top job. Hearing me, Rainmaker? Not 'deputy,' not 'assistant,' not 'under.' I mean *secretary of state.*"

"Sure, Paul," said Greene. "That's understood, hell."

"But not in some theoretical next administration. No. I mean in this one – in the second term."

The room erupted.

Trig Purtly jerked off the doorframe. "What kinda bullshit are you talkin', boy?"

"Hold on now, Paul. You don't have the horses for *that!*" Jannik the media man cried.

"You're going just a little too far too fast, young man," snapped Ted Greene. "You'll have to wait your turn."

"I think Paul has to meditate on this one," said The Rainmaker with priestly sternness.

Mark and Mitch, to whom everything was a joke, were laughing as at a baseball blooper and exchanging high-fives. "Hey, why don't we just make you president directly?" called Mark.

Senator Crick was silent, an unwanted smile of admiration having worked into her lips. Mirage the financial man as well seemed to approve distantly, and Paul knew why: a man who had made three billion dollars in one year understood ambition better than anything else.

Paul ignored the squawking. "SecStates never serve two full terms, and neither will Carlton Mason. I'm up next – and I want that clear before I put my sexy face in the hole at the pie-throwing contest."

Ted Greene coughed and gave him a harsh look.

"And Ted, I don't give a damn about anyone's harassment charges. It couldn't be much worse than what you're asking me to step up to."

"Didn't someone else in this room say very much the same thing?" asked Senator Crick with airy villainy. The Rainmaker looked at her furiously.

"Now just hold the goddamn phone here!" said Trig Purtly. "Nobody's walkin' into the Oval and tellin' POTUS to his face you're his next SecState. There's *politics* here."

"Then *solve* them," Paul said. *"I'm* going to take the public bath, not you. The rightists and the neocons will have a field day with me. Even if I do make SecState, my credibility is going to be seriously damaged."

Panicking, Randy Jannik was looking back and forth like a child watching his parents fight. "But, but, but you're in Doers! You can't do this! This is all set to fall!"

"I wasn't *in Doers* when this was planned," Paul retorted. "I never had my say, I never agreed. And I'm not saying no now. I'm just saying there's a price."

"Paul, what you're asking is totally unreasonable," said Ted Greene. "SecState has a lot of real push behind it. It's not exactly the Postal Service, you know."

Paul turned to a tried-and-true tactic of his: to suddenly agree with an adversary. "All right. Fine. Maybe I *am* being too pushy, and we've all got to be a little reasonable. And I can do reasonable, Ted, no problem. *So:* I'll accept SecState *or* National Security Advisor. If it was good enough for Henry Kissinger, it's good enough for –"

"NSA?" shouted Trig Purtly. "Mitch, Mark: how about we take Paul out back and teach him his place in the world?"

Paul rose abruptly, again catching everyone by surprise. Even the Harmon brothers, still chuckling over the whole scene, fell silent as if chopped in the larynx. "So here's what we'll do," he said.

"You're tellin' *us* what we'll do?" sneered Purtly.

Paul swung his sweater off and started pulling it on; it still had the overpriced smell of the shop where he'd bought it. "I'm going to go outside and get some fresh air. In the meantime, you talk it over, debate, and take another vote on me to enter Doers. If I'm in, fine: I'll play my part in the op, I'll take the guff, the jokes on Facebook, the whole thing – *but* I get SecState or NSA in the second term. On the other hand, if I'm out, I'm out: my lips are sealed, no hard feelings, and my thanks to The Rainmaker for some great pancakes."

"Jesus, Paul: *maybe* we could swing UN ambassador for you," Ted Greene muttered. "Cabinet-level post, all the perks…"

"That's a messenger job. SecState or NSA – one or the other," said Paul, jerking his shirt collar out of the sweater. "That's as reasonable as I'm prepared to get. When you have *habemus papum*, burn something white in the chimney."

He turned and walked out through the back of the house.

29

NOVEMBER 13 (SATURDAY)

I hope the reader is indulging me a bit on my account of the growing relationship between Trudy and Jerry. No, I wasn't there (though at my panicked urging, Joe had been searching high and low for her, and Ian on his rows of computer screens in

Penrith had no better luck, for as mentioned previously a group of concerned citizens, the Guy Fawkes, had been breaking or blacking out security cameras around Manhattan for months; at one point, they said, their work had "reached out" – a favorite Americanism of mine that covers a multitude of sins – to nearly half of all cameras in the Manhattan area. As far as Ian could tell, there was no record anywhere of her leaving the office building with me, and it was only because I told him that she was walking straight down Chambers that he spotted her at all, only to lose her again in Brooklyn Heights). But my sources were, after all, the two concerned parties, and I think my account here faithfully traces the flow of events.

Jerry was still asleep on the divan. He was arriving at two or three in the morning; sometimes he had to wait a half-hour till a street gang – Colombians, by the sound of their music squalling from cell phones – carousing on Pineapple Street moved on before he could move out from behind a stoop.

Trudy had showered and put on the change of clothes Jerry had bought for her, and had a cup of tea with cookies, catching her breath when the pan of water rose to a boil or a cup clinked on the table. She even dipped her cookies in the tea in order to eat them quietly. Then she closed the door of the bathroom and scrubbed mildew out of the plastic curtain, thinking that if she ever survived this, she would happily buy him a new curtain and rod and a soap holder – the kind that sticks on the wall with suction cups – so that he didn't have to lay his soap bar on a washcloth on the floor.

"He is just so great, he is just the best guy in the world," she whispered to herself, scrubbing the plastic.

She dusted the long windowsill and admired the African violets for a while. And all the time, popping into her mind like a pulled muscle she keeps irritating: Where was Paul? Where was Max? How much longer was she going to be a fugitive? Was she ever going to be able to tell her side of the story?

Jerry slept on. It gave her a needling twinge of desire, in a way, to see a man asleep. She had had two serious relationships since high school – both with men little taller than herself, and neither lasting more than a couple of months. Otherwise men had always taken little notice of her. They always wanted more, or different, or better: taller. One sneering fellow had told her that going out with her was like dating a guy, but with longer hair. She could never be just right.

And most men were so selfish – out for the sex, or just for once to go out with a girl who was shorter than they were; but they never troubled to listen to her or discover who she was. But she knew Jerry was right for her. Jerry listened, he was kind, he saw the humor hiding in nearly any situation. How she would love to care for him. If she could find a job, he could go on being a comedian, successful or not. She wouldn't mind that a bit.

Using earphones, she looked at the Internet again. Another hostage from the 1979 embassy crisis was telling his story, this one about how awful the food was: he was served a steak fried a bit on the outside and almost frozen in the middle. "But you had to eat it, didn't you?" the reporter said, nodding in commiseration.

Then came a suicide video of "Gertrude" dressed in a dark burka, her face covered except for the bit around the eyes. It had been found by the FBI in Raschid al-Bousapha's computer and rushed straight to the networks. You've surely seen it: a woman sitting at a table against the usual curtained background, the usual Kalashnikov slouching against the wall like a juvenile delinquent, and the usual claptrap written by someone who could scarcely compose a birthday greeting: I will now go to America and get a job and wait for orders to help my Islamic brothers in committing an attack on the Great Satan; we will avenge the death of Yusef al-Magreb (she held up a printed picture of this former al-Nusra commander), killed by America's drones; paradise awaits me. The actress was the best part, actually, putting real fervor into the lines, punching the air and growling.

Pundits called the video "chilling." 11/9 Truthers called it a frame-up. One fellow handy with math figured out that, judging by the size of the Kalashnikov and the angle of the camera, the height of the woman in the video was between five-foot-five and five-foot-seven: much taller than Trudy. Also, the film would have been shot in Europe – presumably France – before Trudy came to the United States, but the printed paper she held up was of standard American letter size; European letter size, usually called "A4," is slightly longer and narrower. As to al-Magreb, several military websites had reported with glee that he had been killed in mid-September in Iraq: well after Trudy had come to America.

"Oh sure, honey," Trudy sneered. "Why don't you tell them about how I read the Koran ten times a day or whatever it is?"

Jerry woke up, taking a deep breath as if inflating himself for the day.

"Wow – what a sight to wake up to: a beautiful girl sitting in my apartment. And I don't even have to tell her where I've been all night!"

Trudy chuckled.

"Hey, look at that, ladies and gents: I made the lady laugh. C'mon, let's give it up for ol' Jerry Stretch."

Trudy clapped for him, then told him about the video.

Jerry pulled an overbite grin. "I'll watch it after the morning joe. No offense, babe, but you couldn't scare a two-year-old."

Jerry tossed back the covers, swung off the divan, and pulled on a bathrobe. He began swatting the sheets and blanket into some kind of order before folding the bed into the wall. But Trudy had seen how beautiful his body was: well grown, clean and muscular like a dancer's. His ribs stood out at his sides in quick little waves.

"I bought some decent pastries yesterday at Kook-shin's. You see 'em?" He opened the fridge and began moving things around.

Trudy stood watching the curve of the long back, the thin waist, the muscles of his neck standing up.

"You know, I really came up in my performance last night," Jerry said, now fussing with the coffee on the stove. "I walked into the dressing room, and I was really happy knowing you were here safe. I thought of calling you, but I remembered what you said about using the phone. But I'm telling you, babe: I walked out on that stage ready to blow the audience away – and I really did. Second show I gave they wouldn't let me off the stage. Folk-guitar guy for the next act was pissed about getting upstaged."

Slowly, carefully, fearfully, as if he might break, Trudy put her arms around his trunk and pressed her head to his back. After a long moment, he said:

"I'll bet you do this to all the guys you stick up. What a, what a *creep!*"

Trudy laughed. "No. Only you."

Jerry turned and put his arms around her, leaned his head far down and kissed her again and again. There they stayed until the coffee boiled up.

30

MID-OCTOBER

The sky had a few continental clouds floating in it, and the sun dodged in between them trying to brighten life. His thoughts in chaos like kids on a playground – Doers, the Sec-State job, his wife, Iran – Paul ambled around the back lawn of the lodge, glad of the sharp October air: good football weather, as his father always said when they attended a Kansas City Chiefs game. He saw a bull's eye target hung from a tree branch and a bow and quiver of arrows leaning against the trunk. So he took them up and strung the bow and started shooting arrows – there were six – from about fifty feet away, something he hadn't done since summer camp when he was a boy. It was the perfect remedy: the clamor inside him subsided as if the orchestra conductor had tapped loudly on his stand.

"My god, these people are nothing but yokels," he muttered suddenly. "Country bumpkins with money and power, still inevitably thinking in terms of countries and conquest: 'cutting the pie.' *Doers,* for God's sake! All we need now is a shield with a cross on it, like the Knights of Malta."

"How they doin' in there? Jacky gonna finish soon?" a woman called, coming around a small pavilion on the far side of the yard.

This was evidently Jack's girlfriend. She was in her early twenties, he figured, nearly six feet tall with broad depthless shoulders. She wore a belted raincoat above black tights that showed off her straight, slender legs shoed in high boots. Her mass of reddish curly hair shimmered all over and in the light breeze seemed alive itself, sometimes hanging on a shoulder, swinging around to her back, or spilling around her face and framing it. Her face: a cherubic dream with almond-shaped eyes as green and bright as kiwis. The odd thing about her was her shape. She wore the belt of her raincoat cinched up high and tight, and for a long moment Paul couldn't make up his mind if this was some sort of fashion for pregnant women – until he realized that it was her breasts: they had to be enormous. She might have been carrying a medium-sized dog on her chest.

"I'm not sure," Paul said. Then he remembered something The Rainmaker had said when serving him the pancakes. "But someone did mention that everyone had to be on their way by twelve-thirty tops."

"Jacky said twelve," she grumbled. "And he said I can't use my cell. Do you think I can use my cell?" She pulled her phone, turned off, out of her raincoat pocket.

"No," Paul said flatly. "He's right: you could get in big trouble."

She stuffed it right back in. "Trouble? No sir."

Her accent was softly musical, perhaps Tennessee. She hauled up the sleeve of her windbreaker and looked at her watch, which was a single, thick band of diamonds with a gold clock face. "Well, it's almost ten-thirty. How bad can it be, right? Ten hours o' waitin' and ten minutes o' fun – that's what knowin' Jacky's all about. We're goin' up to Niagara Falls later on, then back to ol' Singapore." She was not looking forward to Singapore. "First time in almost two months we've had a whole weekend alone together. With Jacky, you know, you have to schedule everything five weeks in advance. Couldn't even squeeze in an extra day when his brother died last March. We spend a lot o' time in Hong Kong too – Jacky calls it Honkers. Ever been there?" A forearm bounced up and fell, like a puppet's. "Sor-ruh. I'm Tori."

"Paul. No, and it's one place I'd really like to go."

"Yeah, it's okay. Food's weird."

"That's a beautiful watch."

She looked at it as if unsure that she agreed. "Yeah, Jacky gave it to me for my birthday last summer. Nineteen."

Yes – a teenager, with the puttyish nose and jawline of a girl, still the distant glow of schoolbooks and junior proms in her cheeks, nary a crease in her temples.

"Hey, haven't I seen you in a magazine? Like for a movie or some-thin'?"

"No, must be someone else."

Tori didn't register this, but pensively fingered her thick hair, and Paul admired her almond-shaped eyes. This was beauty of a kind he had rarely encountered. "Hey, ah…he, Jack, he doesn't have a wom-an in there, does he? I mean, he told me there were, like, some high-buck businessmen in there he had to do deals with. But sometimes, Jack…sometimes he likes to pull a fast one on me."

"No, no. Just…businesspeople. The only woman in there is old enough to be my mother."

The woman thought this over, then blurted, "He didn't tell you to tell me that, did he? I mean, really, the truth."

"No. No, of course not."

"Sure? Swear on your mother's grave?"

"C'mon!" Paul couldn't suppress a laugh. A few minutes earlier he was being sworn into a secret semi-government cabal, and now he was swearing on his mother's grave to a billionaire's moll whose breasts probably weighed ten pounds each. "My mother, fortunately, doesn't have a grave yet. Nothing to swear on there. But I *am* sure."

"Well, okay." She lowered her voice and glanced towards the house. "It's just that he likes getting in quickies at weird places and then seeing if I can figure out when he's doin' it. It's a...like a sex game we play."

"Quickies," Paul repeated.

"Yeah, like we're at a benefit, and his watch bell rings, and he says, 'I did it out in the alley and you didn't catch me!' I have thirty minutes to catch him, see. He pushes a button on his watch, and it rings when the timer goes off."

"Wow. Never heard of that one," Paul said, scrambling for words. "But...he actually finds a woman at a benefit and persuades her to, to go out into the alley and –"

"No, it's a girl from an agency that's waitin' for him. Agency girls," she sighed. "Some of 'em are pretty sexy. None of 'em have these, though." She glanced down at her breasts as if at her own children. "Jacky had 'em done for my birthday. It was kinda weird at first, but they give me one-up against agency girls, y'know."

"Is that why you wear the belt so high?" Paul inquired.

"Yeah, kinda takes the weight offa my back."

"Right. Good idea."

Then she giggled and tossed back the cloud of her hair, as thick and heavy as pillow stuffing. "But you know somethin'? Last night – well, it would be today, kind of – we were like in a restaurant in Tel Aviv? And he got up to go to the bathroom, and when he got back, I could tell he'd had quickie in there. We were with a bunch of his" – she rolled her eyes – "*business associates,* so I didn't say nothin' right then and there, but I called it on him when we were in the taxi, and guess what: I got him!"

"And he admitted it?"

"Oh yeah, he has to admit – 'cause I just check the timer on his watch to see if it's runnin'. Then he pays the price, see. But if I grab his watch and check, and he *didn't* do it, then *I* pay the price. Or if he does it and gets away with it, I pay." With a wet crack, she punched her palm, startling Paul. "And tonight he's gonna pay up, buddy-boy. I'm gonna have him jumpin' through my hoops till sunrise! Ever try makin' love with your right hand handcuffed to your left ankle?"

"Not my *left* ankle," Paul deadpanned.

Tori giggled. "Drives him crazy. I tease him all over the place. Boy, am I ever gonna have a good time!"

"I'll bet, I'll bet," Paul laughed. He liked Tori – he had a weak spot for anyone with a rich sense of fun. It was only later that he could reflect with pity on how this sweet young beauty had been utterly exploited by a lecher. "And does the game work the other way around? If, ah, you don't mind my asking."

"'The other way around'? Whaddaya mean?"

"I mean, for example, *you* getting in a quickie, starting thirty minutes on your watch, and if Jack doesn't catch you…."

"Oh no no no, I couldn't do that. Jack has exclusiv'ty – whether he's around or not. That's like all spelled out in the clauses." She puffed out her cheeks a moment. "Oh, I'd lose *ever'thing* if I did that. And when he's out, like in Azer-by-John or somethin', heck, I get offers ten times a day. But some of 'em are guys checkin' up on me for him, so I gotta be careful."

Ted Greene came out on the back porch and motioned to Paul.

But before Paul could take a step, Tori grabbed his arm. "Hey, you won't, like, tell anyone about this, will you?" she said quietly. "I also got a, a, a non-enclosure clause, I think it's called. It means I can't tell anybody. I could get in big trouble."

"No, of course not." But Paul needed to swear on his mother's grave to reassure her. "Well, it was nice talking to you, Tori. And you, y'know, you give him hell tonight," he added with a wink.

"Oh, you betcha I will!" she laughed, tossing her hair again. "Hey, lemme try with the bow 'n' arrow."

Paul handed them over and followed Greene into the kitchen before the latter said anything.

"A few people had to call their constituencies and consult, but all right, Paul, you win. In fact, you won bigger this time than the first vote: 9 to 1. Looks like you even impressed Jack Mirage." He stuck out his hand, which Paul took. "And when you're SecState, I bet you make that drunk bum Mason look like a piker."

In the living room, there was again light applause around the circle of chairs, and this time Paul did not do any clowning to acknowledge it. The Rainmaker took his place in front of the whiteboard, taking the black marker and drawing two long parallel lines down its center, hand-width apart. How odd it was, thought Paul, to see a priest in full dress talking to them about national security. Or was security a religion like any other, requiring belief in a devil?

"All right, loved ones, now that we have everyone's career problems solved, let's move on: we're running a bit late, I want to explain the changes that my staff has made to accommodate your critiques" – a glance at Dorothy Crick – "and we've got a lot of ground to cover before the choppers start to arrive at twelve-thirty – which means that Jack will have to vacate the pad by then."

The Harmons sat forward on their chairs like basketball players on the bench; each wore a cross on a chain around his neck; Mitch's fell forward. "This is gonna blow *you* away, Paul," said Mark, jabbing his finger at Paul as if accusing him.

"The theme we chose is, 'Any American street,'" said Jannik. "That's the name of the op: Operation AnyStreet. I've talked to some news editors, and they think it's just *sexísimo*."

"Totally super cool," said Mitch from the CIA, squeezing his enormous biceps.

Out of the corner of his eye, Paul saw Dorothy Crick shift on the sofa, her jaw muscles tight.

"'Cool' – funny how that word has endured. Remember it from the Sixties," said The Rainmaker as he drew little boxes on each side of the parallel lines, one of which he labeled "Hallerbee." Then he put down the black marker and took up the red and green ones. "It's taken us some time to refine the op, but I and my staff have done it. Paul, let me introduce you to Charlesdrew Street in Jersey City, New Jersey. In almost the middle of the block, at number 126, there is now a quiet little Internet digital-advertising company staffed by handsome young adults, many with pretty wives and small children – just the kind of people you want to see grieving on television."

31

MID-OCTOBER
"They're going to burn their agent?" I cried. "Those bloody bastards. Oh, that *is* bad form. Didn't the CIA man raise hell about that?"

Paul shook his head. "Not even a frown."

"Doesn't surprise me a bit. Sod the lot of them."

"The only no vote was Senator Crick, though Jack Mirage certainly wasn't enthusiastic." Paul shook his head. "These are power-mad people, Max. They want to steer the world. You should see the 'futures book' – the future ops that the Doers have okayed for a feasibility study by The Rainmaker's staff. One is a major oil spill near Moscow that will spoil the city's drinking water and discredit the government. A massacre in a Salt Lake City hospital that will make hospitals tighten up security: guards patrolling hallways."

"Indeed. The more people they can get taking a bloody security paycheck, the easier it's going to be."

It was evening, the same day as Paul's Doers meeting, and he was still in shock. We were taking a walk in the cool October air after dinner at my suburban house outside Washington. Our wives, discoursing no doubt on the failure of women's liberation to better their lot, were tidying up after dinner: roast duck with all the trimmings, and for pudding an excellent plum duff, which my American wife had learnt to cook at my mother's elbow. Paul's wife Cindy was using just a walker to get around – truly amazing progress there – and was in charge of rinsing off scraps and loading the dishwasher.

"Getting back to Jersey City, this al-Bousapha fellow – what's *he* been told?" I asked, taking a sip of one of my better ports; we had brought our glasses with us, and I carried a flask in my pocket.

"That his men get it in the forehead the moment they run into the house – *they* think they're legit terrorists striking a blow for Allah and the cause."

"Well, they've got to leave some kind of trail behind them, don't they? Otherwise researchers don't have anything to write about later on. What of the three police cars chasing the van?"

"Bureau guys dressed up, the cars stolen here and there and painted to look like Jersey City Police."

As the inside man, Paul explained, al-Bousapha would stay alive long enough to negotiate by phone with hostage specialists – not in the loop either, except for the SWAT team commander – and then leave quietly through a tunnel running from the basement into the sewer main under Charlesdrew Street. He had been promised a flight on an Air Force transport to Brazil, where Sao Paulo's finest plastic surgeon was going to turn him into a new man. "A full face-lift and a new nose, I hear," Paul added, "and he wants to tweak his cheekbones."

What al-Bousapha didn't know was that he would crawl through the tunnel and find the entrance into the sewer blocked. And rather than three minutes after the warning shot, as he had been informed, the truth was that the explosion would be detonated after only two.

"The bloody, bloody bastards," I muttered and drank more, watching the window curtains of houses along the street to see if any fluttered with curiosity: bloody nuisance these American laws about drinking alcohol beyond the limit of your own lawn. But no problem: the only flutter on the curtains was the dry blue of computer and television screens. "Still – setting his mates up for the kill like that. Maybe he's getting his just desserts."

We walked a block in silence. I refreshed our glasses. We passed an open garage where two fellows under a set of lights worthy of a movie set were lowering an engine block on a chain into a two-seat-er European sports car. The walls were symmetrically mottled with tools, lovingly arranged. Ah, the American with his hobby!

"And the tunnel is ready?" I asked.

"Built over the past several weeks. They even had a couple of CIA engineers working out the physics since there would be cars going along the street. There's also a specially-designed two-headed motorcycle to zip men and supplies back and forth through the sewer system, with bridges built over the junctions. 'The Sewer-Mobile,' they call it. Their op center is a few blocks over on Zilder Street – what to the neighbors is a crack house. So was the one on Charlesdrew till The Rainmaker had it bought and held in reserve for this op. They've had the Hallerbee sign up outside for a few months and a few people moving in and out to convince the neighbors."

"But hang on," I objected. "You said that only one person – one employee – actually goes there for her first day of work – this lass who's been working in France."

"Yeah, a nice-looking blond lady who apparently has no close family. Gertrude. She used to be a gymnast, and they've found sports footage of her at Cornell and located a lot of former teammates and coaches to talk about what a sweet person she was. They want the media to personalize the attack."

"But after the blast, how do enough arms and legs appear all over the neighborhood? All right, you've got the three supposed employees dead outside. You're still missing eight or nine employees."

"Cadavers of homeless people, brought in during the days before," Paul said so quietly I could barely hear, "Two homeless will be taken alive – the ones that escape and get shot. An Oriental woman and a thirtyish man representing –"

"*Oriental,* old man?"

"The media man, Randy, thought that would be the right touch: first out the door will be the Oriental, then Gertrude the blond, and last Hallerbee the boss. The two homeless will be dressed up as office people, pictures placed on the website, then let out to stagger down the steps before they're shot."

"To make a nice little pile of death in front of the house. Bloody hell."

"The media man also suggested placing all the dead bodies upstairs. The explosives will be centered downstairs so that the body fragments fly away hundreds of yards."

"And the cameramen having a field day photographing legs and arms hanging from trees."

"The FBI will set up a fake morgue where body parts will be taken and supposedly i.d.'d, so they'll have that part assured."

"Any bloody American street – Christ," I said, taking out the flask. "May I offer a drop more of civilization, Mr. Under Secretary?" I poured out. "And The Rainmaker – he'll be in there performing *extreme unction?* How on earth can that be possible?"

"Apparently. He wants to give last rites for the dead, and he'll ask the two street people and Gertrude if they would like the extreme unction. The CIA guy told me he just likes to be hands-on during an op, but I'm not so sure. My impression was that he takes his Catholicism very seriously."

"Must be what he calls giving a moral flavor to the thing. Bloody macabre, if you ask me, old man."

"And one more: he held a short Mass before the Doers meeting."

"*A Mass?*"

Paul nodded.

"Bloody hell." I remembered that sodding priest crossing himself at dinner prayers while I was supposed to be down in the basement with one leg turned inside out.

"I almost forgot, Max: I've got some information on him for you. He told me that officially he had been killed in Vietnam. So his name must on the memorial wall."

"Bloody hell. That would make a great bargaining chip if we could find it. I wonder if I could look up curates who died there."

More port, more clop-clopping in the dark. Then Paul spoke in a lowered voice: "What if we could talk to this Gertrude before the event and get her to go along with us?"

"And spike the whole plan?" I looked at him. "Mr. Under Secretary, you are a deep one!"

Paul sighed impatiently.

"All right. Know anything about her?"

"Just the basics. She's a statistical analyst, rents an apartment in Newark."

We walked along the silent streets lined with insipid suburban houses – ostensibly for people, but where zombies would feel perfectly comfortable. Two- and three-car garages dominated the façades as if garages were some kind of architectural marvel. Ahead, a car ripped into our street, squealing its wheels, and by the time it hurtled past us was doing at least fifty. A thick rap beat gushed out of its windows.

"My god, how I'm beginning to hate the twenty-first century," Paul said suddenly. He had pushed a hand up under his glasses and was wiping his eyes. "Can you believe in 1988 President Reagan signed the U.N. Convention on Torture and Inhuman Treatment? After World War Two we were in favor of all manner of international conventions: human rights, laws that governed trade and international affairs, even the Anti-Ballistic Missile Treaty. It seemed that humanity had at long last learnt a couple of lessons. But that was *then,* wasn't it?"

It was then that Paul told me in tears about Tori and the masses of gel Jack Mirage made her carry around in her breasts. Finally, he blew his nose in a handkerchief and got a grip. "Sorry, Max. Let's move on to how we can beat these bastards."

I trickled more inspiration into our glasses.

"Well, we're not going to expose them, old man; any such story would be stifled long before it reached the public ear, and good

Americans would refuse to believe it anyway. The best we can do is –"

"Discredit them, disrupt them, get them closed down," Paul finished. He stopped in an intersection and was looking down another long, straight street of houses dormant under the dumb streetlamps. "Make the op look so bad that they crawl back into the woodwork. We have to let the official narrative come out, and then tear so many holes in it that blaming Iran and Russia loses all momentum and is impossible to try again."

"Hence your plan with the blond Gertrude?"

Paul nodded. "Her and one other person: al-Bousapha."

"You're going to turn *him?*" I asked, incredulous. "Can you contact him beforehand?"

"No." A smile. "I'm a diplomat, Max, remember? The art of persuasion? But I'll need a little help. Are you in?"

"Such a question, old fruit!" I said and raised my glass, which he banged with his own.

PART TWO: THE FINISH

32
And so it came to pass, good reader, that a few weeks after our post-dinner walk, U.S. Under Secretary of State for Political Affairs Paul Klippen found himself in a Jersey City sewer in dress rarely seen at Foggy Bottom and ready to spring into action for the good of his country and much of the planet, with the aid of your servant.

Like me on Charlesdrew Street in my car (I'd left it parked there since the previous afternoon), he had arrived at around six in the morning of 11/9, and spent the first hour lying in a camp hammock slung between two rungs of a collecting juncture at the intersection of Charlesdrew and Warble, well below the level of the sewer tunnel. A LED light clipped to his old bicycle helmet, he was, as usual, reading – from an e-book for logistical reasons – this one on America's invasion of Algeria (then the Barbary Coast) in Napoleonic times. For obvious reasons, he had left his mobile phone in New York.

At around seven-thirty, he heard some whining noises and roused himself to stand on a rung and stare forty yards up the sewer line as men began arriving in the "Sewer-Mobile" with their guns and equipment. The vehicle was a long, low creation that The Rainmaker had described as a two-headed motorcycle, electrically powered for silence, which ran in either direction, the heads connected by a long box. The box was flexible and able to turn: to reach the operations house, several blocks away, it had to make one 90-degree turn. As it approached, its headlamp cast a growing yellowish glow above Paul, who ducked down.

A metallic scraping – a thick brace being loosened – was followed by a sucking echo and a grunt: the concrete plug that separated the house tunnel and the sewer line was pulled out and rolled aside. Paul himself had done this with Trudy three days earlier as they rehearsed possible escapes from the Charlesdrew house, either through the side window, a back kitchen window, or straight out the back kitchen door; as we've already seen, at the moment of truth she chose the first option. Now he heard a humming, and realized that it was the conveyor belt running along the tunnel between the sewer and house, some fifty feet. He had bought a child's toy mirror with a handle, and, holding it above him, got an idea of what was happening: one side of the box was lowered –collapsing in folds, like an accordion – and heavy burdens were unloaded onto the belt: the cadavers.

The agents made five more such trips for equipment, more cadavers, and the two living victims, groggy and whining; perhaps The Rainmaker's extreme unction would soon console them. A woman squawked with a heavy Chinese accent, "Yah, wanna sleep. Whatchoo doin'? Lemme sleep!" Her companion, a man, thundered "Ow!" once, and that was all. Paul shivered.

At about 8'45, the last people and equipment were shipped along the conveyor belt.

"Yeah, this is Janko Ten," a man sang lazily into his radio. "Phase Five complete. Comment? Over."

The answer came in a porridge-thick Missouri accent: The Rainmaker: "Roger, Janko Ten. We're standing by for Goldilocks here. For now, stand away to Bernel. Over." Paul surmised that "Goldilocks" was Trudy, "Bernel" was the opposite end of the 100 block of Charlesdrew.

"Roger that. Standing away."

The Sewer-Mobile sang electrically away up the block, its now-rear headlight still pointing Paul's way, to the bridge they had placed over the junction of Bernel and Charlesdrew Streets. Paul could hear the scratchy gurgle of their radio echoing down the sewer line.

After that, he sat down in the hammock again and tried to read, but he kept looking at his watch and worrying about Trudy. A little after nine, he heard the conveyor belt squeak into action and the profanity of men. And a man moaning:

"Shee-yut, man, I can hardly move. Where are they? Where?"

"They're comin', bro'. Just relax. ETA thirty seconds."

The Sewer-Mobile whined to a stop. A medley of voices commenced, some the two drivers, others the men from the house.

"What happened?"

"Sandusky took a stun gun right in the balls."

Someone burst out laughing.

"It ain't fuckin' funny! Goldilocks got away out the back. Now move him careful!"

Paul sighed with relief.

"Is the op still a go?"

"God says yes."

"You're shitting me."

"Ow! Shi-i-i-it!" shouted Sandusky.

"I'm sorry, man, can you just…ease yourself down onto the floor there? That's all you gotta –"

"O-o-ow. My balls! My…ow! Shit! Be careful!"

"Careful with him – careful! He's real sensitive. Lay him in. Trent, listen: you're gonna be okay, got it? The medic will be waiting for you when you get to Zilder."

"You guys are gettin' a fuckin' stretcher to hand me up those stairs!"

"Hey, you sure? Goldilocks must have seen everything if she ran out the back. And God still says we're a go?"

"Yeah, nobody can believe it. But God has tac command, it's his call. He's putting forty jugheads with badges and packing on the street in Manhattan in an hour. We'll just have to go with two runners instead of three, he says. Middle one's out. Timetable still stands."

"The hell am I gonna tell Janie?" Sandusky yelled, now sobbing. "Would you dumbasses stop blabbin' *and get me to a fuckin' medic?*"

"You're gonna be okay, Trent. Lemme raise this….Watch your leg…There. Now *go go go go!*"

The Sewer-Mobile hummed away.

"Poor guy. I hope they can do a balls transplant."

Twenty minutes later Paul heard the police sirens chasing the terrorist van, and a few gunshots. The Sewer-Mobile returned and picked up more men. Later he could hear the droning crepitation of onlookers gathered at his end of the block. An hour passed, and he heard shots, then screams, as the first "runner" was released, and the other one hour later. Trudy, of course, was to have been the second runner at the half-hour point. Paul wondered if she'd been able to hide somewhere in Manhattan. I had given her several pointers about how to disappear but leave some kind of trail behind to be discovered, but the first twenty-four hours had to be all her own, lest the Doers suspect a traitor.

Now Paul began to limber up after his long wait, holding onto the damp rungs and raising himself up and down in a sort of chin-up helped by his legs on the lower rung. He stuffed his e-book into the big pocket on his thigh, took off his normal glasses and put on the prescription diving goggles he'd used whenever he had a chance to go snorkeling on vacation in Ecuador. He noted that he had become so accustomed to the stench of the sewer that he was hardly aware of it.

The Sewer-Mobile steadily shuttled men out of the tunnel and away to the safe house. Finally just one man exited. He rolled the heavy plug back over the hole in the sewer line and set the brace. Paul watched through the mirror as the man turned the spoked wheel that made the brace's two end-to-end pipes unscrew against each other and, extending, press against the plug on one side and the sewer wall on the other. Al-Bousapha was still inside, negotiating with the police.

Paul looked at his watch: soon the armored car, white flag piously flying from its windshield wiper, would begin to move down the street to the Hallerbee house.

The Sewer-Mobile's light dwindled to a point far up Charlesdrew Street – or rather under it – and he turned his own helmet light close on his watch for several seconds so that its hands would glow. Then he turned it off and lunged out of the collector and, his bicycle helmet scraping the top of the tunnel, walked in the pitch dark towards the brace. The sewer system had surprised him: it was ancient, six feet high and nearly as wide, with brick walling built more than a hundred years ago, and not round, but egg-shaped, with the pointed end at the bottom,. He strode quickly, hands out, and stopped when he ran into the brace, which set at waist level nearly doubled him over.

The Sewer-Mobile, a dot in the distance, now disappeared as it turned the corner. He turned on the light strapped to his bicycle helmet. His hands got a good grip on the two handles that tightened or loosened the brace. He pulled with his top hand and pushed with his lower, and with a sandy scrape, it began to loosen. He kept it just tight enough to brace the plug. For he needed to scare al-Bousapha into believing that he, Paul, was saving him: such is the diplomat's "art of persuasion."

Four bangs – the shots sent by al-Bousapha at the SWAT team's approaching armored car – bounced scratchily through the tunnel.

Two minutes till the explosion. Paul glanced at his watch and noted the exact time.

Soon he heard a scrabbling, and then a frantic banging on the other side of the plug: al-Bousapha, desperate to get out.

Paul twisted the handles, and in a moment, the heavy brace fell into his arms. The plug fell backward, and al-Bousapha, face screwed up from the smell, stumbled into the sewer. He was so short that he didn't have to duck in the sewer line.

"Why is blocked this? Who are you? Where is Sewer-Mobile?" he snarled, squinting into Paul's light.

"It's a double-cross. They were going to let you die. Help me get this thing back on."

"But who are you?"

"I'm saving your life – for the moment that's good enough. C'mon: if we don't get this thing on, the blast will kill us."

The man looked at him a long second, then looked at his watch. "Okay, we got ninety seconds."

"No, we have thirty seconds! They told you three minutes, but it's only two."

Al-Bousapha barked something in Arabic and snatched the fallen plug – no matter that it was made of concrete, weighing more than a hundred pounds – and heaved it into place in one move. Paul held up the brace and told him to turn the handles.

"The other way!" Paul snapped. "Keep going…just enough to hold up the…good enough."

The brace set, Al-Bousapha began to duck under it.

"Not that way – this way!" Paul shoved him back and crawled under the brace.

"But that way is –"

"Run!" Paul snapped, pushing him.

They were twenty yards away from the brace when the house exploded. Inside the sewer, the blast itself was muffled, little more than a firecracker. But it made the sewer jerk under their feet – both men fell to their knees – and a few of the old bricks clattered down from the walls, which gave Paul a jab of panic. He turned around and looked back. At the very end of his light, he made out the brace, fallen but still leaning against the plug, which was tilted back as if resting. Paul ran back and kicked away the brace. The plug fell backwards, followed by a tired wash of debris from the tunnel, which had collapsed. Good enough.

Al-Bousapha clapped him on the shoulder when Paul returned.

"Okay, my friend. Thank you, thank you very much! Now: where we go?"

Paul pushed him along towards Warble, and they were nearing it when al-Bousapha's watch beeped.

"Two minutes! *Moth'fucks!*" he groused. "All they are moth'fucks! But we will kill to them, my friend! They think they kill to me, but is al-Bousapha will kill to them!" he said with a chuckle. The traitorous little fool really thought he would have the last laugh.

33

NOVEMBER 13 (SATURDAY)

It was Saturday night in the secretary of state's office. Carlton Mason had called Paul in to curse him for ten straight minutes, the west-Texan sheriff in him warming with each passing sentence.

Paul and his damn cabal were turncoats, warmongers, bloodthirsty Atilla the Huns who made Hitler look like a damn schoolboy. Paul and the others could all go fuck themselves till their assholes were big as water mains. And he suspected that motherfucker Trig Purtly was one too, because he had heard of him working on the president, telling him that the path was cut and he could go down it fast or slow, but he would go the fuck down it whether he liked it or not. This 11/9 bullshit really ground Mason's balls because for once in the last fifty years there was an administration who wanted a little peace and quiet and prosperity in the world, and he didn't give a shit what he and POTUS had been voting on for a decade in Congress; that was mainly to keep the Israelis and the Pentagon and the arms makers off their asses. It was time to get along with the damn Russians, do business with the Chinese, close down AfPak and the Middle East bullshit. God knew the Army'd been stretched to breaking, with those poor goddamn kids coming home and shooting bullets in their heads at twenty a day. But now the president had no choice but to go along with the resolution in Congress – quickly moving through committees probably thanks to a lot of other fairy-faggots in Paul's group – to authorize the president to go to war because of course he'd look like a lameass shithead if he didn't. And here was Under Secretary of State Paul Klippen with his nice hair and sexy face setting them all up for another nice long run of war.

"And I'll bet for doing the about-face in public after all those women's shows and mag covers they promised you my fuckin' chair into the bargain, didn't they? *Didn't they?*" he shouted.

"Yes," Paul muttered into his glass. Hunched over it, his head was only inches from Mason's similarly bowed as if the two were praying.

Mason hadn't forgotten his manners. He had served Paul two fingers of whiskey as he read over Paul's draft of the change in direction of foreign policy, back to war abroad.

"White House told me to send you out on the road – figured they were grooming you. *Grooming you, like hell!* They were packing you with cred so that fat-assed housewives would accept another ten years o' the neighbor boy comin' home bouncin' off the kitchen walls. Half the fuckin' budget shot out a mortar tube."

Paul said nothing but let another bit of whiskey sear his throat.

"I should've spotted you for the skunk-stinkin' climber you are, Klippen. Nothing but a piece of shit wearin' a silk tie."

"Well, it's no fun for me, either, having to go in front of the cameras singing a different song."

Yes, but he's doing it with a little songbird going in his heart because pretty soon a nice limo was going to be picking him up for a ride to the office, and he was going to have more secretaries than the president of a porno-film producer....

This went on for some time; you get the idea. Paul wondered what to say. He wondered where Trudy was. All he knew from his encrypted Doers phone was that she had not been caught.

"All right, I'm done. I'll scratch a few syllables in the text here and send it out with Parker in the morning. Now get the fuck outta my office, and if you think you're coming to another meeting as long as I'm secretary, you're dreamin' worse than those shitheads that are fuckin' you in the butt these days."

With a sigh, Paul rose to his feet. But as he did, he leaned forward to Mason and murmured in his ear, very low but very clear, "Stall it till Tuesday."

Mason's head jerked up. Even through the whiskey, his senses had turned sharp. He said nothing, just looked Paul in the eye. Still bent over, face not a foot from Mason's, Paul looked back for a long moment and then gave the smallest flutter of a wink. Setting his glass silently on a table, he left.

34

NOVEMBER 13-14-15
Let me then set the stage for you as matters came to a boil on the weekend after 11/9. Here is a selection of the more noteworthy events and passions.

By Saturday, fleets had been launched, alert levels raised, and military home leave canceled. The House and Senate were in conference on bills authorizing the president to take all necessary action to insure a change of regime in Iran; actually declaring war, as the American Constitution prescribed, was still considered passé. The president was making dark noises without committing himself; conservative pundits were openly labelling him a coward. Russia was intimating that it would defend Iran, and again insisted that the International Atomic Energy Agency, as well as Russian and Iranian scientists, be permitted to examine the never-assembled Empire State bomb and particularly its "bullet" of uranium to determine its provenance. The bit of uranium sounded like a pellet of fuel typically inserted in rods used for nuclear power plants, for such pellets are short, round and narrow, roughly like a bullet. If that was the case, the uranium was far below weapons-grade and useless for a bomb.

Ambassador Lori Fischler laughed at this: "And so you're saying that these terrorists died to haul three crates of useless junk up to the fourth floor of the Empire State Building? Tell me another!" So the Russian ambassador did, and Fischler laughed even more:

"I remind my American colleague that the investigators report no trace of radioactivity in the car of the alleged terrorist Gertrude Ingrid Schelling. The police report none in the house used by the terrorists before the attack. The single place where the radioactivity appears is in the vehicle used by the terrorists on the ninth of November. Where did this uranium come from? Did they produce it right there in the car?"

"Gosh, I don't know," said the American ambassador with a mock-innocent roll of the eyes. "Maybe they just bought it on Amazon and put it straight into their van off the FedEx truck. Really, Mr. Ambassador, I would think that we're all adult enough in this room not to chase conspiracy theories." This went down well on nightly television news; Fischler graced the covers of women's magazines for months.

"Ambassador Fischler's sarcasm is well-placed," ran one major editorial I read that Sunday morning. "The fact remains that Iranian and Syrian terrorists thought they were assembling an atomic bomb and would do terrific damage to people and property in Manhattan. The administration's pivot to diplomacy, which this page loudly applauded, now lies in tatters. All that remains is to admit the obvious and get on with other means of defending the nation against Iran – and, if necessary, Russia."

This was the opinion, with a few nuances, of the mainstream media, which like the country had no patience for stuffy institutions like the IAEA. To Americans, the Russians and Iranians insisting on investigation and solid facts sounded like parents insisting on children finishing their homework.

What dissent existed remained largely with 11/9 Truthers, whose theories had made significant noise on the Internet, enough to trouble a syndicated columnist: "At every one of these crises these people come out of the woodwork and do nothing but make the public skeptical. They dishonor the dead. They add nothing to the debate and destroy our faith in our leaders. If you still pay attention to the mysterious 'white-armed shooter' or the assertions of so-called 'bus witnesses,' just look at the big picture.

"First, this is America: everybody talks about everything. Any attempt to falsify an attack like this is doomed from the start. Why? Because you need *dozens,* maybe as many as a hundred people, to pull it off. How many of them would leak? Minimum 10%. Probably more like 30% once the first guy got a book contract.

"In fact, people actually prefer conspiracy theories because they keep the whole thing contained. It keeps at bay the reality that there actually are terrorist elements who wish us harm and are willing to die in the attempt.

"Second, the indirectly-accused guilty party, as always, is the government. But let's admit it: government is government. And government does some things well. But it can't clean a mine without spilling toxic waste into the local river system. It can't spend money with anything like efficiency where the military is concerned. Some auditors estimate there's as much waste as there are dollars well-spent.

"In short, any attempt by big government to do something requiring this kind of fine-tuned operating would be a disaster. Any elected leader giving it the green light would be considered madly reckless. And say what you like about the president, he is not mad nor reckless."

Yes, here and there and everywhere, from pundits, in social-media commentary, among writers on book tours and writers on bathroom walls, Americans were assured that 11/9 conspiracy theories were just that: conspiracy theories. All the news that was fit to print had indeed been printed, and whatever hadn't been was fake. Americans prepared for war; this time Iranians were going to eat those beards, oh yes.

So you can imagine my shimmering satisfaction when during my late-morning Monday class on post-World War II politics, one of my students, finding little illumination in my commentary on Generals Eisenhower and Montgomery, and searching for spicier stuff in his mobile phone, called out that Raschid al-Bousapha, mastermind of the attack on the Empire State Building, was now holed up in a barber shop – hostages quaking at his feet – in the borough of Queens in New York. After a week in the morgue, where his remaining fragments had already been officially identified with DNA testing, it seemed that the poor fellow needed a quick short-back-and-sides in order to make a stunning entrance in heaven.

35 NOVEMBER 15 (MONDAY)

They awoke at the same time on Monday afternoon, with the clean low sunlight reflected from windows across the way. A perfect world. The girls down below were chanting their jump-rope songs. A teapot whistle rose through three or four notes before the heat was turned off. Mrs. Gelling across the way came out of her apartment griping on her cell phone about someone's slovenliness: "She had her grandson waiting *twenty minutes* with her facilitator because *she* couldn't finish her bridge game! Twenty minutes! And then she has the nerve to call Sharon and tell *her* to pick up her son!"

They said nothing for a long time, and Trudy began to worry that Jerry was trying to figure out how to get out of a bad relationship – she always felt that she was a bad lover. She had never been able to bring herself to do a "blowjob"; a guy she liked had once left her just because of that.

Showers, steam, the scrape of jeans, the clank of the refrigerator, the burble of the coffee pot, the clinking gossip of sugar spoons;

now and then a glance at each other as if they were afraid of being recognized. But then he turned and kissed her hair twice, and she knew all was well. All was well.

They sat and began to drink their coffee. Jerry wondered if there was anything going on with her friend the under secretary of state; maybe he was getting things squared away so that she could come out of hiding. Trudy looked at the computer and quickly saw that the answer was no.

Secretary of State Mason said that he had asked Congress to delay a final vote on the war resolution till at least Tuesday, and preferably not until the IAEA's report was in. The media had worked the public into a lather about the "atomic bullet": "Whether the bomb was real or fake, it gave off strong radiation," roared an editorial. "Nobody plays practical jokes on the American public and gets away with it." Though weary of war and sobered by the prospect of taking on a real army for once, Americans as one were steaming angry about the 11/9 attack.

Body parts were still being pulled down from trees, the number of wild dogs roaming Jersey City had multiplied to something like an epidemic, flies were becoming a problem, and the shameless traitor-terrorist Gertrude Ingrid Schelling was still at large.

Then she saw the news about Raschid al-Bousapha, that he had turned up alive.

Trudy groaned. "Oh, this has all gone so wrong! I was supposed to speak out first *before* al-Bousapha! He was the icing on the cake!"

"You *knew* he was going to show up?"

"Well, not exactly what day, but my video statement was supposed to be released on the day *before* to kind of get the doubt rolling."

Jerry drank down the last of his coffee and briefly swallowed his upper lip with his great jaw. "You know what you're supposed to say, right?"

"Yeah, just my story, like I never met either Paul or Max. Just make it clear I'm not a terrorist and that I saw dead bodies and all in that house." She shivered. "It gives me the creeps just to think about it."

"Well, Uncle Jerry has the answer."

"You do?"

"Listen, I don't have a gig tonight, so I was planning to look in on Occupy Madison – at the park? I was thinking I might do another quick gig there. I have a standing invitation from the organizers 'cause of the last time around. I could do five or six minutes of material, then introduce you and you could get up on stage."

"*On stage?*" cried Trudy.

"And then you're in, babe. Two minutes of Gertrude Ingrid telling her side of the story, and voila! You're no longer the new bin Laden. They couldn't suspect you after that – not by a long shot."

Trudy ran her fingers through her hair, still wet. She traced a figure 8 on the table. She hated appearing in front of a lot of strangers; even at gymnastics meets she did her routine and dashed back to her teammates, hoping that the applause would be just the perfunctory little bit so that she needn't take a bow. "On stage. You're sure? I mean, I was just going to make a video at Joe's house and hang it on YouTube or, or…."

Jerry's great overbite grin broke open. "Babe – we're listening to Uncle Jerry, right? Ten sentences from that sweet mouth, and not even the general in charge of splinter-cell anti-terror hang-'em-high Special Ops will believe you're a terrorist. You're the girl who did her boyfriend's taxes two hours before he dumped you. Miss Lake Wobegon."

Laughing, Trudy jumped up, dashed around the table and threw her arms around him. "Gosh, Jerry, I wish I could just stay here forever."

Jerry went mock-serious. "Babe, please: control. Otherwise we're going to end up, you know: getting all sweaty again. First we have to –"

"I'm not very good in bed, am I?" Trudy blurted.

"Oh, so *that's* the little cloud sitting on that brow. I wondered about that. Troodles, look: if there's one thing I've come to hate in this world, it's these girls who go to bed with you and they've got all these ideas from chick mags about 'Six Ways to Make Your Man Wake Up Screaming For More.' You do it sincere. Absolutely sincere. Lots of love. Perfect. Good time had by all, okay?" He pecked her on the lips. "Enough said. I also hate relationship talk." He made a woman's voice: "My boyfriend understands me only skin deep. I need him to understand my core being. I need to feel that I have a soul twin."

Trudy laughed. "Oh, Jerry, you're fantastic. If you can't make the big time, nobody can."

"Hey, thank you, folks. Man, there's nothing like it when you've got an audience behind you. Yeah! Now reach me my notebook over there. Time to fight the forces of evil and pick up a little *publicité* for Jerry Stretch. You know, like" – he used a newscaster's orotund patter – "'local comedian Jerry Stretch introduced Ms. Schelling to the Occupy audience, where she gave them an earful. Let's listen.' Might even get a gig on the *Tonight Show* out of it."

"Yeah, but, but don't say you know me, Jerry. You could get in big trouble. Also we've got to have a way to get out of there after I finish. I mean, word is going to get out pretty quick, you know."

Jerry weighed this. "Point taken. No use doing five-to-ten in Sing-Sing. So let's not go over there till around five when the sun's going down." He slowly turned over a fresh page of his notebook. "But I think the Occupy guys can work something out. They're actually pretty sharp when it comes to cops and all. All right, I'm gonna need about five minutes of material: I can do my three thumbnail gigs, and I'll need something on New York cops; Occupy loves that stuff. And then a nice big bang of a seg-way into Gertrude Ingrid that they'll have to put on the sound bite."

36

NOVEMBER 9-15

Raschid al-Bousapha's return from the dead was more comedy than drama; nevertheless, let's go over the ground here.

After rescuing al-Bousapha, Paul led him through the sewer system, the Iranian vomiting twice along the way. Ten minutes later, the two men heaved themselves out of a manhole in the corner of the deserted staff parking lot of Our Savior's Holy Ascension Baptist Church.

Paul handed al-Bousapha off to my friend Irish Joe and got into my rented car. I drove Paul away before the great terrorist could get a look at him. Not that it would have helped: the bicycle helmet and goggles hid him sufficiently.

And Paul had a meeting to get to. The juggling he had done with his schedule to be both legitimately in New York and out of sight of his security people used to comprise an entire chapter of my account, but a dreary one I've omitted. As Paul stripped off his fragrant plastic overalls and other accoutrements, I drove him to a nameless motel beside the freeway, where he disinfected himself under a roaring shower and changed into new clothes. He arrived only a little late at the United Nations for a meeting with the Foreign Affairs Minister of Cameroon. "But Henri is an old friend from my first State posting and won't take it poorly," Paul told me as I dropped him off. Henri had also kept Paul's cell phone for him and turned it on an hour before their meeting.

Joe, meanwhile, drove al-Bousapha to his home in Newark, New Jersey – actually not far from Trudy's apartment – serving him a fruit juice that would send him into a deep sleep. There the great terrorist remained for the next several days, emerging only long enough to stagger to the bathroom beside his basement room, wonder where he was, observe that he felt dizzy and weak, and nibble a little more of what was making him sleep and feel dizzy and weak. Joe and/or Irene kept a close watch on him via CCTV.

Then, on Monday morning, Joe loaded him back into his taxi, drove him to a park in Queens, and just after 11 a.m., as al-Bousapha was rising once again into consciousness, gave him an injection that would raise his spirits. Joe helped him to a park bench, and then left his taxi with a nearby mechanic – an oil change and lube job – and kept watch from a distance. He was, by the way, deeply embarrassed over losing track of Trudy and determined to do better by us this time.

After some twenty minutes, al-Bousapha found himself amazingly well, alert, full of vim and vigor. He also found two hundred bucks and a small loaded automatic in his pockets – hopeful omens indeed. Al-Bousapha began walking. He first entered a fast-food place, ate a mammoth breakfast and used the restroom. During the latter interval, Joe mentioned to two middle-aged women at an adjoining table that he believed that the man who had just entered the restroom was the evil terrorist Raschid al-Bousapha; could they take a good look at him when he came out? But neither one even recognized the name, though when he mentioned 11/9, one said, "Oh, that was ovuh in Joisey," as if it were no business of theirs.

His luck was little better in the used-clothing shop next door, where al-Bousapha bought a jacket, as a breeze was picking up. Joe pretended to be another customer, and while al-Bousapha was in a fitting room judging whether or not a black faux-leather jacket gave him the proper image, Joe discreetly asked the shopkeeper if that wasn't so-and-so, the 11/9 terrorist, and maybe the police ought to be alerted. This fellow, a Chinese immigrant, went so far as to murmur, "Might-a-be, might-a-be," but was ultimately reluctant to bring in the police before a 75-dollar sale could be made.

Evidently, looking in the mirror to buy the jacket, al-Bousapha realized that he looked scruffy – hair a curly mess and his beard frayed. And no doubt he had enough of his wits about him to understand that he was in serious trouble – on the run, abandoned by the CIA – and a spiffier presentation would surely not come amiss, not to mention a moment to think things over amidst four solid walls.

Walking into a park, he spotted on its opposite side a twirling barber's pole, that of Redoan's Barber Shop, which was actually a half-shop sharing space with a tattoo parlor. In the barbering half, Moroccan immigrant Redoan Sabiri presided, though a few local Muslim fellows always hung around for a chat and perusal of a week-old *Le Matin*, Morocco's leading newspaper. Joe figured that al-Bousapha would be quickly recognized by other customers and run away, but this did not happen. In fact, none of the three inside recognized him. They greeted him in the brotherly way Muslim gentlemen have, and invited him to go directly to the chair when al-Bousapha asked how soon he could get a cut and a shave. (He spoke flawless Arabic as well as his native Farsi.) No commotion having resulted, Joe trotted after a freshly-shorn fellow that came out, showed him the photo from the newspaper, and suggested that the newcomer in the shop was the same man. "There's probably a reward out for him too," he added.

This bloke, an immigrant from Tunisia, eyed the photo again, did some mental calisthenics, and said he would check again. He returned to the shop, made an appointment with Redoan for his brother, and left, surprised not to find Joe anywhere. But if there was a reward to be had, this could only be a convenience.

The rest you surely know: 911 called, SWAT men roused, bullhorns, Redoan and a Jordanian fellow taken hostage, and negotiations ending with a single tremendous sniper shot taken with an infra-red telescope from across the park, this in late afternoon as al-Bousapha crouched over the phone. Both the men in the shop and the Tunisian immigrant were later congratulated by the president for their "vigilance and courage in the face of terrorism." Sadly, no reward had been posted for al-Bousapha – assumed dead, of course – but they were promised front-row seats at the unveiling of Undershall Hick's memorial statue.

So much for the demise of Raschid al-Bousapha. One hopes that in the afterlife he has come across those five colleagues he betrayed on 11/9.

37 NOVEMBER 13-14-15
Corporal John David Paper, Army chaplain from Rochelle, Illinois, was born in 1948, son of Brian and Susan, brother of Rachel, born the year before, and Linda, born two years after. He "died" in a helicopter crash, the result of "hostile fire," in Quang Tin, Vietnam, in March 1972. His name was etched on the Vietnam War Memorial: Panel 2 West. According to the official Memorial Wall website, the body was never recovered. He had been in Vietnam at that point for a little more than a year. There were two comments on his Memorial Wall page, neither from a relative of any sort. A soldier wrote that he was "a standard fixture" in the army hospital while he, the soldier, was injured: "a true man of God. I miss him every day." Another comment, from a fellow chaplain, said that he had made "the Ultimate Sacrifice in the Service of Our Lord and Our Country."

Elsewhere I found a photo from a seminary in Centerville, Ohio: John standing on the steps of the seminary, hands folded over a Bible, his tiny crack of a smile grudgingly performed for some imploring parent. It was taken after his ordination as a deacon, apparently, for he was already wearing the black attire and dog collar.

All of this, of course, came courtesy of Ian in Penrith, who added the chilling note that he had read an exchange between Senator Crick and The Rainmaker, and the latter apparently – Ian could not read The Rainmaker's part due to encryption -- suspected a leak in Doers. Senator Crick replied that The Rainmaker was trying to find excuses for an "imbecilic" operation.

I prepared a file and added my own two items to Ian's fine research: my brief video of Trudy going up to the Hallerbee house and encountering The Rainmaker (Could that really have been just days earlier? It seemed a year.) and a photo, which I took with my mobile phone on my lunch hour, of "John Paper" etched on the Vietnam War Memorial and a screenshot of his page on the

Memorial website. Those would do if it came to blackmailing The Rainmaker.

On Sunday, the day before Joe turned al-Bousapha loose, I wrote out a summary of the information – and Ian's warning – and sent it to Paul through our lavishly paid couriers: my teenage neighbor Ann and his teenage neighbor Chad, who met in a Burger King halfway between our cities. Paul had already informed me through them that the Doers were going to hold an emergency meeting in upstate New York on Monday afternoon, November 15.

38

NOVEMBER 15 (MONDAY)

Senator Dorothy Crick's hard, banging laugh, like a smoker's hack, cracked the thick silence of the room.

"And you're shocked that she turned on her stun gun! Oh no. Oh my word. Only a man would utter such a stupidity."

"Dottie, can we keep this civil?" snapped Ted Greene.

But the senator paid him no attention. Her shoulders shook with mirth. "A young woman with pretty blond hair sees a man – oh, 'just a guy,' I forgot – he jumps out of his truck and comes trotting across the street to her...." For a moment, she couldn't go on, doubled over with acid laughter where she sat on the sofa. "And what was he wearing? A three-piece suit and carrying a dozen roses? No, he was wearing some kind of worker's jumpsuit, am I right?"

"I believe, Dottie, the team's body equipment included –"

But Senator Crick had only refilled her lungs in order to roar at Mitch the CIA man, *What the hell did you expect her to do? Give him her phone number?* Of course she turned on her stun gun! If it'd been *me,* I'd have reached for a *real* gun and popped him right in the forehead! Where would we be then, eh? *Eh?* One man dead in the street, ten supposed Hallerbee corpses already laid out in the upstairs office, every neighbor on Charlesdrew staring out the window and dialing 9-1-1. As it is, we have *ten witnesses* on a goddamn Port Authority bus who can state that the balloon had gone up on Charlesdrew *twenty minutes before* the terrorists arrived! For the moment – *for the moment* – we have been able to fuzz that up, thanks to the good offices of Randy here. Whoever allowed the op to go forward after she escaped – and yes, I mean *you,* Rainmaker – has no business in Doers. If there's a mole in our organization, the leading suspect is *you!* That was madness! The op should have been aborted on the spot!"

Silence. Standing in the doorway, Trig Purtly shifted from one side to the other.

"Still, we really ought to remember the upside," said The Rainmaker, trying to sound priestly. "She provided a more convenient excuse for terrorists to have rifles and explosives."

"Yes, that they carried it all in under their jackets *was* a bit flimsy."

"It was hard as rock. The cops were *our* people," said Mark the FBI man.

"And the neighbors as well, right, Mark?" retorted the senator. "But not to worry: neighbors never look out their windows when three police cars come screaming up their street."

"The time to review the op will come, Dottie," said Ted Greene. "Can we move on?"

The emergency meeting of the Doers, after days of shrill insistence from Senator Crick, had finally come together. And even then nearly all the Doers arrived grumbling that everything was more-or-less under control, that they had had to juggle schedules, cancel meetings, call in replacements, disappoint clients, and even shorten workouts – this from the twins Mark and Mitch. Only Jack Mirage, in Singapore, was missing, but had asked to be kept informed. For Paul, the meeting had saved him from an afternoon flight to Wisconsin, where he was to give a boring speech to a Midwestern investing association.

Paul had boarded the helicopter in New York with former Vice President Ted Greene. Al-Bousapha, still barricaded in the barber shop at that time, was negotiating, for real this time, with a SWAT team; its commander, by good fortune, was the same one as on 11/9, and thus in the loop. Watching the world through a crush of raindrops smeared over the windows, Paul and Greene talked through the microphones hung from their headsets. Greene had been working non-stop for the last few days, heading the search for "the girl." He wondered angrily how things had gotten so fucked up and who had fucked them up.

"There's always someone responsible – never believe that bullshit about how things 'just happen.' If a flowerpot falls off a ledge and hits you on the bean, it's because some idiot couldn't see he had a deadly weapon sitting there – or was too lazy to take it off the ledge, more likely." He was ranting so fluently Paul could scarcely believe this was the pillar of reason that conservative television hosts loved to have on their talk shows.

"And now al-Bousapha has turned up! How in holy hell did *that* happen? I don't know how we're going to keep this under wraps; I hope Randy Jannik and The Rainmaker's people have some ideas." He mopped his face. "They're pretty good at that stuff," he added hopefully.

"It's straight out of the blue," Paul agreed with as much bitterness as he could. "I never heard that the cleanup crew didn't find his body in the tunnel. Why didn't they report it?"

Greene shook his head, making the microphone by his mouth flick back and forth. "Mitch's people have an explanation – CIA, they always do. They could explain God with a PowerPoint presentation if you gave them enough running room." Another shake of the head. "They figured that when he found the tunnel blocked with the plug and brace, he ran back into the house and got blown sky-high. Remember he thought he had three minutes. It's possible."

Paul nodded. "This plug and brace – do you know if the sewer guys found them still in place?"

"No. Looks like the shockwave had knocked them off. But the blast still would have killed al-Bousapha."

"I'm not so sure. This tunnel ran from the sewer into the base-ment *wall*, right? And they surely had some kind of cover across it. Maybe when al-Bousapha saw that he couldn't get out, he crawled back and closed the opening. Or just pulled some heavy object into place, and it stopped enough of the blast to allow him to survive."

Greene waved a weak hand as if shooing away pigeons. "The tun-nel pretty much caved in."

"That's true – though it would depend on where it caught him."

"Dottie Crick said the tunnel aspect was weak a few months ago." Ted Greene grumbled. "God, she's going to be on the warpath."

And he was right.

"Shut it down," the senator rasped now to the rest of the Doers, silent like bawled-out children. "We are playing with fire – don't you see that? Al-Bousapha is alive, which puts *another* hole in the official story. He doesn't seem to have contacted anyone, and we're damn lucky there – far luckier than we deserve to be. But *as I've pointed out repeatedly in the past week,* if this young woman's story

gets out, and she says someone staged Charlesdrew, and ten witnesses on the bus confirm she jumped on in hysterics, then this is
going to get *very* bad *very* quickly."

"But do those people have credibility?" asked Ted Greene quietly.

The hunting lodge was cold and had a senile stale air, as if long
closed and opened just that afternoon for them. There were no lavish
pancakes, just a tall steel pot of watery coffee set up on the dining
table, and alongside it a cardboard milk carton, a tower of Styrofoam
cups and a package of sugar cookies still in their plastic tray. Mitch
had not pulled out Mark's chair. Even before taking off her coat, Senator Crick announced that she could give the meeting barely 45 minutes: with the new developments, she had to get back to the Senate
floor and fight for the war resolution. They sat in the same improvised
circle of chairs and sofas, everyone sitting in the same places. The
only difference was that in the place of the whiteboard stood a large
television screen. With video from two different angles, Mitch had
tried to prove that Trudy, walking up to Hallerbee, had known what
to expect in the house. The Doers were still skeptical. Paul was enor-
mously relieved: apparently Trudy's acting job had impressed them.

If I could only find her! he thought.

General Chet Nicely shifted his bulk to one side of his chair. "Hell,
Dottie, the bus people'd have to make a pretty much pinpoint-con-
sistent case –"

"Oh, forget the matter of the bus," said the senator, wagging her
slack left hand. "That's the least of our worries. A far bigger one is
this: What if this young woman gets it into her head to get one of
those slangy-slick colored-woman lawyers on her side? And that
slangy-slick colored-woman lawyer walks out in front of a hundred
cameras screaming that the evidence against her is all fake news and
makes the –"

"She won't," The Rainmaker said. He was looking far off into the
dining room as if it held the key to the dilemma. The senator stared
at him as if he were crazy, and finally ignored him.

"And if in front of those cameras, this colored-woman lawyer
makes the perfectly obvious case that her client is an innocent victim and that the house was full of paramilitaries *twenty minutes before al-Bousapha's crew arrived*, then, gentlemen, we are looking at a
battle that is not uphill but vertical. *Vertical.* Now does *that* trouble
our little hearts?"

"And the rest of it? What's your narrative?" asked Ted Greene.

"Oh, *narrative,*" Crick moaned, lifting her eyes to the ceiling. "Sometimes I wonder if all government has come down to these days is the telling of a goddamn bedtime story."

"It's what we live and die by, Dottie," murmured Randy Jannik, hunched away from her on the sofa as if she'd punched him in the arm. "In today's society, there's nothing like narrative for sheer hypnotic power. People aren't interested in facts, but they *are* interested in stories."

The senator ignored him as well. "Just say it was a rogue group, Ted. Hackers trying to start a war. Tell the huddled masses that on second examination the atomic bomb was just a half-baked kitchen job that wouldn't have worked, and the bit of atomic material wasn't Iranian at all but turned out to be stolen out of an X-ray machine in Bangor. And Paul Klippen – sorry about your career plans, Paul – needn't do his about-face on arms-v.-dip policy, just a little softening, something for the second term."

"I had a feeling it was a bit of a pipe dream, anyway," Paul said.

"But what about the girl?" Ted Greene insisted.

"Number one? We de-villainize her. When she turns up, I will shove her slangy-slick lawyer out of the room and take her aside as an older woman, tell her this has all been a terrible mistake, I understand how hard it must have been on you, and by the way, six months down the road when this has all blown over, there's five million tax-free and a four-bedroom frame with a pool on Long Island Sound for you." A black stare around the room. "Which, gentlemen, she richly deserves, having shown more guts, gile, smarts and sheer *moxy* than anyone in this room! All that, my dear, if you'll just stand in front of the microphones tonight and say that when you saw the terrorists run up to the front door, you ran out the back way. You saw nothing else of interest in the house. Later, you saw on TV what had happened, panicked, didn't know what to do, so you hunkered down at a friend's place in the Bronx for a few days."

"But what about our narrative?" cried Mitch. "What about the whole backstory we've cut together on her? Paris, her confession vid, the connection to al-Bousapha, picking up the terrorists in Montana? Along with The Rainmaker's people, I've had a twenty-strong staff working this up 24-7. It's baseline stuff on talk shows now."

With a swipe, Crick's bony index finger decapitated all of this.

"Can it – can *all* of it. Wrong girl, wrong photo, wrong everything. The spy world has been selling you fake intel at fire-sale prices. Have the media do stories on how spy people see what they're ordered to see. How budget cuts force you to buy bad intel. Then wipe the egg off your face and get on with life. Won't be the first time – not the first, not the fiftieth. Par for the course. Live with it."

Mitch and Mark scowled together like bookends.

*"Or…*we could just take her down," General Nicely suggested quietly.

"Yeah, that's where I come out," Mark from the FBI blurted, peering around for support. "I absolutely throw in with Chet on that. Depending on your termination scenario, all you'd have to do is layer in to her narrative that she prepared the whole bus scene – the histrionics and stuff."

Mitch turned to him. "We did that, bro'. Don't you remember? Day Two. Acting preparation for sleeper terrorists?"

"Hey, that's right!" And the two exchanged a high-five.

Senator Crick's jaws clenched and she stared at Paul, who rolled his eyes.

"See, Senator? We're practically locked in!" cried Mark.

"Okay, yes yes *yes,* Mark. You *could* kill her off – yes," said the senator tiredly. "But why leave a mystery hanging behind her? Who knows by now what she's told to whom and how many times? By far, *by far,* the most convincing way to tie this off is for her to tell everyone *herself* that it was all a silly mistake: she saw men with guns, jumped out the back way and made a beeline for a friend's place. She saw men inside? Well, they did look awfully Middle Eastern. They must have been confederates of al-Bousapha who were preparing the house as either a fall-back if the Empire State went sideways, or possibly just a post-op safe house. Randy, you could spin that better than me."

Jannik smiled nervously. Dressed in jeans, a black T-shirt and tight brown leather jacket, he looked like an adolescent being asked to sing for his aunts.

"And then what?" Ted Greene demanded. "Call off the attack on Iran? We've worked an awfully long time to get here, Dot. I still say this is a hiccup."

"Ted, my god! You cannot possibly start a war on premises as weak as these." She flicked up a bony shard of a finger. "One: the girl on the loose, whereabouts utterly unknown, who knows the whole Charlesdrew op is a fake." A second finger. "The supposed brains of the terrorist gang, *already officially i.d.'ed by the coroner as among the dead,* has now turned up alive." A third finger. "And these two elements will only increase curiosity about the bomb, which as we all know will turn out to be a Rube Goldberg contraption with a bit of real radiation in it. Gentlemen, are we so allergic to reality that we cannot grasp this?"

Mitch scowled, his whole mouth swerving sideways and making his ears move, Paul noticed. "I still say he couldn't have got out of that tunnel alive."

"Mitch, your inanity sometimes takes my breath away."

"All fine and well, Dot," said Trig Purtly finally, stirring from the doorframe. "But bottom line here, y'know, you're still bound as a Doer to go through with –"

"You needn't remind me of my obligations, Mr. Colorado Rockies, thank you. The op is still on *officially,* and now I will go back to the Senate and fight for war. But I can see the whole thing tottering already, and don't think I'm going to use up the last of my political capital if I see the issue going south. I have to retain *some* dignity."

Finally, Paul saw his opening. He had waited for the moment to give himself the most leverage possible, and this was it.

"I'm afraid I have to agree with the senator," he said, slapping his knees. "And she was, as I understand it, one of the Doers who sponsored this op in the first place. But the issue here could hardly be clearer."

"Well! Finally! A bit of common sense in this room!" cried Senator Crick. She swung to the side on the couch and addressed Jannik the media man, who physically cowered. "Randy, are you listening? You tell the networks that this whole thing *blows over tomorrow.* For good measure, we take down the latest hotshot of al Qaeda or al Nusra or the Islamic State – whoever our baddie-of-the-month is – we swing his head around on a pike a bit, and bury Charlesdrew on page six below the fold."

Silence.

"All right, Dottie, that's one plan," Ted Greene admitted sourly. "But we don't really know what al-Bousapha has communicated to –"

The senator cut him off with a roar: "And then, once we've got this goddamn mess tied off, *by God, we take stock!* We take stock of

Doers, we reform it from the ground up, we cut off the dead wood – Rainmaker, I mean *you* – and we add to this very useful, very necessary group, *civilians*. Yes, gentlemen, I said *civilians*. People like Jack Mirage and I, who were the only two people who voted against this operation from its first draft. Because we are able to look at a proposed op and critique it without the gung-ho enthusiasm of you ungodly blind *experts*." She practically spat the word.

Paul looked around the room and saw faces that were part stubborn and part sheepish. General Chet Nicely was examining his hands as if to see if they had any paint on them. Trig Purtly sighed into his mustache. Mitch and Mark were slouched back in their chairs sullenly as if they'd been caught cheating on an exam. The Rainmaker's meager lips had disappeared into his mouth. Only Ted Greene sat arched and tense, forehead tight in six parallel waves.

"All right, I've said my piece, and I've got to be getting back to Washington. Now: what's our decision here?"

Ted Greene: "We've still got some ways to go here, I think. But we'll communicate the decision to you by vote time."

Crick thought this over and grunted. "Well, I suppose it's better than sitting here listening to everyone make pathetic excuses. Jack is with me, and so is Paul. The motion is to call off the op, and for the moment there are three of us, and we need four more to pass it. Paul, can you take care of that?"

"I think so."

The senator walked over to a large window that looked at the front yard and heliport, where a green military helicopter was waiting. Its pilot leaned against it, thumbing his mobile phone. She rapped sharply on the window, and the pilot waved and got into the machine.

At that moment, in the dining room, the telephones as one buzzed with a message: al-Bousapha had been killed by a sniper, the two hostages rescued safely.

"Well, finally, a lucky break – some of you must have paid it forward with Providence," said Senator Crick, walking to the door. "Paul, don't let these junkyard salesmen run you down. Beat them off with a stick if you have to. Or call in that girl Gertrude – now *there's* someone who knows how to handle men."

39

The mastodon beak of the Flatiron Building, in the rising mauve city evening, looked down on Madison Square Park, its floodlights crawling up its flanks like attackers. It gave Trudy the willies, and as they waited to cross the street, she said to Jerry, "See that building? It looks like something out of a monster movie."

"Never really looked at it that way before," said Jerry, tilting his head back. "Yeah, kinda looks like it's going to lean down and eat you, doesn't it?"

The park was bordered on every side by a rampart of police cars and vans – or long stinking ranks of portable latrines – through which protesters could pass at only three points, and always searched first. The police said this was for the security of the activists, the activists said it was for intimidation by the police.

The Occupy Madison protest itself swayed and swung like a shadowy underworld carnival – posters strung across tree trunks, paper-covered picnic tables lit by all types of electric lanterns where people signed up for activities and clubs, or picked up slices of pizza and soft drinks. Here and there babies squealed, and a parakeet in a cage screeched to a small delighted audience, "Kick the ass of the ruling class!" From a small stage with a microphone stand at one end of the park, people sang protest songs and gave short speeches. The hard-fought agreement with the city dictated that the protest could run 80 hours on Saturday, Sunday, and Monday (72 hours of actual public meeting which must then disperse to allow for an additional eight hours of clean-up operations, which would begin that day at midnight). The city mayor himself had smilingly encouraged people "to participate all they want in this democratic exercise in sharing and caring."

Trudy, wearing her glasses and wool hat, and Jerry passed through a waving marsh of security wands and picked their uneven way through the clumps of people talking, texting, singing, and standing in line for one thing or another. People were quieter near the stage: the police permitted the sound, which came from speakers hung from the trees, to be clearly audible in a semi-circular radius of just two hundred feet. So people had to be quiet to hear anything. A folk band of two guitarists and a singer was performing.

They found the organization's tent behind the stage. This was a ramshackle Army-surplus thing with thick supporting strings running up to tree branches. By the entrance flaps, a cardboard sign hung from one corner: PEOPLE AT WORK, to which someone had appended with a marker, IF IT AIN'T URGENT, STAY OUT.

Jerry stuck his head in through the flap and said, "Hey, can a guy get anything around here except warm beer and cold pizza?"

"Jerry Stretch!" cried a great bullfrog voice. "Where you been, man? Get your ass in here! Great to see you, man!"

Jerry looked back at Trudy. "That's Billy. I'm gonna talk this through with him."

He disappeared inside as two other voices also welcomed him, and Trudy stood by a tree trunk, going over in her mind what she had to say. She would keep it to what Paul and Max had planned for her: what she saw inside, her escape, and the bus.

The tent flap was swatted back and Jerry emerged with a chubby man with graying hair. Jerry called out softly, and when Trudy walked over, the other man stared at her. Jerry motioned her to take off her glasses.

"Sweet Jesus!" the other man gasped. "Okay. Okay, man, you made your point. Sorry. Sorry, ah, Trudy. Hey. Billy Hancock – no relation." He stuck out a fleshy paw to shake, and Trudy wondered to whom or what he had no relation. "Ah, you'd better put that – those – back on." He jerked Jerry back inside.

Two people came out and disappeared towards the street; Trudy hoped they weren't calling the police.

After a good ten minutes, she saw them return and go inside. Finally, Jerry came out alone and called her again.

"Okay, babe, it's all set up. This is the last day of Occupy and nothing's happened, so the police are pretty bored. Billy and his friends have located the police informers in the crowd, but by now there are only one or two left. But when you get up on the stand to talk, they're going to jump them to make sure they don't make a break across the street to tell the cops."

"But if I'm talking on the microphone, won't they hear me?"

Jerry shook his head. "Sound system doesn't reach half that far. Thing is, though, there's a camera streaming everything live, and it won't take long for the news to get back to the boys in blue."

"Okay – I won't take long."

"Just make sure you talk *straight into the mike*. Get it? You don't have to talk loud, just nice and clear *into the mike*."

"Into the mike – got it."

"And you've got your whole gig ready, right?"

"Yeah, I've been practicing off and on."

"Good. Now the hair. Public knows you as blond, and besides you want to look hot for your opening night, right?" Jerry eased the hat off her, and Trudy, reaching up, undid the hairpins and shook out her hair.

"Yeah, like I'm ever going to do this again," she muttered, shaking out her hair and smoothing it down the best she could.

Holding her hand firmly, Jerry led her around the tent to the area behind the stage. It was only fifteen feet wide, and only half as deep. A half-dozen steps led up it.

"When you finish, just turn around and walk back down the way you've come, and we'll zip out of here. Billy's getting a couple of guys to arrange our getaway. We're not going out the way we came in. There's a little VIP entrance for organizers and suppliers, and Billy's guys'll take us out through that. A taxi will be waiting for us, and by the time the police come looking for you, we'll be out of here."

Applause welled up from beyond the stage, and the singers were thanking the audience. Jerry stood on the lowest step, watching them from behind.

"Troodles, we're up. Just let Peter, Paul and Mary get down the steps here." He stepped down and kissed her lightly. "Break a leg, babe. Oh, and don't forget to start by saying, 'Thank you *Jerry Stretch,* Village comic who does me in bed ten ways.'"

"Jerry! You don't want them to think we're, you know, friends."

"Good point, very good. So make it, '*three* ways.'" He kissed her again, waited as the band came down, took a deep breath, and bounded up the steps two at a time.

40 NOVEMBER 15 (MONDAY)

Paul watched with amazement. With Senator Crick gone, the other Doers were inclined to go back to their plan. *This was why Napoleon and Hitler sent their armies against Moscow,* he thought.

Senator Crick's diatribe was taken like the merest bawling-out from the school librarian, and the men stood around in the dining room eating roast-beef sandwiches and beer brought out by The

Rainmaker, who beamed at them like a proud mother. (Randy Jannik, always careful about his weight, found some canned pineapple in the refrigerator and picked at that with a small fork.) No one looked at Paul – the only person to agree with Senator Crick – except Trig Purtly, who edged close and whispered to him that he was a "faggot momma's boy, and your balls are probably made of cheerleader pom-poms."

There was crabby grousing about the nagging of women and their chronic inability – "It's something in the hormones," Chet Nicely averred – to see two sides of an argument. From there they ventured gingerly, like kids wading into a cold pool, into discrediting Senator Crick. They took into account her age, that she was sadly "old school," that "the new century demanded new solutions."

"There are times when prudence is a good thing," said Ted Greene, "and there are times to remember, 'Who dares wins.'"

"Yeah, Dottie's idea's just so fuckin' Plan B," said Trig Purtly, and the others agreed; Paul remained silent.

He had little to say anyway, shocked by what The Rainmaker had just told him, when the two of them were alone in the kitchen making the sandwiches, Prayers the cat winding between their legs.

"You needn't worry about the op, Paul. It can go forward. She won't go to any lawyer," The Rainmaker murmured. He was slicing meat off a roll of cold roast beef.

"You mean Gertrude?"

A knowing smile; again he reminded Paul of his mother. "Just between you and me: I know. Gertrude and I had a little chat at the door. I never told anyone; didn't seem important at the time. But God works in mysterious ways, Paul. When she escaped, I immediately considered shutting down the op. But then I remembered what she told me. She's a good Catholic girl. She goes to Mass regularly, she goes to confession once a year. When was the last time you met a girl like that?"

Paul folded more meat onto the fresh bread, beating his brain for something to say. "That must have been a nice surprise."

"I was moved, Paul, I don't mind telling you." He laid another thin ragged slice on the plate. "She's just a girl, of course; she had to die, it was for the greater good of the nation. Our Lord would take care of her. But it was a *sign*, you see: the op could go forward."

Paul slowly slid his glasses back on his nose. *A sign?* "Well, maybe that and you *wanted* it to go forward."

The Rainmaker said nothing, but Paul had a feeling his dart had hit home, whether The Rainmaker admitted it to himself or not.

"I mean, she *is* a bit of a snag in the op."

A shake of the head. "The snags have been other things." He put down the knife. "And I'll tell you something else: I told her my actual name. She's walking around out there with *my name,* and nothing's happened. Call it a sign, call it a hunch – I don't care."

"How…why did you do that?" (At the time, he didn't know that Trudy had mentioned "John Paper" to me. I had only told Paul in the note that I had a lead on The Rainmaker's identity.)

The Rainmaker told him, adding, "She was going to die, what difference did it make? At first I was worried sick. Now, though, she's been on the run for a week, and unless I miss my guess, she's slipped clean away – which is just fine with me as long as she lies low. Soon as she's under control, I plan to give her a new i.d., a new life, and let her meet some nice fellow and settle down with a couple of kids. God, how we need more girls like *her!*"

By the time the men retook their places in the living room, some with second beers and sandwiches in hand, Senator Crick had been put away like the crazy aunt in the attic that no one wants to talk about. The meeting resumed with a gutsy atmosphere: halftime in the locker room of the team that was losing by several points but was still playing to win.

"All I can say is that I red-teamed this op twice," Mitch the CIA man announced as they began again. "Nothing is flawless – okay – but this op was as steel-reinforced as man can make it."

"Dottie Crick wants to cut off the dead wood?" thundered The Rainmaker. "Well, that damn woman's going to get cut off *long* before I am!"

"As far as *I'm* concerned, the young lady's story gets out if we *say* it gets out," said Randy Jannik, settling his slim buttocks carefully on the sofa. "Internet? There's no truth on the Internet. In today's society, there's narrative. There's who has the best narrative told by the best people. You got facts? You got figs? Great. My narrative is going to tell you how they add up."

"Damn right, Randy," said Mark the FBI man.

Jannik sat forward, his leather jacket creaking. "Dottie doesn't remember that it's *us* that plays with the home-court advantage: people by nature don't want to believe that their government-slash-own-people are behind a terrorist attack. They don't. As long as you give them a solid narrative, they're fine with it."

Paul saw that it was time to enter the debate. "But even still, Randy," he began carefully, "isn't the senator's point pretty solid? You will have a hard time convincing Congress, not to mention public opinion, of the need to go to war if the basis of it is under a strong shadow of doubt. What are we looking at here? The major figure in a terrorist plot, officially pronounced dead several days ago, has turned up alive. This is going to make people wonder. And this, together with Gertrude's eventual story, is going to make it very heavy going."

"Country went to war after 9/11," snapped Trig Purtly, "and there are whole books written by doubters about the Twin Towers."

"But the point is to get to the war, Trig. That's the problem. Serious doubts about 9/11 never surfaced till months and years later."

"Al-Bousapha is a speedbump, Paul," said Randy Jannik. "It's an oddity. In a backward sense, it almost lends cred to the original narrative, especially now that he's dead. And as to the girl, we have control of that, one hundred percent. She's branded out as a terrorist. Anything she says publicly will be seen through that prism."

"Um, Randy, how about putting my mind at rest about something?" said Chet Nicely, shyly raising a hand as if at school.

"My pleasure, Chet. Shoot."

"What about the slangy black female lawyer? If she's even half-decent at her job, she's goin' to be able to spin this one hard against us. Dottie Crick had that one on the button."

"Not a problem, Chet, not a problem. Reporters will divert the narrative; they're experienced professionals, no one needs to tell them what to do."

"You sure?"

"Oh yes, Chet, rest assured. Look, let's say this lawyer goes public, holds a press conf right on the steps of City Hall, says…whatever: Gertrude saw her company staff laid out on the floor. Gertrude saw paramilitaries in the Hallerbee house. Fine." A reporter's voice: "That's interesting, ma'am, but can you tell us *why* you are aiding and abetting a wanted terrorist? Can you tell us where she is? *Are you hiding her?*" Another voice: "And the big question now all across New York is: Where is Gertrude Ingrid Schelling? Will she strike again?"

The Harmon brothers laughed.

"That and the lawyer bitch's looking at disbarment," growled Ted Greene.

"I see. All right," said Nicely.

"Fuckin' right," said Mitch. "My people got a backstory worked up that'll hold a freeway overpass. We're rampin' up the Paris shit, we've got Gertrude in an all-male Arab orgy, we've got her cheating at a poker game a month ago, and we're just about to finish a few traffic-cam vids so that you can follow just about her whole trip to and from Montana to pick up the terrorists. Stands up better 'n sixteen-year-old's dick lookin' at *Playboy*."

Everyone laughed.

"Right: it's black-hat-slash-white-hat – nothing sexier," said Randy Jannik simply. "You black-hat the girl – and nothing does that better than illicit sexual activity. You want to show your audience who the heel is in a film? Just start him off having rough sex. Twelve seconds of footage in the first reel – that's all you need."

"That's why they'll find porn on al-Bousapha's computer drives," said Mark. "Always works."

The Rainmaker chuckled, "Oh Randy, I don't know what we'd do without you." Paul could see that his eyes were misty.

Everyone applauded.

"Save it, save it," said Jannik, dismissing this. "It's child's play. Dottie is forgetting that these are professional reporters and producers: national-network people, seasoned veterans, people who renew contracts for six-to-eight figs every third year. They don't want a revolution, they know what their directors are looking for. Look how well they've done with Shally Hicks – poor Shally, what a sacrifice he's made for our country."

The rest nodded into their beers.

"Deserves every inch of his monument," added Mark.

"And if anyone objects or the Truthers get out of hand, you pull out the old standby: conspiracy theories are a dishonor to the victims and their loved ones. That generally does the trick, and I can't see that it won't here."

"Yeah, but hold on, hold on, just…What about the bus people?" Chet Nicely asked. He looked around for sympathy. "C'mon, guys, you got – I don't know – ten individuals on a bus with her? And they can nail down that she got on in an extremely disturbed frame of mind twenty minutes *prior to* kickoff on Charlesdrew? That isn't goin' away."

"Chet, Chet, Chet," Randy moaned patiently. "Chet old friend, if you want, I have three people on Twitter tomorrow saying they were on the bus with her and her story checks out – and then *recant* when pressed by reporters. Then I've got another fifty saying they were there too but it was a half-hour earlier, and *another* fifty who will say that when the bus crossed the intersection with Charlesdrew, the police were already digging in for the hostage standoff. Don't worry, that story isn't going to fly. All you have to do is drown it. Sorry to repeat myself, Chet, but *we* play with the home-field advantage; Gertrude's the away team."

The general chuckled sheepishly aimed a pistol-finger at him. "Yeah. Got it. Got it. Why you're media and I'm military. And God bless the both of us, Randy."

"Shalom, Chet!"

Ted Greene motioned minutely with his sandwich. "And you can have that up and running quickly, Randy?" he asked quietly.

"If we need it, and with Mitch's team's help, by this evening-slash-night, if necessary."

"Child's play," said Mitch. "We keep thousands of false social-net i.d.s. Twitter, Facebook, Instagram – all of them. In ten minutes, my people can dig out all you need for the Manhattan area. You message-coordinate with them and we're up and running."

"Time, training, and tech," Mark said. "Wins out every time." Another high-five with his brother.

"Plenty of budget never hurts, either!" added Chet Nicely, and everyone chuckled.

The Rainmaker was smiling. "Such good people," he murmured.

Jannik: "Actually, it's not a bad idea to get out in front of that curve today and put out *our* version that *she* has to prove wrong. In today's society, killer first impressions are what move opinion best."

"Damn right – so let's get real," said Ted Greene impatiently. "Real and focused: this is all set to fall. The U.S. Army is ramping up to invade Iran, Americans are backing it to the hilt, Canada is taking shit in their own Parliament to join our security system, Iran is taking major heat on nuclear, since it's now clear they lied about the treaty they signed about their enriched U. What's not to like?"

"Crick was throwing flags prematurely," said Chet Nicely.

Others chimed in, but Ted Greene held up his hands for quiet. "Paul, where do you come out? Are you ready to step up and take more pies in the face?"

Paul knew it would be foolish to put up more resistance; and he had to protect his cover as a full-fledged Doer. "All right, Ted, but with one caveat. I've done my part all the past week pulling for war, have I not?"

"Yes, you have."

"Coulda done more," Trig Purtly challenged him from the doorway.

Paul ignored this. "But to go any further with this, I'm going to need Secretary Mason's support. He hasn't been too happy with my performance, and I'm not –"

All the cell phones began buzzing: the SWAT commander in Queens, New York, was going to make a statement. The Rainmaker fetched his laptop and set it on the dining room table, and the Doers formed a choir circle before it. First came a summary: al-Bousapha had been killed with a single shot from 300 yards that hit him right between the eyes. A photo showed al-Bousapha lying dead amidst a mess of broken glass and blood. His head was propped up because he had fallen against the back wall of the shop. Over him was a full-length mirror whose lower half had been shattered.

"How many of our people do we have on the scene?" Randy Jannik asked.

"Just the SWAT commander," said Ted Greene. "I briefed him by phone on the importance of taking out al-Bousapha."

The television now showed a table with a small forest of microphones and recorders on it. Behind it was a bus-like mobile hospital with people moving back and forth like fish in an aquarium. The SWAT commander, who had an enormous head and the impatient air of a man with better things to do, sat with his arms piled awkwardly before the microphones, squinting into the lights trained on him. He had explained the operation and was now giving reporters short impatient answers to their questions. Yes, he had dealt with al-Bousapha directly by phone. No, he could not reveal the name or agency of the shooter, though he was among "the top of the elite U.S. marksmen."

"Vic McDermott – sent him myself," said Mark, the FBI man.

Yes, the shooter had been helicoptered in from a nearby American base. Had negotiations been fruitful? No, al-Bousapha had asked for a plane to fly him to South America; the commander offered only to take him prisoner without violence and that he would be given the benefit of due process. Had the reality of the recent terrorist attack weighed in his decision to prevent further bloodshed of innocents? Yes. Had the decision to take out the suspect been a difficult one? No.

"Fine," muttered Mark. "Now: thank all the nice people for coming, appreciate their prayers and concern, and close it down."

"I believe now that the two released hostages are ready to take questions," the commander said, turning around awkwardly in his chair.

"*Take questions?*" Jannik blurted. "But you've taken them aside, right?"

Paul was across the circle from him and saw him purse his lips as if about to play a trumpet, tight waves of skin rippling along his concave cheeks.

"Are the two gentlemen ready?" the commander called into the mobile hospital.

"Who the fuck wants to hear from them?" muttered Trig Purtly.

"This is so unnecessary," Jannik groaned. He patted his jacket pockets. "Where the hell is my…The commander's in the loop, right? And he wouldn't allow them to talk without taking them aside, right?"

Trig: "'Taking them aside'? Hell's that mean?"

Jannik found his phone in his hip pocket and took it out. "Who to call? This could be so…" He touched a button and put the phone to his ear – "*so* inconvenient. Is that on all the channels? Can someone check, please?"

It was, even on al-Jazeera. The barber and the other man had lifted themselves down the two fold-out steps and sat looking at the array of microphones. A distant applause simmered briefly. The commander, from behind, asked them to say their names. They were the barber Redoan Sabiri, from Morocco; and Elias bin-Sechnini, from Amman, Jordan, who worked for the Port Authority as a janitor.

Jannik spoke into his phone: "Frank? Randy. This barber-shop hostage thing. Do you know if the commander has taken the two hostages aside?"

Trig Purtly loomed beside him. "Fuck's it matter, Randy? The guy's dead. He's irrelevant now."

But Paul understood it, and one by one so did the others.

"No, it's not life or death, but after all this senseless loss of life, Frank, there's just no point in spreading, you know, hints and allegations that confuse the public," Jannik said into the phone. "Uh-huh. Grant? He's in charge? Thanks. I'll try him." He clicked off the phone and thumbed more buttons. His forehead shimmered with sweat under his high quiff of hair.

"Well?" asked Ted Greene impatiently.

Jannik didn't answer. "Grant? Randy. I'm working on some deadline here, Grant, can't really explain now. Do you think you can get the commander on the line like *toute suite*?... Shit. *Shit.* Okay, start walking *right now.* And if you need to use your elbows, use them. Listen, do you know if the commander has taken these two guys aside?"

41

NOVEMBER 15 (MONDAY)

The crowd roared; Jerry was on a roll. "Hey, no, listen, listen. I'm *grateful* to the NYPD for taking such good care of us. Know what I mean? To protect and serve, just like the song says. I just wish they'd come in and protect us from some of these guys pushing causes around here. Know what I'm talking about?" Jerry shifted the mike to his other hand to set up the new joke. "These guys don't mess around, man. Animal-rights lady jumps me for a contribution, I say no, she tells her cocker spaniel I'm a light post...Guy at the South American poverty booth said for every hundred bucks I donate, I get a free gram of blow...No! Hey, I'm serious!" Another change of the mic. "So I step over to the anti-guns booth, I figure *that's* got to be safe, right? Rescind the Second Amendment? Confiscate every gun in America? Peace and love for all? Like hell! Guy aims a .44 Magnun at my chest, tells me to chuck fifty bucks in the pot for the cause. So I do, guy says, 'See now why guns outghta be banned?'...I mean, where the hell are the cops when you need 'em, man?"

The crowd roared.

"No no no, don't laugh, don't laugh. That is *not* a rhetorical question. It has an answer. Answer is: They're standing around this park feeling up everybody who walks in, that's where...Hey, we're all grateful, *but are you guys gonna protect my ass or stroke it?*"

The laughter and applause rose, rumbled and swayed around, and Jerry shook his head as if at the folly of it all.

"Great, great. Thanks. Always love playing the Occupy crowd: everybody's sober enough to know where the punchline is. So tomorrow take a break from righteous anger and step 'round to Comic Wall in the Village. I'm on at 8, but not to worry: I do four shows in case you've been busted for disturbing the peace. Come in, buy a drink and help Jerry Stretch pay his rent, okay? Well now, next up, we've got a – let's see – a *special mystery guest speaker* who's coming up here. Spooky, huh? She's a mystery to me too, but the Occupy high-and-mighty tell me she has something to say that will make you forget all about Jerry Stretch. *(That is, Jerry Stretch who's on all this week at Comic Wall, right?)*" He slipped the mic onto the holder and with a practiced hand lowered the microphone stand, bending down. "And I'm told that she's about five-one in lifts, but let's not hold that against her."

Jerry turned back, half expecting to see a blank stage, but no, there was Trudy, her hair glowing like a golden shawl over her shoulders. She stood with her feet together, her hands gripping each other like terrified passengers on a sinking ship. Jerry motioned her forward, wondering if she was able to move her feet. She performed short steps as if coming to receive communion, and Jerry waited till she stopped at the microphone, which was a good thing because she had obviously forgotten his advice about speaking into it. He'd lowered the stand just enough, and now he tilted the microphone nearly to horizontal till it aimed at her mouth.

"Okay, babe, let 'er rip," he said in her ear, wondering if she would say anything at all.

Trudy cleared her throat. Again. *Just get it over with,* she told herself, looking at the sea of faces in front of her – and a light that stared at her from a tree branch like a dirty old man on the bus. How did Jerry manage to concentrate like this?

"Thanks, um, thanks. Hi. Okay, um, first off, I'm Trudy Schelling." And waited for the gasp. Jerry had told her to wait after saying her name.

Nothing. The hum of the crowd, if anything, rose a little out of boredom. "I'm Sherry Smith, so what?" someone giggled to her left.

This irritated Trudy – and broke the ice for her in one great smash. "Um, let me start again. My name is *Gertrude Ingrid* Schelling."

Now a true shockwave of silence rolled away from her as if a giant powder puff had fallen on the park. Far away, she heard the parakeet: "Kick the ass of the ruling class!" and a few people laughed nervously. She took a breath and began: "I'm not a terrorist – I'm not. I just want to tell you the truth about what happened in Jersey City the other day."

42

NOVEMBER 15 (MONDAY)

At least once a year since 11/9 I replay the press conference with Messrs Sabiri and bin-Sechnini; each time I find a different nuance to savor about their statements. They duly review the situation in the barber shop – them cowering in a corner, al-Bousapha waving his gun and negotiating on Sabiri's cell phone, that sort of thing. And then they get into a few of the juicier details that al-Bousapha had related: the fake bomb in the Empire State Building, the CIA's knowledge of the event and their double-crossing him. Some two minutes into their statement, the SWAT commander behind them is bothered by an underling to take a phone call, which he refuses, listening petrified to this unexpected testimony. Then a reporter shouts the question on every mind from Maine to Hawaii: "Did al-Bousapha tell you how he got out of the house alive?"

He certainly had: the CIA had a tunnel between the house and a "sewer connection on the street" – the two men need to consult each other on that term in English – and al-Bousapha crawled out just after the explosion. The CIA had blocked the tunnel, trying to – now another consultation on terminology – "treason" al-Bousapha. But the explosion opened the way – just how he never quite explained. Al-Bousapha also said that the bodies in the house were already dead, and were not Hallerbee employees, the whole event having been plotted by the CIA long ago.

It is a tag-team press conference: bin-Sechnini, with philosophical surges, brings up each new charge, and Sabiri, the barber, gives the details. This was fortunate: the latter's English is far smoother. And towards end, Sabiri adds with catty satisfaction, "So maybe it seems not only the Muslims are terrorists, but also we have some terrorists here in U.S.A., eh?"

Then the reporters all begin shouting, a barrier holding them back on one side falls over with a crash, and though local police are quick to help up those fallen and restore the line, nothing but journalistic cacophony can be heard, and the commander, not so commanding now, leans down between the two men and splutters into the puddle of microphones that the FBI's investigation is only beginning and that the men will have to continue their statements in "more secure surroundings." Then he plucks the two men from their chairs and propels them back into the medical bus. Bin-Sechnini turns back to the cameras and shouts that he'll "express more information" later. Like many immigrants, he had a rather grand idea of what freedom of expression meant in America, but this would presently be whittled down for him.

I listened to the original press conference in my car on the way home from Georgetown, and was no sooner in my bedroom taking off my tie than my wife shouted up the stairs in her classically abbreviated American English: "Max, that terrorist girl is on live in New York at that Occupy thing, in case you're interested."

I was, but first I called Irish Joe and told him where he could pick up his old objective; he said he was hardly four blocks away in his taxi, and he would shoo away his fare and get on her trail. Two hours later I was landing at La Guardia Airport. I wished I could call Paul, but I didn't dare.

43

NOVEMBER 15 (MONDAY)
Trudy's speech: another jewel.

For set design she has the grave checkerboard of lit office windows sliced by the naked branches of trees, and the cement silence of her audience. Lights are blasting the stage and making her squint. But they also lay an angelic glow on her lovely blond hair that lies with virginal symmetry on her shoulders. She stands concentrating at the microphone with her hands gripping her forearms, her legs tightly closed – she reminded me of my son at the school spelling bee. She speaks with "ands" between her sentences and "ums" in the middle of them, and tells of her experience just as Paul arranged it with her long ago. She winds up:

"And that's, y'know, the whole story: I just walked in, saw all these military people and some dead people lying on the floor and only one or two alive – like that Chinese lady who got shot – and um, this one tall guy attacked me, and I zapped him with my stun gun, and I got away and went to a friend's house. Well, except for that guy who tried to pick me up. Okay, so I'm not a terrorist, okay? I've never done anything like that ever, ever, ever. I mean, people have been saying some, uh, pretty creepy things about me, and I just wanted to, um, to get everyone informed on the right track. And well, that's all. Thank you."

"What about that guy's gun you took?" someone shouts.

"Oh. That. I was scared. I just panicked and took it. But I threw it away."

"What about the poker game?"

"Yeah, I'm a pretty good poker player. I make, um, statistics? That's my job. And those guys I played with that day, they were, um, y'know, pretty bad." This elicits laughter from the crowd. "Um, thank you. Bye."

A few other people shout questions, but they crowd and garble each other.

Now Trudy turns back and grabs the mic, speaking fast: "Oh, and Mrs. Disner, would you please water my bonsai trees? Just take a good look at the serissa foetida, okay? Before you water it. It's probably pretty droopy, but it gets upset if you give it too much water, but try and do the ficus retusa and the Chinese elm today, okay? Tonight if you can. They're probably pretty miserable. If you haven't done it already. Prateek, can you let her in with your key, please? Thanks. And thanks, everybody. And please don't believe what those creeps are saying, okay? Bye. Thanks."

44

NOVEMBER 15 (MONDAY)

One big helicopter conveyed the Doers back to New York. The Rainmaker phoned his staff, Randy Jannik the news producers, Chet Nicely the oil markets, Mark the FBI, Mitch the Company, and Trig Purtly the White House. They spent most of the time, Paul observed, yelling into phones that they could barely hear. Ted Greene informed Jack Mirage what was happening, and he had no trouble hearing Mirage's answer. When Greene clicked off his phone, he turned to Paul. "Jack's even pulling out of Doers – said if we wanted financing to go to the Red Cross. That cocksucker! God Almighty, the sky is falling!"

Paul nodded understandingly.

Indeed, the sky had fallen; Trudy's speech had just hit the airwaves as well. Hawks in Congress were falling silent, doves unwontedly roaring, Iran and Russia sneering, the United Nations Security Council grumpily adjourning without any vote being taken. Only the Doers still had some fight in them. As the helicopter flew along, a roll-call vote was taken on Senator Crick's motion to cancel the operation, and Chet Nicely alone ("Has anyone else here seen where barrel prices have been going in the last hour?") joined Paul, Senator Crick and Jack Mirage. But there was still hope, Paul thought: the two Harmon brothers said that they had to check in with their offices, though for the moment were staying with the go-ahead group.

Randy Jannik, as they landed, said, "Everybody keep cool. This is all contained – after all, these are professionals; they know what to do. The tunnel stuff will be kept low-key and the Gertrude story controversial. But Jesus, folks, we have to find her and get her to, to *moderate* her story. And for God's sake, don't anyone even think of taking her out." This with a glance at the Harmon brothers. "That would be the last nail in the coffin. Otherwise, I don't know where this is going. I'm heading for a studio right now." He then trotted from the helipad to his limousine through a quiet rain. The other Doers were picked up or caught taxis; the vice president's Secret Service detail was waiting for him. The hasty dispersal reminded Paul of a boys gang caught breaking windows.

Mark was going to look for the Occupy organizer William Hancock, who lived in the city of Nyack. The Rainmaker was going to track down the comedian that had introduced Trudy; his people had already traced his address to Brooklyn Heights. Paul trotted after him as he strode to a Navy Intelligence car: Brooklyn Heights was where Trudy had last been spotted. It was as good a chance as any.

"Rainmaker, why don't you let me do it?" he said. "If persuasion is necessary, perhaps a diplomat is more the man for the job."

The Rainmaker hesitated – and then his deep-set eyes sharpened into suspicion. "We'll *both* go."

45

NOVEMBER 15 (MONDAY)

You would think that the re-appearance of Raschid al-Bouspha and Trudy's little speech, with its resounding sincerity, would open the door to doubts about the official narrative. They did among everyday citizens, but the official narrative simply swallowed these items and slithered on its way. Paul later observed to me that Randy Jannik's confidence in reporters was well-placed; the pros did indeed know what to do with hiccups like these.

A sheepish, puling statement about al-Bouspha was released to the media by county forensics, saying that experts had only had a few fragments to work with and questionable DNA to compare them with, these taken from the safe house where al-Bousapha and his men had stayed before the attack. And forensic examiners had been working under "extreme time pressure from FBI authorities, which inevitably compounded our mistakes." Reporters called them "hard-pressed public servants" who had "burned the midnight oil" to get answers for the public. Mistakes were inevitable.

Next came the comments of the two barber shop hostages. Reporters wrapped al-Bousapha's revelations about 11/9 in phrases like "the two men alleged that…" or "al-Bousapha reportedly told them that…" or "There were linguistic issues here, so it's also possible that they two men misinterpreted the *precise nature* of al-Bousapha's statement referring to…." They might have been talking about children rather than grown men. This continued until panels of experts could be corralled and dabbed with make-up and arranged on stools to declare that the al-Bousapha "confession" was just a last-ditch effort to throw 11/9 into doubt when what had happened was already clear beyond all reasonable doubt. The matter of the tunnel to the sewer was flayed to pieces. A tunnel? Really? Surely the two hostages had that wrong. Maybe they had been referring to the service alley out back. "I'm sorry," said one panel host, his milky visage absent of any sorrow, "but this tunnel thing is just a total joke."

Yet within hours, post-explosion aerial photos of Charlesdrew began to appear on various websites, yellow arrows pointing out what to me had already been obvious: a vague but visible trench, perfectly straight, now filled with debris, which bisected the sidewalk and ran into the middle of the street. Indeed, the linked barriers quickly erected around the three wrecked houses (too quickly, one Truther would later discover, the barriers having been ordered by some local official three days before 11/9) formed the shape of a letter envelope with the flap open, the flap reaching into Charles-drew to include the sewer line. Mainstream news reporters, faced with the aerial photos, merely opened their tool boxes of ambigui-ty: "possible," "potential," "ambiguous," "what may or may not be." One called it a natural-gas line that had exploded. Nonetheless, the idea of the tunnel stuck in the public mind. (According to Paul, Ted Greene later groused that if it had occurred to someone to park a vehicle over the visible part of the trench, "we might have got past those two damn Arab blabbermouths.")

Thus experts bit with far greater gusto into The Shot Heard Round the World: the one that "took out" or "took down" – basic decency forbade the terms "murdered," "killed," or "assassinated" – Raschid al-Bousapha from across the park. The shooter's technique was speculated upon, as well as his history with the agency, his choice of weapon, and his "other possible important takedowns." Outdoing everyone, one network went so far as to bring in a "certified mafia hitman" – one wonders what government agency issues certifica-tions – who sat in prim silhouette behind a screen, his voice distort-ed as if he were gargling, to offer his sublime insight into long-dis-tance assassination. Yet the only expert that spoke with authority, I felt, was homemaker Matilda Fernandez, of Puerto Rican heritage, who proudly admitted being the one who allowed federal officers into her apartment, which faces the park. "I am very happy for do-ing this. We gotta face up these fackin' terreests," she screeched.

And Trudy? How did her performance fare? About as well as al-Bousapha's. Her presence was prefaced with the terms "a wom-an reportedly calling herself Gertrude Ingrid Schelling," or "Ger-trude, or whoever that was." Terrorism experts reiterated what they had said all week: terrorists had intense training in propa-ganda and psy-ops. In that regard, Gertrude had genius on the level of Osama bin Laden, this according to no less a luminary than Randy Jannik, the man who had practically reinvented movie promotion in the Internet age:

"As an old ad man, I really have to give all the credit in the world to this 'Gertrude'" – here he scratched two quotation marks in the air, making the high wave of his hair wiggle – "especially the 'wa-ter-my-bonsais' riff: hands-down the masterstroke. And that body language! The gripping her arms, the legs set together, not a single gesture from start to finish, looking scared. That practically shouted, 'I learned how to do this at terror school in Beirut.' My take? Snake oil, one heck of a salesperson – but this woman is more than ever a danger on any American street."

"Absolutely, I have to agree with Randy," said an ex-NYPD police chief. "Hell, if she's as innocent as she says, why didn't she turn herself in? What does she have to hide?"

"Isn't that always the man's point of view?" an earnest congresswoman despaired, one finger raised, either for emphasis or to see which way the wind was blowing, which indeed all of Congress was now doing. "Just turn yourself in to a roomful of men and hope for the best. Some option!"

In the credit column, however, I must add two items. First, a local radio station soon broadcasted a conversation, echoingly recorded, with Mrs. Emily Disner, Trudy's neighbor. A retired first-grade teacher, she confirmed that the building super, Prateek, had keys to Gertrude Ingrid Schelling's apartment. She was unable to enter, however, because the apartment had been sealed by police. "It just makes me sick to think of those lovely trees in there dyin' o' thirst. Trudy took care of 'em like they were her own family – had a couple of 'em since she was fifteen: the um, the um, the serissa and the ficus, I mean. Now the Chinese elm, she bought that a little later, but it was just seven years old at the time, y'know. When she went to France and back, goodness me, the red tape with the Agriculture Department she had to go through to bring 'em with her! And don't you believe what everybody's saying about Trudy being a, a, a, a bomb-thrower or something. She's just the nicest young lady in the world!" Local plant lovers, enraged that good bonsai trees were going without water, deluged the police department with calls, and the next day the police allowed Mrs. Disner "supervised access" to Trudy's apartment to water the trees.

The second item: one New York rag had the temerity to publish the headline, "11/9 Terrorist Loves...*Bonsai Trees?*"

Trudy and Jerry, by the way, slipped out of Madison Square Park just before the police closed in; others were not so lucky. When the NYPD got word about her presence, they immediately closed off the openings to the park and started to herd everyone – "herding" being the correct term here – into its center, the idea being to let them out one by one in a search for the dastardly terrorist. The police were already miffed that she had slipped in past their noses and were in a vile mood. As the crowd got denser and denser towards the center of the park, they kicked Occupiers along, whacked them with batons, and then a Gandhi-esque idea occurred to someone: "Lay down! Everyone just lay down!" This became the rallying cry – on recordings a nasal pedant can be heard loudly quibbling with the use of *lay* for *lie* – and in a question of seconds, some two thousand people had sat down as if at an open-air concert.

The police, few of whom wore helmets, took offense at this lack of citizen cooperation, and began swatting at the recumbent with their truncheons – swinging with abandon as if they were workers cutting a field of sugar cane. It was a bad tactical mistake. The Occupiers had by now been corralled into a space, said one reporter, the size of a baseball infield, and the thirty-to-forty police officers that manned it were thinly dispersed along its perimeter: easy targets. The outraged protesters – and there were many – now fought back. Groups of men, and some women, tackled cops and stripped them of their truncheons. More protesters fought their way from the center to the perimeter and joined the fight. Two people, having snatched away cannisters of pepper spray, largely turned the tide all by themselves, spraying the stuff directly into every police face they could find. One fellow – his identity never discovered – achieved YouTube fame for his martial arts expertise by splitting a truncheon in half with the heel of his foot and then slicing through three policemen; he was looking for another when the video stopped.

Some two dozen officers ended up injured, and two were found stripped naked and barely conscious. Sirens – mainly ambulances – began to sound, and among the protesters the idea swiftly spread that fate would smile on those who dashed while the dashing was good.

In ninety seconds, the Occupiers dis-occupied the park, an act which reflected the other tactical mistake of the police: they had left no reserves in the rear. The Occupiers slid over the boots and bonnets (*trunks* and *hoods* for Yankees) of police cars and made for side streets. Traffic squealed, radios buzzed, and reporters mooed. After ten minutes all that remained of Occupy Madison were the homeless, the injured and the innocent, the latter of whom bore the burden of guilt. Neither Occupy Director William Hancock nor Gertrude Ingrid Schelling was found anywhere.

46

Jerry's name got a few mentions on news reports, and a fellow comedian called to congratulate him on the PR coup. But that was as far as the good news went. In his apartment again, he and Trudy sipped beers and with growing disgust watched news reports, which included a few innocuous excerpts of her speech, quickly overwhelmed by the more colorful footage of the protesters' "violent revolt." Trudy kept muttering, "those creeps, those creeps," and Jerry just shook his head and said, "I wasn't really expecting this, babe. I really wasn't. I saw this all differently."

Jerry's manager called to say that he had taken several phone calls asking if he knew "the girl" or knew where she was, and the manager had said no; that was correct, right?

"You know, babe," Jerry said, hanging up, "since they're still making you look like Jack the Ripper in panties, I'm starting to think that maybe the best thing is for you to sleep over at a friend-of-mine's. Bet you anything NYPD's going to be along first thing in the morning asking about you, and if we move you now, so much the better. The heat will have died down by tomorrow night."

Jerry picked up his phone, then put it down. "Just a sec'. Just to be on the absolutely, totally safest side, I'm going to go across the hall to Mrs. Gelling and make the call. She won't mind, and you never know about those nosy guys at the CIA. Get together your knapsack for the night, okay?"

Trudy did, and when Jerry returned, he grabbed his jacket, "Okay, Troodles, here's the play: my friend Mary Jane walks the line between straight and lesbo, but I explained the deal to her and she's totally cool. Only one rule in her house, and that's that you remember at all times that her cat Greta is a person: manners, place at the dinner table, kiss good-night, the whole deal."

Trudy giggled. "Okay, I get it. Jerry, I'm going to miss you, even for one night."

"Know what you mean, babe. Know what you mean."

47

By the time they arrived on Pineapple Street, neither the NYPD nor anyone else had located the director of Occupy Madison, William Hancock. Jerry "Stretch" Strajenska – name and address provided by his manager – was the only possible trace, and Paul had a queasy hunch that this was something. Beside Paul in the back seat, The Rainmaker spied on him as he checked his messages. Finally, Paul said, "Rainmaker, I'll let you have my cell phone as soon as I'm finished with it. But do you mind not leaning over me so much?"

The Rainmaker grunted and moved away.

Their driver was a thirtyish officer from Naval Intelligence. He let them out on Pineapple and said he would wait at a nearby parking ramp.

It was night, and amidst the bored blurry drizzle and general ashiness of New York City street lighting, the going was not easy. Number 32-and-a-half seemed to jump back and forth along the street as if afraid to be found out. But finally they found the gate, threaded their way hesitantly through the canyon of the two neighboring buildings – this lit by a single shy bulb under a sort of Chinese coolee hat – and emerged into the interior patio, whose lighting was little better.

"Paul! Hey, am I glad to see you!"

And then Trudy was stretching up to throw her arms around his neck, and Paul was watching The Rainmaker's face wheel and teeter through a series of emotions that started with shock and ended with rage.

"You…you traitor! You *Judas!*" he snapped, jerking out his mobile phone. "I'll have you –"

"Yeah, well, look who's talking, Father John!" cried Trudy, going up to him. "You creep! You gave me your blessing and then you just let me walk in there knowing those guys were going to kill me! What kind of priest are you?" And before anyone could stop her, she rammed a righteous fist into his midriff. With a spectral guffaw, The Rainmaker doubled over, his knees collapsed, and he knelt to the pavement, his cell phone clattering. "Take that, it serves you right!" she snapped.

"God, I'm injured. Call a medic," The Rainmaker gasped. "Paul, goddammit, call a medic!"

Indeed injured. At that moment, a tiny rupture in his spleen was pouring poison into his system, and The Rainmaker was looking at a very poor night ahead of himself.

Which was when your reporter stepped out of the shadows of an electrical transformer box; I had arrived some ten minutes before and, having seen lights on in both top-floor apartments, been wondering what to do.

A great teary reunion with hugs and cries of joy was probably in order at this point, but now that The Rainmaker had discovered the connection between Trudy and Paul, there were lives to be saved and haste to be made. With a quick hello to Trudy and Paul – a handshake to Jerry – I snatched up The Rainmaker's phone and whisked everyone except The Rainmaker down the canyon to the sidewalk. Paul gave me a quick rundown on the situation with the Doers and The Rainmaker's driver, and I called Joe, who after following Trudy and Jerry from the park had remained nearby in his taxi. Our heroes dispatched, I returned to The Rainmaker, who was already in the canyon, crawling after us like a bear with a hangover. I stopped him and made him sit against the wall – which must have been damnably uncomfortable in that trickling rain. I introduced myself, fishing a gun out of my pocket and screwing on a suppressor. Joe had built the latter himself, and he had assured me that a fired shot made no more noise than a stapler.

"What are you…Oh no." Terrified, The Rainmaker drew up his knees and threw his hands over his face, trying to stop the bullet. Then he bunched them into fists as if they might protect him more. I have always suspected this of men who torture, and even more of those who have others do the dirty work for them: they are cowards of the commonest type. "I have clearance – higher than the president. You can't do anything to me. You'll pay for it."

"We've met before, you know. The Yucatan? Cancún? The MI6 fellow tied up under the table?" I briefly lifted my newsboy cap and let him get a look at me without the shadow across my face. "Don't remember the beard? I need it, you see – covers up the nail marks given me by Hano and his friends. Dear Hano, may he rest in peace. And then I escaped, remember?"

He did, oh yes.

48 AFTER NOVEMBER 15

By the next morning, matters had changed completely: the military was standing down, the administration would wait for the result of the IAEA investigation of the Empire State bomb, and Trudy was no longer a terrorist but a "person of interest"; Jerry would later joke to me that, for him, this took the zip out of their sex life. The media hastened on to fresher meat: an important leader of al Qaeda had been wounded and captured entering Turkey from Syria, and suddenly all the news cameras on earth were pointing at a dusty little field where a mummified body was being loaded into an ambulance. Turkish soldiers in red berets were charging at the camera wagging fingers like scandalized mothers who had caught boys spying on their daughters in the changing room.

About a week after my re-encounter with The Rainmaker, the FBI issued a complete retraction of its accusations against – we use that three-legged name one last time – Gertrude Ingrid Schelling. At a full-dress press conference, the director read a formal apology and grumpily ended by reminding Ms. Schelling that if she had quickly turned herself in to the police much of the confusion could have been avoided. Trudy, ankles together and face white with nervousness, accepted his apology in a brief statement that she read without ever looking up.

They left the podium to Assistant FBI Director Mark Harmon, who explained that "the expedited press of events" and "enormous information inflow" had contributed to "the overly triggerish drawing of conclusions" which were "in retrospect insufficiently red-teamed." Taking a breath, he added, "And the fact that the terrorists were so quickly able to install incriminating evidence on her computer is a red flag to a whole new level of sophistication on their part. They probably had ready the entire list of IP addresses for the Hallerbee staff, and the minute one escaped, boom! They triggered their emergency procedures and had a virus sent to that computer such that the moment it was turned on and connected to the Net, the information installed." An amazed laugh. "I mean, this just takes it to a whole new level, folks. We're going to need a lot more resources to deal with that kind of stuff."

He then presented his brother Mitchell Harmon of the CIA, who denied political pressure in making decisions and explained that "Sally Brown" had been on and off the CIA's radar for two years. "She had already travelled way up *our* flag paradigm," he said, as if every Tom, Dick and Harry had a flag paradigm. "Everyone just assumed that we finally had her on-screen. I mean, the intersects with Sally Brown were just incredible: blond, short, Paris, American, terrorist-dating. Coincidence is just the bane of an intelligence analyst's existence." Reporters in attendance asked toothless questions; one that I remember was, "Will the admission of this mistake mean a difficult period of self-examination for you and your agencies?" Both Harmon brothers, with the crumpled faces of teammates who've lost a national championship game, admitted that it meant just that.

The clearing of Trudy's name had begun when Paul Klippen introduced her to Senator Crick, explaining that Trudy had quietly contacted him at his office because she had seen him on TV and, as Trudy said, "he seemed like a really nice guy who would listen to me." Senator Crick then told the under secretary of state to take a hike and gave Trudy a private chat "as an older woman." As a result, Trudy, in benign questioning by the FBI – Crick sitting beside her, shooing away any question she didn't like – recognized that the dead bodies must have been Hallerbee employees; she couldn't be sure how many were dead and how many alive. And yes, the men in the house could indeed have been from the Middle East. Well, the Bureau had suspected as much, hadn't it? And yes, it had been her in the department store and who jumped off the roof; but the man didn't identify himself as a police officer, so why not? Through the good offices of Senator Crick, all of this – except the department-store matter, which was an embarrassment for the NYPD – leaked out to the media.

So the late-discovered tunnel served the new story as well. The men Trudy had seen in Hallerbee had apparently "egressed out through the tunnel," as Mark Harmon later put it, during the hostage standoff. Two nights later, they slipped out of Port Newark at night on a fast boat and were never seen again. Port Authority security admitted its poor vigilance and said the incident proved not a lack of effort but a lack of funding.

In time, the entire story of 11/9 turned around.

About three months later, a special commission was convened, headed by two ex-members of Congress; they named White House aide Trig Purtly as executive director of the project. (Much criticism attended this appointment, pundits wondering how a president's right-hand man could maintain any objectivity.) The Istles-Verde Report, as it would be called, was marred by the resignations of several staff members, who said that Purtly had presented them with an outline of their conclusions almost on the first day of work, and that their job was mainly to fill in the story. Mainstream media reporters inferred that staffers preferred to quit rather than stay and fight to produce a proper report.

The report's publication, moreover, was preceded by a rolling thunderstorm of leaks, revelations, rumor, chatter and hint. Istles-Verde would turn our understanding of 11/9 on its head, sources said. Istles-Verde would rewrite the whole story. Raschid al-Bousapha's computer was providing investigators with a "wealth," a "gold mine," a "cornucopia" of material. One headline read that the Charlesdrew standoff, not the nuclear bullet, was the point of the whole operation. Reporters' scoops shot across the public stage like fireworks, each one more breath-taking than the last; lucky was he who didn't need to breathe. The families of the victims, now well-known faces on TV, pleaded for clarity about the matter. (Not that they were in any hurry. Each one posted a website about their deceased husband, girlfriend, brother, or sister, and beside the slideshow of photos a little "Donate" button allowed Americans to demonstrate their commiseration in a more substantive way. Charity-experts' estimations of the donations generally ran to a million dollars per victim.)

Thus to great éclat did appear *The Final Report of the National Commission on the November 9 Attacks Upon the United States,* which ultimately became the bible on the events of that day. (The addition of the word "Final" in the title raised eyebrows among journalists: had there been previous reports unknown to the public?) Its conclusions did indeed differ from the previous narrative, mainly on two crucial aspects. First, the terrorists, it turned out, were not working for either Iran or Russia, but stateless al Qaeda, that obliging repository of planetary blame, a fact that the group's website confirmed: "Yet again have our brothers delivered another crushing, disorienting blow to the twin Satans of the United States and Israel. Despite the failure of our martyrs to effect the release of our illegally held brothers in Guantánamo and other sites, the Americans have been exposed as unable to defeat us. They have proven themselves a wounded imperial giant, now blindly lashing out at Russia and Iran, enemies that they can scarcely perceive through the corporate blindfolds tied tight across their eyes."

There's nothing like Islamic rhetoric, Paul later observed to me, even when it's forged and inserted on the al Qaeda site by Mitch Harmon's subtle aides.

Second, the real target of the terrorists was indeed not the Empire State Building, but "a hostage-based contingency that was to involve significant nuclear blackmail," according to the Final Report's prologue. The uranium was indeed Russian. The terrorists had got hold of a nuclear pellet used in one of their nuclear power plants. The IAEA's team said that the pellet had been produced in the 1990s in Russia and used in the Balakovo reactor in the region of Saratov Oblast, then extracted from the reactor tube for study, then discarded at one of Russia's overcrowded, under-guarded radioactive dumps in the Arctic. "Robbery was not terribly difficult, although most likely the pellet had been purchased on the black market," their report said. It was far too impure and degraded to be used for a bomb, so the terrorists' idea was to assemble a mock-up in the Empire State Building – one that stank of radiation and would appear dangerous until experts could examine it.

Meanwhile, the bomb would allow al-Bousapha to dictate terms: the immediate release of all prisoners in Guantánamo, others being held at CIA "black sites," and several Palestinian activists in Israel. The SWAT team commander, who had handled the initial call to al-Bousapha, confirmed this. For every hour of delay in compliance, one of the Hallerbee hostages would be publicly executed. Hence the murder of the two hostages exactly an hour apart, a point that 11/9 Truthers had harped on. So they had not escaped, but had been released and shot in the street for greater effect.

"And if this plot had succeeded, it would've been game over, no question," added former senator Jim Verde at the report presentation. "It was supposed to *look like* a bomb involving radioactive material, and had the bomb been properly assembled, our people would not have been in a position to ably and quickly approach near enough to the bomb *itself* to make a positive determination as per its supposed authenticity re: a WMD or just as a so-called 'dirty bomb' that would extend and propagate radioactivity all throughout New York City."

"And what were the negotiators supposed to do?" added former congresswoman Rita Istles. "Say the usual, 'We do not negotiate with terrorists'? And then the Empire State Building falls through midtown Manhattan crushing out hundreds of lives? No. Sorry. Unacceptable. Unquestionably, nuclear blackmail is going to be an issue going forward, and it is an issue that this administration is going to have to *address* going forward."

Yes, the public's understanding of 11/9 was completely changed by the Final Report, a veritable nova of enlightenment that required 937 pages. Some examples:

The terrorists entry into the United States from Canada – on false passports but otherwise legally, and not through Montana but from Windsor, Ontario, into Detroit, Michigan – occupies 98 pages. Their black-market purchase of the uranium "bullet" could come to no specific conclusions after 187 pages. Their leasing and surreptitious occupation of a "safe house" requires 45. The "inordinate and unwarranted" pressure put on local forensics to produce reports – including al-Bousapha's, considered faulty – is described as a major error in 83 pages. But the question, *How did our security services fail us?*, fills 346 unputdownable pages. No detail was without its footnote, scarcely a footnote without its lame appendage: "For more information, see Annex 2...." Critics noted angrily, however, that many of the annexes were heavily redacted.

And yet other questions, such as how and why Raschid a-Bousapha chose Hallerbee, are dispatched in single phrases: "The terrorists were looking for an easy target." Who built the tunnel and when? "An itinerant band of al Qaeda operatives, most likely those who entered the country and escaped by sea, completed the tunnel between the sewer line and the basement of 126 Charlesdrew in the three weeks before the attack, working secretly at night to avoid detection." This "itinerant band," by the way, later receives but four terse paragraphs, which is a true snubbing in view of their feat of entering the United States undetected, digging a proper tunnel under a busy street in total secrecy, and stealing away into the night from Port Newark two days after 11/9, when ports and airports and border crossings were still on high alert.

Then there is the question of how, if the terrorists' objective was a hostage standoff, they expected to draw the police to the Hallerbee house. Had Shally Hicks not walked up, had the three boxes been successfully pulled up to the fourth floor of the Empire State Building, no police would have been called. As on many sticky points, Raschid al-Bousapha's bountiful computer came to the rescue, and the report dashes off the explanation in a sentence: "Upon arrival in Jersey City, Raschid al-Bousapha was to exploit his vehicle's potential as a machine of death and destruction, and drive/run over pedestrians at random, although avoiding areas adjacent to Muslim shrines (see Maps Appendix), thus drawing the attention of local authorities."

Only 11/9 Truthers troubled to extend this tortuous nonsense to its nonsensical conclusion. Having mown down pedestrians, al-Bousapha was supposed to linger long enough for witnesses to spot him, and then arrive at Hallerbee with, first, the police chasing him but not blocking the way; and second, with enough time for him and his men to run up to the house and get inside.

At MI6 we used to call that kind of plan a "low-plausibility contingency." But let's not be judgmental.

The narration does answer the question of why al-Bousapha shot at the front door while running up to it; that is, why his cohorts, already inside, didn't simply open up for him: "Pursuing police officers could have interpreted a door opening as a sign of a confederate-inhabited abode."

Lost to history is what the pursuing police officers thought of this gesture to verisimilitude: they are not mentioned anywhere.

All in all, the Final Report earned the praise of television pundits, who intoned sagely that it held many a lesson to be learnt. Terrorist experts confirmed that they were re-writing their manuals, security agents that they were adjusting their software. The sniper who shot al-Bousapha published a book (*The Shot*), as did the SWAT team commander (*The Burden*). Money was made all around, oh yes.

The 11/9 Truth Movement dismissed the Final Report as "five-and-a-half pounds of bovine excrement." They noted that it neglects entirely al-Bousapha's six-day disappearance, or Trudy's supposed rooftop escape, which brought half of the NYPD dashing to the department store and later to the adjoining office building. (The security tapes from the department store have ended up as classified material.) Who was the "itinerant al Qaeda cell" that had dug the tunnel? Where were they? How did the FBI locate the safe house on the day of the attack and not a week before? Why didn't al-Bousapha escape with the other men by sea? (*The Final Report* was particularly harsh in its criticism of the CIA for drawing such a total blank on them.)

Then there was the matter of the "Barber Shop Confession." The two men who heard it fell silent directly after their "fifteen minutes" of fame. Truthers speculated that they had been threatened with the removal of their residence visas if they said anything more. Elias bin-Sechnini testified to the Committee but had nothing new to offer, other than that al-Bousapha had asked for a shave as well as a haircut. Redoan Sabiri, the barber, flatly refused to cooperate with anyone, moved back to Morocco with his family, and died not a week later in a rare terrorist event in that country: the bombing of a restaurant committed by one of the rising Boko Haram factions in Africa. Truthers said that the death proved that Sabiri had more to say about 11/9. For the sake of his children, his wife implores everyone to believe that this is not so.

At the end, among the public, 11/9 has lapsed into that sizzling purgatory of wonder inhabited by UFOs, sightings of Elvis, and the succulent mystery of Area 51. An 11/9 Hollywood movie came out a year later. The three movie stars, burnishing their patriotic credentials, ably created their characters by consulting still-grieving family members, and I must say the young woman who played Ellen Nguyen was wonderful. *Charlesdrew* was a fairly obvious production about a hostage standoff and featured a poignant scene in which Steve Hallerbee, just before making his dash for freedom, begs for but is refused the forgiveness of one of his female employees, whom he had accosted sexually just a week before. The issue had been raised by his wife, interviewed on a network news show one week after the attack, to whom Hallerbee had tearfully confessed his sin. According to her, he had gone to work on 11/9 planning to make amends with the employee, whom she refused to name, giving rise to great speculation on social media.

Truthers, incidentally, say they can find little in the way of a public record for this Mrs. Hallerbee, and the network that did the interview refuses to reveal where they found her. Hallerbee neighbors along Charlesdrew attest that they did see people going in and out of the building in the time after their sign was put up several weeks before the attack, yet no significant paper trail is available for the company, Steve Hallerbee, or any of the employees of the company – neither death certificates nor registrations on the Social Security Death Index nor mention in the FBI Crime Report for that year. Every funeral was with a closed coffin and every burial site secret.

At best, a few large corporations – all of which, Truthers discovered, did handsome business with the Departments of Defense and

Homeland Security – attested to contracts with Hallerbee. Truthers reply that neither department has any particular need for digital advertising. They further accuse the government of having hired actors to play the roles of bereft family members, and indeed one fellow had a certain reputation in the Chicago, Kansas City and Minneapolis theater communities. And Ellen Nguyen's mother can apparently be spotted in several mid-90s Chinese martial-arts films, normally in the role of ferocious heroine.

Most surprising to me has been the absence of scholarly interest in 11/9. Besides the two previously-mentioned "books" – an august term for such rubbish – 11/9 gets at best a chapter here and there by scholars writing about the event's impact on international relations. None calls into question the official story as told in the Final Report. At Georgetown, I am told, to do so is career suicide.

11/9 controversies continue to bubble and crackle on the Internet, videos on YouTube bloom big and brash like orchids and are often removed as "fake news." The social media give Truthers no quarter, and even important progressive websites ignore them as "conspiracy theorists." Top progressive pundits, if drawn at all on the matter, say that if the government had been behind the attack, "someone would have talked." They neglect to say just who might have listened, much less reported the information imparted.

49 THE YEARS AFTERWARDS

According to Paul, the cover-up of 11/9 was the Doers' last real operation, a careful, if rather improvised, concerto directed exactingly by Senator Crick, with the brothers Harmon playing first and second violins. When it was all over and the Final Report written, the military and security agencies withdrew their support for Doers; Jack Mirage, who paid for Doers operations, had already told them all to go to hell. Senator Crick and Vice President Ted Greene tried to keep the flame going and had some rather pointed meetings with top agency officials, Paul as their acolyte, but everyone, he said, was running scared and acting as if they had never seen them before in their lives. At best, they were told a new Doers would have to wait a few years.

That is the main reason Paul has kept quiet about 11/9: if a new Doers is mounted, he wants to be there to head it off. Another consideration was that if he came forth with revelations, he would immediately be smothered in sexual harassment charges, if not murdered outright like poor Redoan Sabiri; and his story would go nowhere. It's sad to have to agree with a seedy sodomite like Randy Jannik, but he's right about public truth: "There's who has the best narrative told by the best people." Such is the twenty-first century.

The Rainmaker, however, will see no more of it. His last task as a Doer was to collaborate with me. I helped him to a café down the street and showed him my telephone: a short documentary about his true identity, including footage of him walking out of the house on Charlesdrew and talking to Trudy. I told him, "Either this shows up on an 11/9 Truth website, or it stays with me. Your call, old fruit." It scared him to the depths of his scrotum, and he called Mark Harmon, he of the FBI, and told him that he and Paul had talked to Jerry Strajenska, who said he knew nothing about Trudy. Then The Rainmaker told Mark that he was getting heavy static from his constituents in government and the private sector and that finally he had to agree with Dottie Crick: the operation had to be closed down and tied off.

So much for Operation AnyStreet.

The Rainmaker having fulfilled his purpose in this life, I sent him on to the next one. He was having a soft drink, still in pain from Trudy's blow, and when he went to the bathroom to throw up, I mixed the contents of a pill into his glass. Joe had provided it, in addition to the gun, in case the latter proved too noisy a weapon. When we had finished our business and The Rainmaker had no doubt about my threat, I left, and he called his Navy Intel driver. An hour later he suffered a stroke, went into a coma, and died before sunrise. Paul says that the autopsy revealed nothing odd because the Navy driver testified that The Rainmaker got back into the car alone and with stomach pains.

Paul went back to his campaign for diplomacy, and much strengthened. He argued that 11/9 had shown that he – and the administration – could be flexible in the face of changed circumstances. The administration's foreign policy has since met with wide support, enough to put the warmongering conservatives, mainstream news networks, and even the Pentagon on the defensive. After nuanced apologies were made, relations with both Russia and Iran have turned civil, with talk of a "collective security" arrangement for the Middle East. During a Cabinet meeting and after the media had left the room, the president said that the foreign policy boat had turned in a new direction, and anyone who didn't want to row that way should start looking for a job elsewhere. Trig Purtly did just that, and now blows his horn once or twice a week on one of those right-wing news shows that trafficks in fat, brainless certainties.

"The only thing is that I would rather have been part of the truth than part of the lie," Paul said to me in my office over a couple fingers of magnificent scotch – a gift from Carlton Mason that Paul found on his desk, complete with a ribbon around it, the day after the war bills died in Congress.

"Indeed, old fruit. I'm preparing a full accounting of it. In time, it ought to come out. But we staved off a war and did in the Doers, and that in itself is not bad for a single op. Well done us, old man."

We clinked our glasses together.

"Still, we were lucky, when you think about it," Paul went on. "Trudy's talk and the re-appearance of al-Bousapha weren't enough to make the Doers back down. If you hadn't threatened The Rainmaker, we wouldn't have made it."

"True enough, old man." I drank. "You know, I still wonder which frightened him most: the prospect of losing his life, his security status, or his name etched on the Vietnam War Memorial."

I could go on and on about the ramifications of 11/9, but I do hate an account that pads and fills and stuffs and inflates; I've tried not to do that here. To finish up, then, I give you news of Trudy and Jerry.

They married just a few months after 11/9 and now live in a lovely house on Long Island, fruit of Trudy's talk with Senator Dorothy Crick. They have a son and are expecting a second visit from the stork as well. Her bonsai collection has grown to a dozen trees which, I recently observed, she waters with a special watering can with tiny holes in the spout that emit thread-like rivulets – Trudy being a rainmaker herself. Jerry maintains his humbler collection of African violets on a window sill.

Things have gone well for him too. His Occupy Madison riff went viral on the Internet, and his career quickly moved up a couple of levels to the better clubs, even Las Vegas, where he recently made a recording of his monologues that is now selling well enough for him to forgive the many copies downloaded for free. His stand-up comedy has come up in quality as his themes have darkened. His standard riff is "My life can't be happening – impossible." He must repeat it fifty times a show, in a fast mumbling drum-roll, almost a mantra, often complemented by a rictal mugging with that monumental lower jaw: very effective. He told me that he made up this line after his experience with Trudy and 11/9 – about which he has never said anything in his monologues, except in the following story, which provides a fitting end to my account – not to say "narrative."

"No, man, my life can't be happening – impossible. No way. The other day I'm in the park with my kid. He's bustin' a gut on the roundabout with some other toddlers, and I'm sittin' on a bench, right? But it's made of cement and it's pretty cold, so I take the Sunday magazine out of the newspaper and put it down under my butt. And I'm reading the sports section, which is the only half-honest part of a newspaper.

"Lady comes along pushing a baby carriage, sits down at the other end o' the bench – big blond democratic-type lady in a track suit. Points at my ass and says, 'Excuse me. Are you reading that?' I swear! My life can't be happening – no way. So I say, 'Matter of fact, I am,' and I stand up, turn a page, and sit down on it again.

"No no no, man, don't laugh, don't laugh. It gets worse. Lady says, 'Okay, if you're readin' that, what's it about?' And I say, 'Remember that terrorist from 11/9? Al-Bousapha? I'm reading an exposé about how he was actually on the CIA's payroll.' Lady just looks at me – you'd think I'd asked her how much she charges per hour. Then she says, all indignant, 'I *refuse* to believe that!' Gets up and walks away. Which just goes to prove, man, which goes to prove: people will believe you have eyes on your ass before they'll believe the government plays dirty."

THE END

*

www.ingramcontent.com/pod-product-compliance
Lightning Source LLC
Chambersburg PA
CBHW020113180626
46812CB00006B/2582